TOP OF THE HEAP

TOP OF THE HEAP

Michael Marmesh

Michael Marmesh (signature)

Cover art by
Kate Marmesh

Acknowledgments

First of all I want to thank both my parents for passing on their love of books. The "Story Lady" reading aloud from a hammock during vacation is a treasured memory.

I would like to acknowledge my transcribers, those brave family members who deciphered my handwritten manuscript from its yellow pads and transferred it onto the computer.

Thanks to my manuscript readers, a tough bunch. Two librarians: Judy Orr and Janet Blum, and four teachers: Kathy Bowker, Pat Singleton, Claire Kirk and Clara Gardano (who also helped with my elementary school and schoolyard Spanish.)

Thanks to my family editors including my mom, Sarah, my in-laws, Jan and Herb, and my daughters, Kate, Liz, and Mo. These folks were all helpful with their input and criticism. And, yes, I know that some of the sentences were not complete.

Thanks to Carol Ewing, without whose help with graphics and layout, this project could have been stalled indefinitely.

A special thank you to the faculty and authors from Florida International University's writers' workshops in Key West and Seaside. These experiences were insightful and encouraging.

Most importantly I need to thank my wife, Nancy, my biggest supporter, without whom this book would never have come to fruition.

Finally, there is my beloved South Florida, an insanely rich source of material for so many writers because there are so many less than sane people on the loose down here.

Many of the locations used in this book exist in South Florida, including Mt. Trashmore, but they are used fictitiously. The unique political, historic and geographic situations that exist in this area and the characters they seem to attract have served as an inspiration for this novel. However, this book is a work of fiction. Names, characters, places, and incidents are either the product of the author's imagination or used fictitiously. Any resemblance to actual persons, living or dead, or to actual events or locales is entirely coincidental.

 **Prologue**

Tracer bullets from the machine gun mounted on the old Soviet personnel carrier arced toward the go-fast boat. They stitched a line just in front of the starboard bow, sizzling as they hit the water. None of the five men on board heard the bullets' hiss.

The roar of three 250 horsepower outboards rammed to full throttle drowned out everything else.

The coyote at the stern was encouraging the captain to "get us the fuck out of here." His three-man cargo huddled against the transom was thinking the same thing.

The captain didn't hear a word his one-man crew was shouting. But, with fifty caliber motivators being sprayed his way and the possibility of rotting away in a Cuban prison if captured, he was doing his damnedest to grant their request.

Obviously this smuggling run was not going off as planned. Unexpectedly heavy seas, with ten-foot swells, had forced the captain to cut his speed on the southbound leg of the run. When the smuggler, the coyote, had complained that they would be late for the pick up, rather than argue the captain had pushed the throttles full forward. The twenty-five footer's bone-jarring slam into the first swell knocked the smuggler off his feet. The slam into the second caused him to crack two teeth on a rail as he was trying to stand up. Before they could hit a third he was signaling to slow down.

"Bastard."

"It'll teach you to question my judgment. The $15,000 we're getting for each of our passengers will leave you plenty to fix your teeth."

A clogged fuel line had to be flushed out and further delayed them.

Instead of reaching the Playa de Los Hermanos on the eastern end of Cuba at midnight, they arrived at the GPS coordinates at four a.m. Fortunately their three passengers were still waiting for them.

The three young men rushed from the dunes as soon as the pre-arranged signal was flashed toward the beach. As they splashed into the water, a floodlight suddenly switched on and started sweeping the shore behind them. In seconds the light's operator had focused on the splashing and was illuminating the three men climbing into the speedboat.

Fortunately, the personnel carrier was undermanned. There was only the driver and his private. The light man yelled for the driver to stop and join him in the truck bed. The big diesel powered carrier angled to a halt atop one of the dunes.

The private moved to the 50 caliber and uncovered it. He released the safety and swung the barrel toward the water.

The driver dropped into the truck bed and grabbed the light that had swiveled on its gimble and was now aimed skyward.

"¿Adonde?" The driver asked the gunner.

"Ayer," was the response, the gunner pointing in the last direction he'd seen the boat.

As the driver rotated the big spot around there was a rusty snap as the whole mount cracked off at the base and fell useless in the sand.

"Mierda," the driver cursed. The whole country was turning to shit. The loss of Soviet foreign aid with the fall of the USSR, together with the U.S. embargo, was causing an ever-increasing rate of economic decay. There was no money or parts to maintain this old piece of Russian crap.

The moon having set, it was pitch black and neither man could actually see the smuggler's boat. The gunner took his best guess and loosed his first fusillade at the fleeing craft. It was the barrage that raked just in front of the bow. He aimed again and fired a second burst.

On the boat the smuggler was stupid enough to stand up to see how far they were getting from the beach. A bullet whined by his head passing through the GPS monitor and the console windscreen lodging in the bow deck. He put a hand to his face and thought he felt a gouge in his cheek.

"I think I'm hit," he yelled. He was already soaked from the rough trip down. His hands were wet. But he thought he could feel the stickiness of blood on his fingers.

The captain, crouching down between the bench seat and the console, reaching up to the wheel to steer, yelled back, "Get down you asshole!"

As the smuggler squatted to the deck, the refugee in the center touched his face and turned his head. "I don't see anything. You're ok."

A sickening "chunk" came from the machine gun. It had jammed. They were done for the night. The gunner didn't even bother to curse. Equipment failure was becoming the norm. Why waste his breath.

"¡Gusanos!" Worms. The driver hurled the epithet into the darkness. It was the term the old Barbuda in Havana used for those who fled the island. In his heart the driver was beginning to wonder if maybe they had the right idea.

After three minutes of running northward, timed on his digital watch, the captain stood up. A veteran of the first Gulf War, he knew the risks he was taking and planned accordingly. By now they were close to three miles off shore and out of machine gun range. In another ten minutes they'd be in international waters. The Cubans were unlikely to mount any further response. His boat was too fast and they wouldn't want to burn a lot of fuel, an increasingly precious commodity on the island, trying to find him in the dark.

He looked at the shattered GPS navigational system and the large starred hole in the center of his windshield. "Jesus! That was close!"

"Sí," came the affirmation from the middle of the knot of refugees in the stern.

He hadn't really expected a reply. He motioned for the men to come forward and seated then in the best positions to balance the boat.

He didn't ask their names and didn't introduce himself. That was his policy. The less they knew about each other the better. If they were caught at either end of the trip, they would be able to give little testimony against one another.

The smuggler handed out granola bars and bottled water to the bearded young men.

"¿Que es eso?" one asked.

"Desayuno. What passes for breakfast in America."

The refugees munched their dry cereal bars and sipped the water. They were starving after waiting all night and it tasted like manna to them.

Without a GPS system for guidance, the captain took a best guess compass heading for the northward leg. At least the compass hadn't been shot out.

Just after six, as they were passing to the west of the Bahamas Cay Sal Banks, the sun started peering over the horizon. There wasn't anything prettier than dawn at sea. Even with his nerves ground to frayed edges, his boat shot up, illegal strangers spread around his deck and potentially more trouble ahead, he took a moment to watch the sunrise. The pinks and oranges lighting up the dark blue sky. The blinding white path across the waves from the sun's reflection on the horizon burning right to his boat. God it was beautiful he thought.

"Sí," he heard in his head. Maybe he was getting punchy?

It also meant trouble. The sky was clear and cloudless. Right now he would have preferred clouds and rain. The weather would provide no cover. Unknowingly he'd already been exposed. The Coast Guard's drug smuggling interdiction Black Hawk patrolling the Florida Straits had picked him up coming off the Cuban coast. For now it was just monitoring his progress. If he didn't veer east to the Bahamas, the chopper's crew would eventually radio ahead to arrange his interception. He didn't know any of this.

For now it was just a more or less routine boat ride. Mostly less. As the sun rose, they all warmed up and dried out some. The seas had died down, the swells only about six feet now. It wasn't enough. The granola bars ended up feeding the fish instead of nurturing the refugees.

"Poor bastards," the captain thought. Sure the money was good, forty-five grand for a tough day's work. Plenty left, even after expenses, as he looked over his battered boat. But there was satisfaction, too. Bringing people to freedom, a freedom he'd fought for, that was a real kick.

He looked at them again. They were thin, almost emaciated. All were looking forward. Maybe just for landfall and relief from their mal de mar. But, he thought to himself, it's more than that. They're looking for their freedom. And he was going to give it to them.

Around nine o'clock he nudged the helm more to the west.

Orders were radioed from the Black Hawk.

As they approached the South Florida coast the first structures the refugees saw were the tall cooling towers of the Turkey Point nuclear plant.

The second appeared to be a short, emerald green mountain with houses on top.

"What's that?" one of the young Cubans asked.

"It's where rich people live," the captain replied.

"I didn't know you had mountains in Miami."

"That's not actually Miami. We're still too far south. And it's not actually a mountain."

All three gave him a questioning look.

"It's a garbage dump."

"That rich people live on? I don't understand."

It's called Mont Basura Harbor. It's a long story."

"Tell us."

At that moment, the Black Hawk swooped down for its first pass.

"Shit. Later. Put these on," he ordered reaching under the bench and throwing them life vests.

The race had begun. South Beach was the place he could take them in closest without risking running aground. He jammed the throttles full forward one more time.

TOP OF THE HEAP

 **Chapter I**

Mont Basura Harbor, the most exclusive residential development in South Florida, Rogelio Negro appreciated the sheer audacity of his own, newest real estate venture. No one could accuse him of false advertising on this one. Mont, from the French for mountain, and basura, from the Spanish for garbage. Yes, his newly planned community was being constructed atop a 150-foot high flat top pyramid of residential waste. The locals in the southern part of Miami-Dade County had long referred to the site as Mount Trashmore. He'd made a mountain out of something even less than a molehill. As for the harbor part, well, every new housing development in South Florida had to have some mention of water or nature in its name. On top of the garbage mesa there was a fabulous view of Biscayne Bay and the Atlantic to the east, and in the distance, the Everglades to the west. He'd even found a local amateur archaeologist who would attest that the present Mount Trashmore was built over the top of a Tequesta Indian shell mound. In other words, the place had been a refuse pile for over a millennium. And no doubt the Native Americans had at one time beached their canoes on the nearby shoreline, so it had also truly been a harbor of sorts. This was as honest as land development got in this part of the world.

You just had to know how to sell. Over the years people had told him he could sell freezers to Eskimos and sand to Arabs. He knew they were trying to insult him, meaning he was sticking people with things they didn't need. But he took their comments as compliments. To him selling was an art.

He had first learned about selling by accompanying his old man door to door in the '60s. His father sold The Encyclopedia Americana. In that decade Miami was just beginning to transform from a sleepy southern coastal town, America's winter playground, to the international financial and cultural crossroads of the western hemisphere, America's Casablanca. This was due in large part to the influx of Spanish speaking professionals fleeing Castro's repressive Communist regime. The new refugees arrived with education, skills and a drive to succeed. To many, this was a frightening invasion of foreigners who spoke a different language, who worked very hard for meager wages. In short, who provided very stiff competition. Many of the old southerners left town. To Rogelio's dad it was a golden opportunity, new customers who needed to learn about American culture. He learned Spanish, pressed on, and watched his sales sky- rocket.

Rogelio learned about talking your way into a customer's confidence. He learned about how to be rejected in two languages and not take it personally. He learned about setting goals and then acquiring the knowledge and skills to pursue them. He watched the Cubanization and Latinization of Miami, his hometown.

So in 1974 young Roger Black set off to the University of Florida to pursue his career. He had already picked up Spanish from his Cuban friends in junior high and high school. In college he polished it so he could use it at the business level. By 1978, having pushed himself, and having changed his name, Rogelio Negro was granted his M.B.A. He headed back home.

His timing couldn't have been better. He hit town at the same time that the money flowing up from South America started arriving in torrents. Brickell Avenue, an old oak and Poinciana shaded street hugging the shore of Biscayne Bay, just south of Downtown Miami, used to be lined with the mansions of the city's original movers and shakers. Señor Negro would be pivotal in their obliteration. On the bay side, he helped finance, build and sell the giant condos that now completely block the bay view. On the west side it was the office towers, almost every one home to at least one bank, that helped turn Brickell into the Wall Street of Latin

America. Rogelio helped build the buildings too, and was instrumental in moving funds into the banks. More importantly, he made connections in the local government and financial communities.

Today Brickell Avenue is still a cool and shady street. One can even find the occasional oak or Poinciana tree. But most of the shade now comes from the assortment of skyscrapers that have turned the historical old road into an urban canyon.

His work done there, when there was no land left to build on, Rogelio needed to move on to new pastures. Or, more correctly, not pastures but farmland. He acquired several large parcels in the southern part of the county. Most of it was acreage that produced a large part of the nation's winter vegetable crop. The farmers could live well and not work nearly as hard off what he paid them. He also picked up some low-lying undeveloped marshland toward the coast.

La Vida Buena, his development company, became one of the biggest developers of tract housing in the county. He became a prominent member in the county's Hispanic Builder's Society a group that, through political contributions and connections, carried tremendous clout.

Then came Hurricane Andrew. Hundred fifty mile an hour plus winds with tornadoes spawned on top of them roared across South Dade, right through where La Vida Buena had sold so many customers on the good life. The shit they built, literally hit the big fan.

No local power base was going to save his ass now. The national news media, The Miami Herald, state and federal inspectors all swooped down. And everyone was out to nail Rogelio's hide. Tie-down straps to hold the roofs on, plywood instead of pressed wood for roof sheathing, nails instead of staples to hold the shingles down, storm shutters to protect the windows and all that crap cost more money and added to construction time.

How was a builder supposed to turn a profit and still build homes that buyers could afford? Life wasn't always fair. La Vida Buena immediately declared bankruptcy.

Fortunately for Rogelio, the few parcels he hadn't yet developed were separate from the company holdings. He would hang on to them for future consideration.

He decided to try his hand at sports promotion and he had what seemed to him to be the perfect concept. It would be a variation on the indoor arena football game—women's indoor flag football. The players would come from the girls who didn't get selected in dancer and cheerleader tryouts for the city's pro football and basketball teams. After all most of them would be in good physical condition and it wouldn't be hard to teach the basics of the game. Still, some would balk at the one other requirement for being a player in the latest pro sport. But this was after all a business, and how much of a live gate or cable audience could you actually expect to watch little more than amateur women play flag football. That is, of course, unless the official team uniform was a thong bikini. Thus the National Tushball League was formed.

The league was a success right from its inception. There were eight teams the first year and twelve the second. All the teams were in Sunbelt cities. Player recruiting was easier where the girls had longer bathing suit seasons. By the third season the franchises actually had monetary value, some approaching eight figures.

From the beginning the ticket prices and TV money covered the players' salaries and league operating expenses. By the third season they had become a significant revenue stream. Rogelio Negro had made money right from the start. There was the merchandising—the usual team calendars, pennants and T-shirts, and also the knock-offs of the team uniforms that men would buy their girlfriends in hopes of playing a little touch at home. But the big money was in the international re-broadcast rights. The foreign market was huge and, as far as the audience was concerned, an understanding of the rules of the game was optional. The collector's video of the pay-per-view league championship Hawaiian Tropic Buns Bowl, played in Honolulu, was a big seller both domestically and overseas.

Rogelio was, naturally, accused of exploiting the young women. The truth was that most of them were to some degree already exhibitionists. They'd worked hard to develop their bodies and didn't mind showing them. Negro paid them well and saw to it that the teams were well chaperoned. Any fan attempting to jump onto the field during a game was immediately bounced from the arena.

Occasionally there would be a moment of embarrassment when a thong bottom would start to fall off when a string broke as the flag was snatched from the side of a suit. Adjustments in the tensile strength of the string ended the problem.

The truth was that most of the women liked the job. Men got to admire them without mauling or coming onto them. It certainly beat being a stripper or working at Hooters. There was even some local recognition, with some players getting spots in commercials for businesses in their team's city. One player had even managed to catapult herself into a role in a prime time TV series.

Lindsey Lee Olson, quarterback and captain of the Miami Coconuts for the team's first two seasons, managed to make it to Hollywood. She gained national attention in the Coconuts' second year when she was unexpectedly pressed into service as head coach, after the original head coach was fired for trying to teach several of his players about scoring after practice. Close-ups of her standing on the sideline, her hard body glistening with sweat, her face a mask of concentration, as she led her team to victory in the second Buns Bowl, captured the attention of a couple of national television producers.

While the rest of the Coconuts were in training camp the next year, Lindsey Lee was the latest in a line of physically talented young women saving lives on a fictitious California Beach on the world's most popular television series. Unlike some of the other starlets on the show, she'd even had previous acting experience, having appeared as one of the orphans in her high school's version of Annie. And she even knew how to swim. Within two years she'd become one of the central characters, with story lines centering on her. She'd also appeared in a couple of "B" action movies. She hadn't seen Rogelio Negro for years, but their paths were destined to intersect again.

After five years the NTL was still going strong, but Rogelio could see problems in the near future. Though ESPN2 had carried the championship game live for the first time, competition was in the offing. Thong beach volleyball was about to make its cable debut and there were rumors of a topless tennis series in development. They would definitely dilute his audience and cost him market shares. So when he was offered 55 million for his interest in the league he took it.

It was time to get back to real estate. Again his timing was impeccable. And fortunately the public's memory was short-lived.

Miami-Dade County had a big problem, its government landfill was nearly maxed out and the local politicos were desperately looking for a new site. Not surprisingly, no one wanted Trashmore II anywhere near his or her property.

Enter Rogelio. It just so happened that out of several parcels of his undeveloped property one lay just south of the original Mount Trashmore. His intent had been to develop the acreage into a golf course. When he learned that the county government was interested in his property for the new trash site, he decided to see how much he could extract from them.

He accompanied one of the county's land appraisers when the man was going out to determine for the government what his holding was worth. On a whim, they drove to the top of Mount Trashmore to get an aerial view and assessment of Rogelio's property. It was then that the inspiration struck. It was a clear, sunny day, with a fleet of cotton ball clouds in the sky. Looking east, the afternoon sun glinted off Biscayne Bay and you could make out Fowey Lighthouse, out near the edge of the Gulf Stream. Far to the west you could see the border of the River of Grass, The Everglades. Even the landfill itself didn't look bad, its sides covered with sod, an emerald, flat-topped pyramid. There wasn't another location with a remotely comparable vista in the whole southern half of the state. In a place where the average elevation was less than 5 feet above sea level, this was a virtual mountain with captivating views.

The public rehabilitation of Rogelio Negro was about to begin. The once despised developer, who had foisted shoddily constructed houses on an unsuspecting public, made the magnanimous gesture of swapping his undeveloped land for Mount Trashmore. Other developers were sure he'd lost his mind.

They just didn't have his vision.

Included in the swap were two provisions. The first was that the county would four-lane and landscape the access road that led from U.S. 1 to the fill. The second was that the county would green-light the residential development of the top of the pyramid, including providing water, sewer and power connections.

Thus did Mont Basura Harbor come into being. Good marketing just required spinning negatives into positives. The greedy land developer, who had taken useful farmland and built crappy homes on it, was now the county's savior, taking useless landfill and changing it to one of the most desirable and ecologically forward thinking communities in the state. A 150 foot trash heap, sure. Now it was 158 feet since he'd covered the top with a four-foot layer of gravel and then a four foot layer of soil. But it was the only place in the southeast quarter of the county that was not going to be worried about flooding when a hurricane threatened. The methane percolating up from the decomposition of organic matter in the fill was no problem. Special collectors were in place under the gravel to scavenge the gas. Basura Harbor produced enough methane to provide gas for cooking and heating water and swimming pools for the homes built on its summit. And projections showed it would do so for the next 10 years. It was the ultimate in politically correct recycling.

Recycling was the hook he would use in his advertising. That's where Lindsey Lee Olson came in. Like all young actresses she had to have a cause to devote herself to. Others on her show were saving whales or backing animal rights. She was into safe garbage and recycling. In fact she had recently appeared for a tasteful Playboy layout shot at a San Diego dump. In the photo spread she started out in a bikini made of plastic 6-pack holders. The holes were strategically placed so you could see that she had pink areola and was indeed a natural blond. In the last photo in the layout she appeared to be twirling the plastic holders around her finger, the only part of her body left covered.

Rogelio contacted her when she was in Miami to promote "Caribbean Commandos," the sequel about a team of elite, endowed, female agents who fought drug and alien smuggling throughout the islands. She was glad to hear from him and seriously interested in his latest project. He offered to build her a luxury home on the prime southeast corner of the Mont if she would help him promote the development. She happily agreed.

Both the print and television ads showed Lindsey Lee in upper torso shots. She was shown bare from the top of her cleavage up, spinning a plastic 6-pack holder on her right pinky. She invited potential buyers to, "Reach new heights. Expose yourself to the best lifestyle South Florida has to offer." She mentioned that if the homeowners association wanted to vote to make the portion of Mont Basura where her house would be a "clothing optional" area, she would be extremely happy. Finally she pointed out the advantages of living in a recycling community with a "fabulous view." The spots were shot on top of the Mont and the background images were indeed spectacular.

Rogelio hadn't named a minimum price in his advertisements, waiting to see what the public response would be. The broker inquiries, phone calls and website hits soon let him know he had a real winner. Allowing for a sales model, a small park, a community activities center and the requisite streets, he figured he could still squeeze about 75 luxury homes on ¾ acre lots on the top of the landfill. He set his minimum price at 1.5 million knowing full well that by the time he'd talked the buyers into added amenities there wouldn't be a house that sold for less than 2 million.

Lindsey's ads really brought them in. He figured most of the customers would be white Anglo mid-westerners who had no idea what the community's name translated to, but who wanted to live near a beautiful movie and sports star. He also thought he might get a few of the rich cyber geeks who wanted to demonstrate their P.C. devotion to recycling by purchasing a luxury Florida vacation home. What surprised him was the local response from the Cuban community. There was a rumor circulating that the word 'basura' had been suggested for the development's name by an agent of Fidel Castro. The reason--to keep Cubans out of the best living arrangements in town. Rogelio did nothing to squelch this story, because he knew it would make them all the more eager to buy. If, for the one time in his life when he was up front, people wanted to think he had ulterior motives, let them. As long as they had the cash to buy.

The project sold out within four months.

 **Chapter II**

The chopper swept down closer. Close enough for its crew to count the occupants on the speeding boat. Five. One at the helm and the rest in life jackets, clinging to the side rails. They could see the driver looking up at them.

Damn, the captain thought. How long had they been tracking him? It didn't really matter. They were on his ass now. This whole freakin' run was snakebit. The previous six had gone off without a hitch. Law of averages he guessed. Well, he still had to finish this one.

The Coast Guard copter zipped ahead, climbed in a big hundred eighty degree arc and swooped back down toward him. It slowed up as it closed on him and he could see the co-pilot motioning him to stop. Screw him.

The three young Cubans stared at the captain, their eyes wide with a combination of exhilaration and fear. Freedom was close, but if they were caught at sea it would be back to Guantanamo and repatriation to Cuba. They would no longer have jobs and face endless government persecution. In a way their very lives were at stake.

They could see the Black Hawk was armed with a machine gun and rocket pods. These days drug smugglers often carried heavy firepower. It could be suicidal to go up against them without defenses.

"Will they shoot?" One of the refugees yelled to the captain, trying to be heard over the outboard whine and chopper blade whup.

No. At least we have that going for us, the captain thought. The tracers from the Cuban beach earlier that morning were still a vivid memory.

This whole situation was so fucked up.

Cuba. Just ninety miles and a half-century back in time from Florida. If he'd gone down there on a pleasure cruise, like so many Americans did, he'd have been welcomed in any of half a dozen ports on the north coast, including Havana. He'd have enjoyed the good rum and cigars, the friendly welcome for tourists, and the museum-like atmosphere of a country whose cars and architecture had never left the 60's. Slip in. Have a good time. Slip out. No one making a fuss at either end.

But now, pick up a few passengers and they shoot at you as you leave. And chase the hell out of you when you try to get home. What a friggin' mess.

Nothing to do now but run for it. He couldn't go up Biscayne Bay from the south. Too many shallow sea grass flats, like the Featherbeds. There was a big risk of running aground. In which case their ass was grass. Same problem with the seaward approaches to Key Biscayne, the closest populated landfall. Off Miami Beach the water was deeper much closer in to shore. He took a straight line heading for South Beach.

The Coast Guard helicopter came around for another pass. This time head to head, lower, directly toward the go-fast's bow. A collision course.

Bull shit, the captain thought. No way they're dumb enough to wreck a multi-million dollar piece of equipment and possibly get themselves killed. He held his heading.

They were closing in on each other at warp speed.

At the last possible second the pilot pulled back on the stick and the chopper banked hard right. The skids on the aircraft missed catching the boat's fiberglass T-top by inches.

In the boat the coyote pissed himself. The refugees let go of the side rails, reflexively covering their heads with their arms, and went caroming around the deck. A few seconds later, realizing they weren't dead, they grabbed back on.

What balls, the chopper pilot thought, with no small amount of admiration. Brass ones, big enough to sink the boat he was driving. Whoever the captain was, he'd called his bluff.

He'd like to have fired a shot across the son of a bitch's bow. But they were too close to shore and bucking procedure. That could cost him his commission.

Instead, as he circled around to take up the pursuit again, he clicked on his helmet mic. It was time to call for reinforcements.

 **Chapter III**

There are, of course, always problems with being the pioneer in a field. Residential development on top of a landfill certainly was no exception. Initially Rogelio had wanted to build a couple of condo towers like the ones he put up on Brickell Avenue. His structural engineers quickly squelched that concept. There was no way the dump would support the weight of huge buildings. And driving pilings deep enough to support the apartment buildings would pierce the layers sealing the bottom of the fill, allowing potential contamination of the underlying groundwater. Although the county appreciated his taking the dump off its hands, they would never go for this. So luxury housing was the solution.

The next problem was that the methane collector wasn't a hundred per cent effective. At least ninety-five per cent of the time there was a breeze blowing across the mesa, usually out of the southeast. But on the rare day when it was dead calm, the development had a distinct odor. Even the paving of the streets and planting of large numbers of flowering shrubs in landscaping couldn't completely cover the smell. It got so that brokers would check the weather report for projected wind speed and direction before taking prospective buyers to tour Mont Basura.

Señor Negro's solution was rather ingenious. At a bankruptcy auction he purchased a small company, Scents of Class, which had produced knock-offs of designer perfumes. With the company's chemist he concocted a not too offensive combination pine and floral mixture. They made gallons of the stuff. Next he purchased a used mosquito control truck. Whenever the weather was calm, the truck circled the development spraying perfume into the atmosphere under the guise of insect control. Several residents commented on how surprisingly wonderful Basura Harbor smelled when the wind didn't blow.

Then there were the animal pests. Rogelio knew what the old pharaoh felt like when the plagues descended on Egypt. First there were the rats, then the snakes and finally the seagulls.

It wasn't exactly big news that rats hung around trash dumps. Rogelio had hoped that the eight feet of cover would bury the problem, but it wasn't like the rodents had anywhere else to go. Besides they could still burrow, and there were places on the sides of the pyramid where they could easily tunnel and reach pay dirt.

Where one species does well in an ecological niche, it is rare that nature doesn't send in another to challenge or exploit it. The snakes from the surrounding marshland found the plump well-fed rats to be an excellent supplement to their diet. The occasional rattler, water moccasin or copperhead gorging on a furry varmint had been a common- place event ever since garbage had started to be dumped on the site.

However, this sight did not sit well with the newest millionaire residents who had recently staked their claim on top of this pre-existing food chain. The new denizens considered the chance to encounter a poisonous snake helping nature take its course an opportunity they would as soon live without. They complained vociferously.

Rogelio turned to nature for the answer. Ferrets. They were better than traps. They could chase rats right down their holes. They were efficient, tenacious exterminators and they worked for what they ate. They were also quick enough and had a broad enough palate that they could branch out and kill some of the smaller snakes. Plus the ferrets you brought from the pet shops were already neutered. That meant they wouldn't proliferate later and become a problem of their own. Two hundred ferrets sprinkled liberally around the top of Mont Basura reduced the ground dwelling pest problem to manageable levels. Best of all, if a ferret were seen scampering across a street or yard, the residents thought it was cute. The animal's reputation secured by one of those warm and fuzzy Disney animal movies.

The seagulls were a problem he was still working on. They too had scavenged the dump when it was still a work in progress. Not being one of the brightest lights in the avian firmament, they still returned to their old feeding grounds. It wasn't just that the birds would swoop into a new east side homeowner's patio when they were trying to enjoy a breakfast with the sunrise, stealing food right off their plates. Or that the same thing happened to west side owners barbecuing and watching the sunset. It was that the damned birds didn't leave after they ate. The flocks of gulls deposited the processed food the same place they acquired it, as well as at other locations atop Mont Basura. He was tired of calls from irate buyers complaining about bird poop on their terraces, patios, Mercedes, Lexuses and luxury sport utilities. With the help of one of those Seminole Indian guys, Rex Panther, Rogelio would again use nature to solve the problem. And, if he were lucky, raise his standing in the community another few notches.

He'd missed one opportunity when he was plotting home sites and it probably cost him at least a million dollars. He shouldn't have put Lindsey Lee at the southeast corner. Sure, she was happy. She had a fabulous view of the Atlantic and Bay to the east, and of Card Sound and the Keys to the south. But he hadn't realized her full marketability as a spokes-model. Location, location, location. Buyers were willing to pay a premium to live near her. Especially after the southern third of the development was voted to be "clothing optional" in the community's new by-laws. As situated, Lindsey Lee's house had one neighbor to the north, one to the west and one diagonally across the street. If he'd given her a site in the center of the development, there would have been eight homes (counting those diagonally located around her) that he could have gotten an extra 100 grand to a quarter mil for. As it was, the three houses around hers offered an interesting trio of success stories.

Diagonally across the street lived Florio Flores, the head of the Colombian flower cartel. It looked like Rogelio Negro wasn't the only one who'd changed his name. Approximately eighty per cent of cut flowers that came into the U.S. passed through Miami. The lion's share of them was grown in Colombia. It wasn't as lucrative as the narcotics trade, but the flowers had made Flores a rich man. And, if once in awhile one of his flower shipments was seized because cocaine was found in it, well that was the price of doing business. No one had ever directly linked the illegal drugs to him. More importantly, he was willing to pay an extra 200 grand just for the privilege of living so close to Lindsey Lee.

The house to her west had been bought by the first round draft pick for the Miami Heat, Hamilton Patrick, also known as "Big Sky." The nickname had dual implications due to the fact that Patrick had played for Montana State University and that he had the best sky hook since Kareem Abdul Jabbar. He had helped lead MSU to the Western Athletic Division conference championship. The W.A.D., derisively known as "Who Are Dey?" was an eight-team conference of second tier state schools in Wyoming, Montana and the Dakotas. A seven-foot three white boy, he had been recruited by Division I-A schools. But he was a country boy, fresh off the farm and he liked the animal husbandry program at MSU.

Now he was the Heat's new hope. They would use Patrick with the established heat center, Riley Leonard, in an effort to duplicate the success the Spurs had with twin towers David Robinson and Tim Duncan.

Unlike the San Antonio situation, where Robinson took Duncan under his wing, The Heat did not expect Leonard to be a mentor. In fact, off the court, management felt that the further Patrick stayed from Leonard the better. Riley "Is it morning already?" Leonard was a scoring threat both on and off the court. His nickname came from the time he was stopped for speeding on McArthur Causeway, coming back from South Beach the morning after a game with the Bulls. He held the unofficial NBA record for most illegitimate offspring. He played great but, as with so many other modern athletes, he was no role model.

When the kid wanted to move into a gated community ten miles south of the lights of the big city, the team was delighted. When he was willing to pay an extra 300 thousand so he could live next door and "maybe get to see the pretty girl naked," it seemed like a good investment. If it kept him away from the fast women, alcohol and drugs on South Beach and in the Grove, he could concentrate on his game.

On the house north of the girl's, Rogelio didn't make an extra nickel. He was surprised when he received the request for the home site. The guy who wanted the place usually wanted to be as close to the action and limelight of the urban center as possible. But he owed Reuben Elias a lot, no pun intended. And if Reuben wanted to live next door to Lindsey Lee, it was the least he could do for an old friend.

Reuben was one of a few people, besides his parents, who knew Rogelio when he was Roger Black. They had roomed together at the University of Florida. In fact, it may have been Reuben's idea to change Black's name to Negro so Roger would have better entree into the Hispanic business community. Reuben had gone on to law school.

By the time Rogelio needed his help Reuben Elias had become pretty good at his chosen profession. After Hurricane Andrew the authorities looked for someone to prosecute, someone to make an example of in hopes that shoddy construction practices would no longer continue. Elias kept Negro out of prison. He managed to deflect prosecutors onto several of Rogelio's subcontractors. He even managed to shift a good deal of blame onto the county itself. The investigation showed that there were multiple instances of building inspectors signing off on houses after being given gifts or envelopes containing cash. If some subcontractors cut corners and inspectors took bribes not to notice, how was Sr. Negro to know? There was no proof that he had provided any of the illegal compensation.

Reuben Elias was best known for his willingness to take cases that seemed to be losers and sometimes win them with extraordinarily outlandish defenses. Perhaps his most famous case was that of the nympho prostitute. The tabloid headline had read, "Hooker Humps John Until He's Gone." Police found a jewelry salesman nude and dead in a Miami Beach hotel room. They found Elias' client in possession of the man's wallet, sample case and credit card, which she had used. The police wanted to charge her with felony murder since the man died during the theft of his valuables.

Elias' defense was unique. He claimed that his client wasn't really a prostitute, just a nymphomaniac. She was just trying to make a living doing something almost everyone really enjoyed. She enjoyed sex—a lot. If the guys she had sex with wanted to give her gifts afterward she wasn't going to be impolite and say no. She claimed she would have intercourse with men for free. In the most recent situation the guy died while she was riding on top, apparently of a heart attack. Otherwise there would still have been a smile on his face. Before they'd started he told her he was going to give her a big gift when they were done. When his heart popped off before he did, she just decided to honor his wishes and take his belongings as gifts. After all he wasn't going to need them anymore.

The prosecution heaped scorn and skepticism on this defense, citing the defendant's previous arrests for solicitation and asking why she had used the victim's credit cards.

Elias's redirect was a masterpiece. She stated that the credit card thing was just for a new wardrobe she was sure the guy would have appreciated. The solicitation charges were just proof that she wanted sex. Reuben asked how often she felt these sexual desires. She responded, having been locked away from men for several weeks, she would like to do the judge and whole jury right there and then. The prosecutor howled an objection. After he demurred her offer, the judge denied the motion. She walked after only fifteen minutes of deliberation. Rumor had it that she did indeed show several jury members her appreciation.

What people didn't know about Rogelio's friend Reuben was that he was also a successful writer—at least after a fashion. During a failed attempt to clear a man whose performing name was Andy the Anaconda from an assault charge, Elias was exposed to the world of professional wrestling. The Anaconda had a special hold that supposedly squeezed his foes into submission. Unfortunately he used it on a police officer outside a bar. Though he didn't save the big snake, he got hooked on the sport. For the last three years Reuben Elias had written scripts and story lines for the pro wrestlers to act out.

Now he wanted to branch out. He had written a screen treatment of the nympho/ prostitute story. He thought maybe Lindsey Lee Olson could play the lead. If not, at least she had Hollywood connections. Maybe she could get someone to give the story a look. Living next door to her would give Elias the opening to show her the script. Rogelio knew not to bet against him.

Mont Basura Harbor was so popular that Rogelio decided to move in himself. He converted the model home on the northeast corner for his own use. Other members of the Hispanic Builders Society told him he was nuts to live in the same place as his customers. He was leaving himself open to all sorts of harassment.

But sitting there on his terrace after sundown, sipping a Cuba Libre, Rogelio felt great. Looking north, he could see the warm orange glow of downtown Miami ten miles away. He'd had a big hand in turning that city into the modern metropolis it had become. It didn't bother him that the orange color came from the sodium vapor in the anti-crime lighting. With progress there was always a trade off.

He was safe perched on top of his secure pyramid. He'd provided a wonderful new environment that made a bunch of rich powerful people very happy. He felt so proud he was starting to think of himself as El Rey de la Montaña—The King of the Mountain. Some people would have put the word Loco before Rey.

It had been a long time since Rogelio had played the children's game, King of the Hill. He didn't remember what the object of the game was, but he would soon be reminded.

Chapter IV

The helicopter had dropped a couple hundred yards behind the speeding boat and seemed to be content to match its speed. No more intimidating passes to try to make it stop.

Drug smugglers would be happy with this situation. Punch holes in the contraband. Dump it overboard. Let it sink in deep water. The evidence is gone.

This was not a feasible solution for those who dealt with human cargo, at least if you were a smuggler with a conscience. And there were those out there who had none, as attested to by the bodies that occasionally washed ashore.

The captain knew that the chopper laying back was not a good sign. A principled man, he would never consider dumping his cargo. He'd do his damnedest to deliver them. He had an idea of what was coming.

So he wasn't surprised when he saw the Coast Guard cutter, its distinctive white hull slashed by a diagonal orange stripe amidships, steaming full speed out of Government Cut, the deep water channel connecting the ocean to the Port of Miami. An impressive sight, it didn't really worry him. There was no way a vessel its size could match his speed or maneuverability.

The two solid orange-colored craft flanking the cutter, then speeding ahead of it, were another story. With their semi-rigid inflatable hulls and twin outboards they were fast. Their air-filled pontoons made them lighter than the solid fiberglass construction of the speedboat, almost making up for their engine power deficit.

The captain knew they were nearly as fast as he was and that they were driven by highly experienced seamen. And there were two of them. It would be some duel.

Looking back over his shoulder he saw the chopper had pulled closer. The pilot was smiling and giving him the finger.

Formulating his plan on the fly, the captain turned his bow toward the space between the stern of the cutter and the end of the channel jetty, which also happened to mark the southernmost point of Miami Beach. At his present speed less than five minutes away.

The two Coast Guard chase boats which had been making a beeline straight toward him suddenly veered apart. Each boat made a rapid half circle turn so that when they converged they were running a parallel course to the speedboat. They moved into his path to intercept, trying to catch him in a pincers move, with one boat along each of his sides.

The captain could see that besides the driver each boat had three sailors carrying sidearms. As the three raced along, the chase boats were trying to squeeze in closer. If any of the sailors managed to jump aboard and put a gun to his head, the game was over. The captain started to zigzag to make them keep their distance. He had less than a mile to go.

Even if he kept them from boarding him, they'd still grab the refugees as soon as he slowed to try to land them. He had to delay them.

As he neared the cutter, the captain zigged hard right, right toward the big boat's stern. The speedboat passed less than ten feet behind the big ship, momentarily going airborne over its wake. The starboard chase boat had to throttle down and veer off in a big circle to the right to avoid slamming into the steel hull.

That left the chaser to port.

The captain motioned for the coyote to come to him at the helm. The man quickly staggered over, the captain bent toward him as if to talk directly into his ear.

The whiny little coward was more trouble than he was worth. He'd bitched the whole trip south, nearly gotten shot off the Cuban beach, and then wet his pants when the Coast Guard showed up. He picked the little bastard up by his life vest and tossed him over the starboard rail.

 **Chapter V**

The damn seagulls had to be dealt with. The residents were really pissed. Most of the people who lived on the Mont had earned their fortunes one way or another. They'd fought their way to the top and they'd arrived. Their cars were an expression of their success. Shit on their Jag or Rolls and it was almost like shitting right on them. People in South Florida took their cars personally. You dis' them in their cars and they often took a shot at you. The seagulls had to go.

He consulted the same biologist who'd given him the ferret idea. It turned out what he needed was a bird of prey, one of the raptors: an eagle, a falcon or a hawk. The problem was there wasn't any readily available source of these animals. Plus you needed both state and federal permits to keep them. That's when Rogelio thought about the Seminoles living in the Glades. They'd probably be able to get a couple of the birds for him.

He called Mitchell Gold, the lobbyist who'd helped him push through some zoning variances he'd needed from the county. Mitch also did lobbying with the state for the Indians, something to do with water rights and gaming problems. It was Mitch who hooked him up with Rex Panther.

The one thing Mitch told him was to get his story straight. Panther wasn't a Seminole. The Seminoles had been forcibly removed from Florida in the 1800s. Panther was a Miccosukee and didn't take kindly to people who didn't know the difference. His people were some of the last Native American descendants left in the state. They took pride in the fact that they had never been captured by, nor surrendered to, the federal government.

Gold had arranged for Panther to meet Negro at his office in the development's community center. The meeting was set for 9:00 am on Monday.

Promptly at nine there was a rap on his office door. Rogelio opened it and was momentarily surprised by what he saw.

"What the heck kind of Indian is this?" he thought to himself. The man before him wore a gray silk Armani suit, what appeared to be a custom shirt and Bally shoes. He was just over six feet tall with a tan, rugged look and razor cut hair worn slicked back. He looked more like a Mafia Don. The only fashion acknowledgement of Miccosukee heritage was a small finely beaded necklace in place of a tie.

"Good morning. I'm Rex Panther," smiled the man, showing a perfect set of capped teeth. "Behind me is my brother, William," he said extending his hand.

William was more like what Rogelio expected. He was about the same height as Rex, but was wearing a denim shirt with the sleeves rolled up, worn jeans and beat up work boots. The only article of clothing he had in common was a similar beaded necklace. This is how Rogelio felt someone coming out of the Everglades should look.

"Good morning, Rex. Nice to meet you, Billy."

"It's William."

"He don't like Billy. Thinks it's a patronizing thing the white man uses to put the red man in his place," Rex explained.

"Sorry, William. No harm intended," Rogelio replied. "Please sit down." He motioned to two leather chairs in front of his desk.

The brothers each took a seat.

"You got a lotta people going nowhere fast out there," William commented.

It took Rogelio a second to understand what he meant. Then he realized that they'd walked by the health club on the way to his office.

"Yeah. In fact, we just added five more stationary bikes and four Stairmasters. When we made the southern third of this place clothing optional a lot of residents wanted to get in better shape. Funny thing is that it's the 'clothing-on' bunch that're doing most of the exercise. What can I get you guys to drink—coffee, juice, bottled water?"

"No thanks," they replied in unison.

"Mitch Gold said you have a problem we might be able to help you with," Rex said.

Rogelio explained all the bitching he was hearing about the damn seagulls crapping on everybody's luxury rides. Then he detailed the plan for using birds of prey to reduce the seagull population naturally.

"Rich people and their fancy cars," William commented.

"You know, you could keep that Navigator a lot cleaner," Rex pointed out, referring to the black Lincoln SUV that William chauffeured for him.

"It's just a tricked up truck."

"He doesn't understand the image thing," Rex said to Rogelio. "I'm not sure how we can help you. It's not like we can just go out and catch some hawks and eagles and give them to you. There's permit problems and besides they aren't that easy to catch."

Of course Rex knew what the problem was before the meeting started. He was just trying to milk the moment because eventually he would want something in return.

"Well, Mitchell said that you might have a solution. Maybe he was wrong." Rogelio knew he was being worked, but figured he'd give the Miccosukee another opening.

"Perhaps there is one way."

Rogelio arched his right eyebrow in response.

"You know they're expanding the science museum," Rex continued.

"Yeah, so?"

"To make room for more hands-on stuff and computer simulations they've got to take out some of the older exhibits. One of them is their raptor rehab center. It was a place people could bring injured hawks and such. The museum wildlife staff would repair the ones they could and then turn them loose. With the popularity of all the new electronic shit, the natural stuff has to go. So the birds are out of there."

"So I could take over the rehab program and put the birds to work."

"Not quite that easy. See we've already made arrangements to move the center to our operation on Tamiami Trail. It'll be a good addition to the alligator show and the Glades animal exhibits. It's a natural fit to what we already have. And it's good P.R. for us to help out the museum and fix up the poor birdies."

"Couldn't I just borrow them for awhile?" Rogelio asked.

"Well, we haven't moved them yet. I suppose we could say that we're building a state of the art facility and it won't be ready for, say about ten months."

"But we're ready for them now. We've got everything all set up," William jumped in.

"Yeah, yeah. But we don't have to let anyone know. We're trying to do our friend Rogelio here a favor. We let people know he's graciously offered to house the animals while we put the finishing touches on our set up. They'll have their own aerie here on top of the mountain. More favorable publicity for Señor Negro."

"It's not good for the birds to keep moving them around," William complained.

"They'll live," Rex shot back.

William glared at his brother. The man had no respect for the animals.

"Sounds fine to me. I'll talk to my biologist and we can probably set up a suitable temporary enclosure within a couple of weeks."

"Fine," Rex smiled.

Rogelio decided to get right to the point. He knew Panther was an operator. He wasn't doing this favor out of the goodness of his heart.

"For this assistance you're giving me, what can I do for you?"

"You own the land there east to the shoreline, right?"

"Yes. It's about a quarter mile from the base of the development to the water. I'm not giving you all that land just for borrowing a couple of birds."

"No, of course not. I just want you to listen to a business proposition I have for you."

"Go ahead."

"As you know, the tribe owns a large bingo hall near Ft. Lauderdale. And we have the big new casino out in the Everglades, the so-called big gamble in the swamp. Both of them are doing quite well. But we'd like to consider expanding our holdings."

"What'd you have in mind? Where do I come in?" Rogelio asked.

"How'd you like to be partners? We'll develop that strip of land into a waterfront resort with a marina and casino."

"No offense, chief, but what've you been smoking? There's no way to pull that off. The state don't allow casinos and the feds won't allow you to change the shoreline, the mangrove trees are protected."

"Mr. Negro, you and your kind have been exploiting the native peoples for over 400 years. We've learned a few things, like how to use the system. It's time for you to start thinking like a member of the tribe."

Rogelio ignored the comment about the Spanish exploitation of Indians. He didn't think that confessing that he wasn't really Hispanic and that all his ancestors had emigrated within the last 75 years was really cogent to the present discussion.

"How would a member of the tribe get around these problems?" he asked.

"First of all, you transfer ownership of the land to the Miccosukee nation. This can be done either for monetary consideration or for a percentage interest in the resort. I figure with your history in development and with a casino on site, you'll go for the percentage."

"I'm beginning to get the picture. You turn the land into a reservation, right?"

"That's the idea. Federal law basically recognizes native reservation land like that of a sovereign nation. Essentially we become like our own country within U.S. borders. Kind of like the Vatican in the middle of Rome. Once we designate the property as reservation land, we can develop it any way we want. How do you think we put that casino in the middle of the Everglades?"

"So you can build your casino and alter the shoreline any way you want."

"Right. That's one reason bay front property is so desirable. We can clear the mangroves, put in a beach and dockage for yachts. Make a more upscale type property. With the rich folks living here on your mountain it'll already have fancy neighbors."

"You mess with the shoreline and the tree huggers and gator lovers will be looking to nail your hide to the wall. Plus the people up here aren't going to want their view ruined," Rogelio pointed out.

"We've dealt with the environmentalists before. They're not easy but we can handle them. After all we're the original conservationists. As for the view, proper architecture and landscaping will enhance it."

"We could offer yacht club privileges to my development people."

"Now you're beginning to see the potential, thinking like a modern Indian. Give the White man what he wants and charge him well for it. Everyone is happy."

"This is unreal," William, who'd been observing quietly the whole time, had had enough. "You're talking about ripping out mangroves, the hatcheries and nurseries for so many marine species. You're going to put in a marina. That means dredging. Tearing up the bay bottom and turtle grass, more pollution. I want no part of this. Rex, you're not only trying to take advantage of them, you're becoming one of them."

"William, I bring you along because you are my brother, next in line to head the tribe should something happen to me. But you seem to have no idea of the burden I bear looking out for the welfare of our people. Your natural ways will not put food on our tables nor provide money to educate our children."

"So we sell tax-free cigarettes on our reservations, cut-rate cancer for nicotine addicts. We open casinos for the risk takers who are too stupid to know that in the long run the house always wins. Help the losers stay losers."

"We've had these arguments before. Nobody makes them come to us. If we didn't provide these options someone else would. And, if we have an advantage doing it, then good for us and our people."

"And if we exploit the weak and addicted so be it," William remarked sarcastically.

"Most of them don't see themselves that way and would be offended at the description. William, it's just business."

"Bad business. I'm going for a walk. I need some fresh air."

William stood and walked to the door.

"Come back in about an hour," Rex called out. "We've got some details to work out."

William slammed the door.

"Rex, your brother doesn't seem to have your vision. Is he going to screw this project up before it even gets started?"

"No. He doesn't have the stomach for the business and political decisions. He'd rather be out in the swamp somewhere. The tribe will back me. They all like getting their dividend checks from our business enterprises."

"If it's not too nosy, how much do they get?" Rogelio was naturally curious about how successful the Indians' operations were.

"Each member over age 16 gets a share. Right now that's a little over 500 people. Last year's pay out was a little over $31,000 each. And that doesn't include the salaries they earn working at our sites."

"Impressive. You take care of your people well. As chief, do you get a larger share?"

"I do well enough. Most of my income comes as CEO of the casino operation."

"I won't ask anymore. You know we're still going to get a lot of heat from the county commission."

"Don't worry about it. We'll be bringing jobs to an economically depressed part of the county. They've never completely recovered from Andrew down here. Mitch is a good lobbyist. He'll be able to sell it to them. And if we need some extra convincing, the members of my tribe would be willing to contribute a hundred bucks each to the campaign chests of undecided commissioners. They know you gotta spend money to make money. Do the math and it comes out to about 50 grand. We're sort of like our own PAC."

"I can see I'll have to join the tribe."

"No problem. We're a democratic group. We elect new members, no blood relation necessary."

Rogelio smiled. He could work with this man. He appreciated someone who could see an opportunity and make something concrete happen. He'd had no trouble becoming Hispanic and he would have no trouble becoming a Miccosukee.

They got down to listing the details necessary to make the project go. Each would take the list to their own lawyers to make sure they weren't getting screwed.

*   *   *

After slamming the door, William walked down the hallway past the spa. There were still at least a dozen people walking or climbing nowhere. It was a beautiful day, temperature in the 70's, with the same high cumulus clouds billowing like a fleet being blown in off the ocean by a ten-knot southeast breeze. It was the kind of conditions they pushed in all the advertising to bring the tourists to Florida. Yet William knew that if he waited and watched the people come out after they finished their exercise more than half would be getting into a car to drive home. This, even though none of them lived more than three quarters of a mile from the health club and it was optimum weather for a walk outdoors.

He decided to kill time by taking a stroll through the development. He started south on the appropriately named Bayside Boulevard. This was indeed a place for rich people only. In some ways it was beyond his comprehension.

Admittedly the landscaping was beautiful and lush. There was an assortment of palms, varied species of hibiscus, every color of bougainvillea, and other native flowering shrubs, all precisely arranged on neatly manicured lawns. Definitely a big improvement over an open mound of garbage. But, to someone used to nature's helter-skelter arrangement of flora in the marshes and hammocks of the Everglades, where the discovery of a flowering wild orchid in the arms of a mossy bald cypress is a pleasant surprise, the order here was too regimented. William didn't like life to be so well planned.

Then there were the houses. He viewed them with a mixture of awe and disgust. The small ones had a good six thousand square feet of living space. Most were a variation on Mediterranean style with tile roofs, stucco finishes, brass or iron lamps used for exterior lighting. There were a few ultra-modern ones with big windows that took advantage of the light. They were painted white with bright basic color accents. They appeared to be well constructed. Most of them were occupied by singles or couples, very few by families with children.

While his older brother embraced the glitz and the ritz, the younger Panther didn't comprehend it. What did one or two people need with six, ten even fifteen thousand square feet of house? When a house got that big did you own it or did it own you? Just maintaining a living space that large was a continuous project. Of course most of the houses had staffs to take care of them. But to William, a house staff was just something more to worry about. One or two generations ago, most of the Miccosukees lived in chickees, raised platforms with thatched roofs and no walls. It was a much simpler life and William still kept a chickee in the River of Grass.

About ten minutes into his walk William reached a ten-foot tall ficus hedge that appeared to stretch east to west across the complete width of the development. The sidewalk he was on angled sharply to the left through a leafy tunnel in the hedge. At the entrance to the tunnel a small sign was discreetly posted at eye level. It read "Clothing Optional Beyond this Point. If nudity offends you proceed no further."

William went through the hedge. A body was nothing to be ashamed of, clothing or not. Miccosukees generally were not into so called "naturism." They had nothing against nature. In fact they were in favor of it. But, between insects and saw grass, a Miccosukee found it prudent to keep most of his body covered. William thought most people looked better dressed, clothing covered a multitude of sins and the natural wear and tear that a body goes through as it's used throughout life. But seeing a naked one wasn't going to offend him.

The ficus tunnel was only about fifteen feet long and opened with a sharp angle to the right. When William emerged he felt disappointed. He laughed at himself. The houses and landscaping were similar to the other side of the hedge. But he had half expected there to be an au naturel greeter to meet him coming out of the hedge. He felt let down when there wasn't and then realized how ludicrous the idea was.

He continued on his path down the boulevard. Soon enough he reached the southeast corner, and, although he didn't know it, Lindsey Lee Olsen's house.

There he finally saw his first naked person. Standing at the door to Lindsey's house was a man holding two large bouquets. It was a backside view, but, even with the flowers, it wasn't pretty. The guy had saggy cheeks and William wasn't seeing the ones on his face. Although the guy was balding, nature had been much more liberal with hair for the rest of his body. There was enough black fur on his back to qualify as an SPF 15 for sun protection. There wasn't quite enough to style, but certainly enough to brush into a pattern, which somehow the guy had apparently managed to do.

William could hear the house's doorbell chiming, but hadn't seen the man pushing the button. It reminded him of the old joke about New York cabbies—If they drive gesturing with both hands, what are they steering the car with? He didn't want to take that thought any further regarding pushing the doorbell button.

What he was watching was an almost daily ritual. Florio Flores, in an effort to make an impression on his beautiful neighbor, would have arrangements made from the freshest of his flower imports and try to present them to her. Initially she had graciously accepted them. But after two straight weeks of daily deliveries by the naked florist, she had gotten tired of it. She really had no interest in seeing him socially, or nude, and told him so. However, like a persistent schoolboy he kept bringing the flowers anyway. When she stopped answering the bell, he left the arrangements in front of her door. He hoped she would eventually realize in what high esteem he held her and decide to go out with him.

William didn't know about any of this. He saw Flores squat down to place the flowers against the front door and decided he didn't want to be there when he turned around. He quickly cut between Reuben and Lindsey's houses, staying on Lindsey's property. Behind the house he came out on a verdant lawn with a three-foot Barbados cherry hedge bordering the top edge of the trash pyramid.

He had to admit to himself that the view from the heights was impressive. South Biscayne Bay and the Atlantic to his left and the Florida Keys stretching out straight ahead—it was indeed an awesome sight. No wonder, that in spite of all the problems in South Florida, you couldn't keep more damn people from flooding into the state. His thoughts were interrupted by a woman's voice.

"Excuse me, are you one of the landscape maintenance crew?"

William looked to his right. There was a large limestone paved terrace surrounding a swimming pool. There was a woman sitting in a chaise lounge beneath a big blue and white striped umbrella. She was wearing a broad-brimmed straw hat, sunglasses and a one-piece navy blue tank suit.

"No Ma'am."

"Well then who are you and what are you doing in my backyard?" Her tone wasn't nasty or imperious, just one of somebody looking for an answer.

"My name's William Panther, and I was just enjoying the view."

"Pretty spectacular isn't it? Is that why you came back here on private property, for the view?"

"No." He walked over closer to her as he explained about the hairy, naked man with the flowers. He mentally appraised her while he was talking. She was a beautiful woman with an athletic figure, blond hair and penetrating green eyes that he saw as she lowered her sunglasses to evaluate him. Despite sitting outside on her terrace, she was barely tan. Obviously she spent most of her time in the shade.

"That's Florio. He lives across the street and brings me flowers every day even though I told him to stop. And believe me, the front side is no better than the back. You didn't miss anything. You really don't know who I am?" she asked.

He answered honestly, "No. I feel like maybe I've seen you somewhere before, but I don't know who you are."

"You watch much TV or go to the movies?" She was trying to help jog his memory.

"I don't go to movies very often. Occasionally I'll watch the news or a sports event."

"Maybe you've read Playboy or watch the junk sports on cable."

"Don't have much use for those so-called men's magazines." But her prodding had finally rung a bell for him. He broke out in a big grin.

"You were that girl quarterback on that flag football team." The memory of her in the thong uniform was what had made him smile. "You were a pretty good passer." Diplomatically, he left the "for a girl" part unsaid.

"What's your name? Did they pay you enough money for playing flag football that you could afford a house up here?" he asked.

She found his combination of directness and naiveté refreshing. Now that she was famous, men were rarely straightforward with her. They were either literally almost drooling over her because they wanted her physically, like Florio. Or they were trying to finesse her, using her status for their financial gain, like Rogelio.

"I don't play flag football any more. My name's Lindsey Lee Olson."

There was no recognition on William's part.

"I'm an actress now."

"I don't think I've seen you in anything."

Lindsey had no illusions about the quality of her roles. It wasn't Shakespeare. It was actually a favorable commentary on William's taste that he hadn't seen any of her work.

"Well acting pays the bills a lot better than football did."

It was her turn to evaluate him. Obviously he was from one of the local Indian tribes. The high cheekbones, straight black hair and dark brown eyes that held her in a steady gaze were clues enough. The beaded necklace was the clincher. He was what would be termed ruggedly handsome, different from those body-conscious narcissistic actors she spent time with. She figured he was about four or five years older than she.

"What tribe are you from and what brings you to the top of the trash heap?" she could also be direct.

"I'm Miccosukee. My brother is president of the tribe. He's here working on a deal with Señor Negro. We're going to help him set up a raptor rehabilitation center here." He was ashamed of their plan to rape the nearby shoreline and didn't mention it.

"That doesn't sound like Rogelio. What's in it for him?"

This young woman is sharp, William thought to himself.

"You know Señor Negro?"

"We go way back. He started the flag football league you saw me playing in. But I knew him even before that. I got this house on top of the heap for helping him promote his development. He wouldn't be doing the bird thing unless he saw some benefit to it."

"Well, there's the obvious benefit to the birds. And it's good public relations for the top of the heap," he replied, borrowing her term for the development.

"Listen, I'm involved in animal rights work and it's wonderful to rehab the big birds. In fact, if you need any help, I'd be glad to chip in. But that's not enough for Rogelio. As we say in the acting biz, what's his real motivation?"

"The truth. The seagulls that used to scavenge the dump are still coming back. Apparently they're leaving excessive amounts of guano on the precious luxury vehicles of your neighbors. The idea is that hawks and ospreys will scare them off."

She smiled at his obvious distaste for the foibles of the wealthy. She was beginning to like William. When she thought about it, it seemed like she was spending an extra amount of time hosing off her Jeep Wrangler. But it didn't bother her. Birds, like every other living creature, had to dump their waste somewhere.

"That's more like Rogelio. But you and I both know that they won't just scare the gulls away, they'll take a lot of them out. I don't like this pitting one species against another."

"It's better than indiscriminate use of poisoned bait. Besides nature is always pitting one species against another," William said pragmatically.

"Then we should let nature do the pitting, not man."

Without knowing, he had hit one of her animal rights hot buttons. She was ready to give him one of her lectures about what right did man have playing God and making decisions for other species.

They would have clashed. He would have pointed out that even the decision to leave other species alone was still a decision that affected their existence. In a way it was just like a lioness deciding which antelope in the herd she was going to kill and then deciding she wasn't hungry enough to hunt yet. Maybe a cheetah would end up eating the antelope the lioness had selected. Species would still interact, just in different ways. Mankind was after all just another species, though with planetary dominance. It was impossible for humans to exist without interaction with the hosts of other species.

Before they could even start their discussion they were interrupted.

"Lindsey, is that man bothering you? Should I call security?" It was Reuben Elias. He'd been sitting on his terrace working on a screenplay for Lindsey to star in. He found it inspirational to view her while he was typing. So whenever he saw her reading on her terrace or swimming in her pool, he'd grab his laptop, move out to his patio and work on his story for her.

Lindsey wasn't thrilled about being Reuben's muse. But she wasn't going to hide inside and avoid him and he'd never tried anything with her. Eventually she got used to seeing him.

Reuben had seen the Indian come into the backyard and had seen him strike up a conversation with her. He didn't recognize the man. After watching this admittedly good- looking stranger talk to her for at least ten minutes, he began to get jealous. That's when he decided to butt in.

William turned around to see a man striding toward them. This one looked to be in his mid-fifties, tall and thin, sort of chicken-chested, with a full silver mane of hair and a salt and pepper beard. As he got closer, William recognized him. On the news the man was always wearing a three-piece suit and representing some scumbag or weirdo with a novel or twisted legal defense. Now he was just in his birthday suit, representing no one but himself.

"Mr. Elias, Miss Olson and I were just having a conversation."

Reuben smiled. He was always pleased when somebody recognized him.

"He's right, Reuben. There's no problem. This is William Panther of the Miccosukee tribe. They're going to help Rogelio set up a raptor rehab center up here."

"Oh. The seagull thing. Pleased to meet you, Mr. Panther."

Reuben reached out and they shook hands. Here William was, shaking the hand of a locally famous, eccentric, naked lawyer in the backyard of a movie star he'd just met. Who said the rich and famous were no different. William didn't think the situation could get anymore surreal.

Of course he was wrong. Lindsey Lee could have predicted what would happen next because it seemed to happen almost every time Reuben Elias set foot on her terrace to speak with her.

William had hardly unclasped hands with Reuben when he heard something come running up behind him. As he turned, the first impression he had looking over his right shoulder was of an approaching sweaty, giant, red, praying mantis wearing a jock strap and tennis shoes. Since he did occasionally watch sporting events, William quickly realized it was the Heat's new center/forward, Hamilton Patrick.

It turned out that, as part of his conditioning program, Hamilton would run laps up and down the side of the trash pyramid. He wore the tennis shoes to protect his feet and the jock to keep his male equipment from slapping and flapping as he jogged.

William could see the practicality of the outfit. He often wondered why nature had designed man so his favorite and most sensitive parts were hung out where they could so easily be traumatized. He also thought the kid should be buying sunscreen in five gallon buckets. Judging from the almost white buzz cut hair and the ice blue eyes, Hamilton was one of those melanin challenged individuals who would never tan. With sun exposure his color options would always be pink, red or redder.

Lindsey was happy that Patrick was at least wearing the jock strap; otherwise William would have seen another reason that the appellation Big Sky was appropriate. It was like clock work. If Reuben stepped into her yard to talk to her, Hamilton would usually show up within minutes and vice-versa. And even though she always came outside clothed, hoping they would get the idea and follow suit, they always showed up nude or close to it. They were like a couple of jealous mongrel dogs, trying to win the favors of an alpha bitch. The way they acted and the way they were undressed she wouldn't have been that surprised to see them sniffing around on her shrubbery trying to mark their territory.

"Hey Lindsey, what's going on? Who's the guy in the clothes?" Hamilton puffed, still breathing hard from his hill climbing.

Despite the fact she couldn't keep him off her terrace, Lindsey still liked the big farm boy. He reminded her of a Labrador puppy, klutzy, easy going and trying hard to please. She introduced William and filled Patrick in on the plans for the raptor center.

"Cool. You know. I took a lot of animal science courses in college. Maybe I could help," he responded showing genuine interest.

In spite of the fact that his initial question had made him feel like the odd man out for being dressed, William appreciated the ballplayer's enthusiasm for the project. He'd figure some way to include both Patrick and Lindsey in his plans.

He also couldn't help thinking that, of the three people here he was talking to, only one would look really good naked, and she was the only one dressed. Those were the breaks.

Lindsey looked at the three men around her and wondered if things would ever change. She'd had trouble with males of the species since she was a young girl. As early as sixth grade she'd had to start fending off the boys. By high school she was classifying men into two groups: those who wanted to get into her pants and those who put her on a pedestal and worshipped her. With stardom she had expanded her thinking to include a third group of men who wanted to use her fame for their gain, like Reuben. But there were also still members of the second group, like Patrick. Her father was the only male figure who had treated her like a person. He knew there were brains under his daughter's beauty. He also encouraged her athletically, even teaching her to throw the football. But her parents had broken up in her sophomore year and her father had moved to the west coast, leaving her mother full custody. She was pretty much left to learn to handle men on her own. Her main way of coping turned out to be avoidance. She submerged herself into athletics and her studies. She got a full tuition scholarship to the University of Florida for playing volleyball. This was where she met Roger Black.

Throughout her life, Lindsey Lee Olson had never had a steady boyfriend. In fact she rarely dated. The truth was that the woman who had played football on TV in a thong bikini, who had appeared nude in a spread for Playboy, who had played a lifeguard in a TV show that helped sell millions of provocative posters and calendars, and who was probably America's hottest female sex symbol, was still a virgin.

She hoped that someday this would change. It was so hard for someone in her position to even look for the right man. Beauty, fame and fortune were wonderful things to have. But they forced her to be suspicious of the motives of the men she met.

Someone who didn't know who she was, who wasn't overwhelmed by her looks and who wasn't consumed by the acquisition of wealth was all she was looking for, just someone who would get to know her for her. She looked at William and had the brief hope that maybe "that someone" had just stumbled into her backyard.

She realized she had zoned out when she looked at the men again and they were all staring at her as if awaiting an answer.

"What was the question?" she asked.

"We were just trying to decide what would be the best location up here to put the rehab facility," Patrick replied. "I thought maybe that bare strip of land on the other side of my place would be good."

"That's a right-of-way for an emergency exit road Rogelio's supposed to build. Right now there's only one way up and down off our little mountain," Reuben put in.

"It's only a temporary facility, till we get the one in the Glades finished," William added.

"You mean till the gulls are no longer a problem," Lindsey said. "Still the far south end here without a privacy hedge would be much quieter with less traffic to bother the birds."

"I'll suggest it to Rex and Rogelio when I get back to the clubhouse," William said.

"You mean Rex is here talking to Negro right now?" Reuben asked.

"Yeah, he's my older brother. I drive him to some of his meetings."

Reuben Elias knew who the political and economic powers were in South Florida. He knew the kind of hustler Rex Panther was.

"Nothin' personal, William. And not that saving the birds isn't important. But what's your brother doing here? This seems like the kind of thing that, to tell the truth, he wouldn't be that interested in. A small something he'd delegate to someone else to handle."

William wasn't a very good liar. Besides that he didn't like what Rex was scheming and didn't feel like covering for him.

"My brother's cooking up something with Rogelio."

"Like what?" both Lindsey and Reuben asked.

William described the creation of the new reservation immediately followed by the development of the casino resort.

"That son of a bitch. There's nothing Rogelio won't do for enough money," Lindsey said with disgust.

"Slick too. His archeologist has already verified that historically this was once an Indian habitation site. Gives Rex a claim for tribal lands when he changes it to a reservation," Reuben observed.

"Damn. How can he just go in and tear out all those trees, destroy that habitat?" Patrick threw in his two-cents worth. He was still a country kid at heart. The scrubby, flat mangrove coast was a long way from the forests and mountains of Montana. But it was still the most natural thing in these parts and the young man felt nature had to be protected.

Reuben may actually have been the most upset. True he had saved Rogelio after the Andrew disaster. But then he had felt that it wasn't fair that Rogelio had been singled out for prosecution. They weren't the best houses in the world, but they were ones more people could afford. He could justify his defense to himself.

But even Reuben had a sense of ethics and morality. Sure he defended what society would call the oddballs and the losers. He at least partially believed in his successful nymphomaniac defense. He was actually shocked when his Internet intoxification defense failed for the sixteen-year-old girl facing the attempted murder charge. If you left a young mind unsupervised, allowing hours of viewing violent hate group websites day after day, how could it not be warped? These were the kind of people who needed him. If he weren't there, who would defend them? They'd get an overworked, underpaid public defender who would look at their case for an hour and plead them out. He truly believed that everyone deserved the best defense available.

To hear that his old friend was considering the deliberate rape of the shoreline pissed him off. And a casino. It was bad enough that the state was sucking money out of poor people's pockets with the lottery. A casino was just another option for the people who could least afford to lose money. Reuben could feel the acid in his stomach eating a new ulcer.

"I'll talk him out of this," Reuben said.

"Fat chance," Lindsey responded.

Reuben knew she was right. It'd be easier trying to snatch a bone out of the mouth of a pit bull.

"It's time for me to get back," William said.

He got the phone numbers of the three neighbors and promised to keep in touch about the rehab facility and with any news he could scrounge on the plans for the casino.

He headed back north toward the clubhouse.

 **Chapter VI**

The little bastard skipped across the ocean's surface like a flat rock across the ripples in a pond. Of course at close to sixty knots he was moving a little faster when he started, but he landed on his back and the life jacket had cushioned a lot of his ride.

The port chase boat slowed and changed course to pick up the man who'd gone overboard. Just as the captain knew they would. After all, the Coast Guard's primary mission was to preserve life at sea. And the captain really had nothing personal against them. In fact in other times they'd come to his aid. They just didn't see eye to eye on this refugee thing.

He'd delayed the two pursuers. But not for long.

He turned the boat toward the beach, decreasing his speed as he cut inside the warning buoys that were supposed to separate swimmers from boaters. He shifted the props into reverse long enough to bring the boat to a stop parallel to shore, right off of famous Ocean Drive.

"This is as close as I can come. Over you go," he said as he headed for the port side.

"Gracias," each man said as he jumped into the water.

"Por nada. Buena suerte mis amigos," he murmured, not even loud enough for them to hear.

The pursuit boats were nearing fast. It would be a very close contest on whether or not they made it to shore. He'd hoped they'd get to the beach, be welcomed ashore by the tourists and bought beers and T-shirts at the Clevelander Hotel's outdoor bar, like the group three weeks ago.

But he couldn't wait around to find out. He aimed his bow east and mashed the three throttles full forward again.

Good luck my friends.

The captain set his course for Bimini, the nearest point in the Bahamas. The chase boats didn't follow. They wanted the refugees.

The chopper followed for a little while. But, low on fuel, it had to return to base. As it banked back westward, the speedboat captain returned the one finger salute.

In less than an hour, he was pulling the boat into the channel at South Bimini. He'd tie up at a Bahamian fishing buddy's dock on one of the canals, walk to the airstrip and hook a ride back to Miami.

In a couple of weeks he'd fly back with parts and repair his boat. Then he'd bring her home.

He was going to catch hell from his sister for dumping his nephew overboard. But the little wimp needed a lesson to make him a man.

 **Chapter VII**

Rex and Rogelio's timing for the land deal and site designation as a reservation turned out to be impeccable. What little mention there was of it was in a small article on page nine of the local section of the Herald.

It wasn't that they had connections with the media and could suppress unfavorable coverage. It just happened that their questionable machinations took place during the so-called "second coming" and their story, like any other taking place in South Florida at the time, was considered much less newsworthy.

To understand the "second coming" one has to understand some of the unique cultural and legal aspects of the Miami area. In this situation, most of the points revolved around the special character of the local Cuban-heritage population.

First of all, Miami was one of the few American cities where local politicians needed to have a foreign policy platform. The platform had only one plank--being as anti-Castro as possible. If you were more vehemently against Fidel Castro than your opponent, then the Cuban American population carried you through at the polls.

The second aspect was the practice in Hispanic, not just Cuban, society of naming male children Jesus. Pronounced "HEY ZOOS", it was not an uncommon name for Cuban boys. In fact there was the old joke that if a born-again Christian really wanted to find Jesus all he had to do was come down to the corner on S.W. 8th St., aka Calle Ocho, in Miami's

Little Havana section and yell the name. He would likely get several responses.

Thirdly, there was the unique U.S. government policy regarding Cuban refugees, the wet foot-dry foot policy. It was played like an obscene game of hide-and-seek. The refugees would try to make it to base (dry land), where they would be allowed to stay. But if the Coast Guard or Immigration people caught them while they were still at sea, wet foot, then they were repatriated to Cuba.

Finally, with the large Catholic influence in the Cuban population, there was the habit of reading religious inferences into the sometime miraculous tales of survival that arriving Cuban rafters told.

These things combined to color and influence the events around the "second coming."

It started on a bright Wednesday morning on Miami Beach in the hip Deco district along Ocean Drive. A high-fashion photographer, known professionally only as Al, was working with a group of models on the beach at 12th St. He was momentarily distracted from arranging his lighting by the sound of a helicopter and powerboats close to the shore. When he turned he saw the Coast Guard chopper and two high-speed inflatable boats pursuing three men through the surf. He swung his camera around and started shooting.

The images he captured would end up on the front page of every major newspaper and news magazine in the country.

The first pictures showed the three thin, bearded young men reaching and staggering across a sandbar a hundred yards offshore. This was where the legal controversy would arise. It was low tide and some of the sandbar was completely exposed. The question would be whether or not they had stepped on this part and did this then qualify as a dry foot situation that would allow them to stay.

The rest of the photos showed how the two inflatables, in a pincering movement, came around the sandbar. And how the Coast Guardsmen captured the three refugees before they could reach the beach. The last shot was of the two boats headed out to a cutter standing offshore in deeper water.

If the Coast Guard ship hadn't developed engine trouble, perhaps the situation would never have gotten out of control. It could have headed out to sea and turned south toward Guantanamo to return the three men to Cuba. Unfortunately the ship ended up having to put in for repairs at the Coast Guard base on Government Cut, at the tip of South Beach. This was less than fifteen blocks, as the crow flies, from where the three men had tried to come ashore.

Then there was the vacationing Colombian couple who had been making out in the murky wave backwash near shore as the two inflatables swept in to cut off their targets. They both said that the lead man cried out, "Somos Jesus, Pedro y Pablo. Por favor. Libertad!"

That was the caption that ran under Al's photo. The media almost all used the same picture, the close up of the men coming off the sandbar, their feet barely wet, like they were walking on water.

Jesus, Peter and Paul, the master and the two disciples struggling toward land, asking for freedom and ending up as captives of the U.S. government. It was like hitting a jackpot on one of those big multi-million dollar slot machines in Vegas. The media, the militant anti-Castro groups and the religious fanatics all lined up seeing a big payoff.

The anti-Castro groups, being the best organized and the most sympathetic to incoming refugees were there first. They blockaded the Coast Guard base by land and water. They brought traffic on MacArthur Causeway to a standstill, cutting off the southernmost access to South Beach. They ringed the docks of the base with a flotilla of around a hundred small boats.

The media wasn't far behind. With the traffic tie-up cutting off the broadcast trucks, they came by helicopter and boat. There were even a couple of small time free-lancers on jet skis.

The trifecta was completed the next morning when The Miami Herald ran its front page with the "Second Coming?" banner headline and Al's photo. The religious zealots came by every mode available from foot and rowboat to chartered yacht and the new blimp, shared by several fundamentalist Christian denominations. It was known as the Ark and capable of flashing religious messages to participants at outdoor rallies. Some went to the Coast Guard base and some kept a vigil on the beach at 12th Street.

An understanding of "Cuban time" explained the vigil on South Beach. Castro's revolution sent this country a large group of people who knew how to work hard, play hard and get the most enjoyment out of life. Unfortunately in a certain percentage of this group there is a trait, certainly not bragged about but nonetheless readily acknowledged by the group as a whole, of not being able to arrive at a planned meeting on time. When planning a social function that includes written invitations these people are often sent a notice that shows the starting time as one or two hours earlier. This is so they don't arrive on "Cuban time." The vigil, which lasted four days, was being held with the hope that perhaps some of the other ten disciples would just be showing up a little late. To the believers' great disappointment no one else ever came. When they gave up at the beach, they moved over to the blockade around the Coast Guard station.

Among the religious protestors was Barry, the estranged son of the lobbyist Mitch Gold. In denouncing his father and the way he earned his living, he also renounced Judaism, his father's religion. He was now a fervent member of Semites for the Son, a relatively new sect for Jews who'd converted to Christianity. Their group owned a fifty-five percent interest in the airship Ark.

Between these religious groups and the "Down with Castro" bunch, the causeway adjoining the Coast Guard base leading to South Beach was still closed a week later. It was virtually the only news being covered by the local media since there were so many story lines available. This was great for the chief and the developer. They filed their building plans and started to acquire their construction and dredging permits while nobody was watching.

Politically, the refugee situation was a nightmare. The mayors of the city of Miami and of Miami-Dade County knew they couldn't afford to offend their large Cuban-American constituency. But by the same token they couldn't let a mob, even a well-organized one, take possession of a major public thoroughfare indefinitely. The hotels and clubs were screaming about lost business. And, to make things worse, some of the richest people in the area, and in the country for that matter, were complaining about being denied access to their homes. Unfortunately, the Coast Guard base was only about a block from the loading dock for Fisher Island, possibly the richest community in the country. Fisher Island, the exclusive enclave where people like Oprah and Rosie kept condos, was accessible only by ferry. And now some of the wealthiest people with not only local, but also national political pull, couldn't reach their homes. The local politicians were squeezed between their voting constituencies and some of their wealthiest contributors.

Florida's governor and the state's U.S. senators and representatives all took a hands-off approach. In election years they all solicited campaign contributions from the two groups involved in the protest as well as the rich celebrities and business people who were being denied access to their private island. The safest thing for them to do politically was to dump it back on the local politicians and the U.S. Justice Department, which was responsible for asylum cases.

At one a.m., the eighth day after holy men were taken into custody, a convoy of three black Chevy Suburbans and ten squad cars containing federal marshals left the Justice Department offices in Downtown Miami. They headed for the MacArthur Causeway. They hadn't even reached the first bridge before word of their impending arrival had been relayed by cell phone to the crowd keeping watch at the Coast Guard station.

Immediately, most of the mob began moving west to intercept the convoy and prevent it from reaching its destination. The news helicopters and the Ark quickly followed. At about two a.m., as soon as the air space over the base had cleared, a matte black Coast Guard Black Hawk helicopter, normally used for night tracking and interdiction of drug smuggling go-fast boats, swept in from over the ocean. It landed at the base and the three men were quickly hustled aboard. The chopper then delivered them to the Naturalization and Immigration detention center at Krome Ave., on the eastern edge of the Everglades.

While they could just as easily have been flown to a cutter offshore and returned to Cuba, that would have been political suicide for the administration when it came time to seek votes in South Florida in the next election. In the rural detention camp, the lawyers could hash it out and the story would fade from the national spotlight. At least that was what the administration hoped for.

Reuben Elias had something else in mind. He didn't have any experience with immigration law. In fact he didn't know squat about it. But like a bee to nectar, or more accurately, a fly to dung, Reuben was attracted to the bizarre cases that made the news. Somehow he would get himself added to the "holy men's" defense team.

Lindsey Lee had seen it coming of course. She had seen Reuben seek the public eye too many times before. It was a shame because Lindsey, William and Hamilton could have used Reuben's media contacts to help publicize Rex and Rogelio's plan to rape and exploit the adjoining shoreline. But Reuben would be working those contacts for all they were worth.

Lindsey had contacts with the animal rights people. But the media often looked on these groups as nuts on the fringe and didn't give them much credibility. Hamilton, as the Heat's 21-year-old rookie center, hadn't proved himself on the court yet and didn't carry much weight with the local news people, not even the sports correspondents. William, although second in line for leadership of the Miccosukees, had studiously avoided any media contacts and carried no weight at all. As long as the "second coming" was the major story locally, the development of an Indian casino in an obscure corner of the south part of Miami-Dade County behind an ex-garbage dump wasn't going to make much of a splash.

At least the construction of the raptor rehab facility was almost complete. Lindsey and Hamilton Patrick had input on the design of the structure. They made sure that the nesting boxes were big enough to accommodate the large birds of prey. There was also enough indoor horizontal flight space to exercise the birds to allow them to build up their strength and stamina before they were released to the outdoors. William would be in charge of the transfer of the birds from the old facility to the new. Lindsey felt a strong desire to see him again. She also hoped there would be some news coverage at the dedication of the new facility so that she might get a word in about the development plans.

Rex and Rogelio were ahead of her. When the birds were delivered, they were there for the dedication.

The media coverage was minimal. For the six o'clock news only one local TV station sent anyone, the weather girl. Hoping to break into harder news, she realized you had to start with fluff pieces. The Herald sent a college intern from the local page, who not only wrote the text, but also did the photography. Not exactly the in-depth heavy hitters Lindsey had hoped to talk to.

The two seasoned self-promoters handled it well anyway. They showed up wearing matching colorful hand sewn shirts that the Miccosukees were famous for producing. They posed shaking hands while each held a hooded hawk.

Rex spoke, "For his assistance in providing this temporary housing while we finish our rehabilitation facility, the Miccosukee nation has voted to make Rogelio Black a member of our tribe."

"Thank you, Rex. I'm honored. In appreciation, I'm offering the land from the base of the east side of this development to the bay to the Miccosukee Nation for use as a reservation," replied Rogelio.

Not mentioned was the fact that the offering was contingent upon Rogelio's receipt of thirty percent of the profits from the development of the yacht club, the resort and the future casino.

"We gladly accept your generous offer," responded Rex, thinking to himself that it would have been more generous if Rogelio had accepted twenty per cent. Still, some of the casino's games could be adjusted to improve the house's odds and make up for the bigger share Black was taking.

"As this was once a Native American habitation site, it seems most fitting to me that it become one again," was Rogelio's final sound bite.

The video and still cameras, both tightly focused on the two new tribal brothers, didn't pick up the scowling faces of William and Lindsey Lee in the background. The implication of the new reservation and the alliance with a major developer was completely lost on the two young reporters. They couldn't see that the two most rapacious birds of prey were not the feathered ones wearing the hoods, but the smiling brightly garbed twosome holding them.

As soon as the video lights were off, Rex and Rogelio put them away. It was dusk and time for them to go to their new nests.

"Rex, I'd like to stay for awhile and see that the birds get settled in right," William suggested.

"How am I supposed to get home?" Rex asked.

"No problem. I'll give you a ride. Whaddya say we have dinner at Joe's. I'm in the mood for some stone crabs. We've got some things to discuss any way," Rogelio offered.

"Okay. Fine. William, just have the Navigator back home by 10 am tomorrow. I've got some meetings to get to," Rex replied.

"Sure," William sometimes didn't understand his brother at all. William liked stone crab, caught them and cooked them for himself on several occasions. But Joe's Stone Crab Restaurant was a noisy place on 1st Street on the southern tip of Miami Beach. It was the place where celebrities and power brokers went to be seen and deal and it always had a long wait unless the maitre'd knew you. It would be the last place William would choose to enjoy a simple crab claw meal. And Rex's house was an eighteenth floor penthouse, with its own pool, on top of a hotel casino complex. Not exactly your simple Miccosukee chickee. William just didn't get the attraction of all the trappings of financial power. He was a simple man of simple tastes. He didn't feel a need to have more or consider himself better than anyone. And by the same token, he didn't feel that wealthy people with all their possessions were any better than he.

He was having these ruminations, as he was carefully placing each of the birds in its new nest. He was so lost in thought, that at first he didn't hear Lindsey speaking to him.

"William?" (pause) "William?"

"What? Lindsey, what is it?" he replied.

"Nice to see I'm not the only one who zones out," she said, referring to the time they'd first met in her backyard.

"Yeah. That's true. What's your question?"

"How many birds are there? And is there anything I can do to help?" she asked.

"Four osprey, two falcons, seven hawks and three eagles, sixteen in all. I'll move them. We don't have the right equipment to protect you," he answered, looking down at the heavy leather gloves he was wearing. Without protection, the talons on some of the bigger birds could cut human flesh to ribbons.

"Who's going to take care of the birds?"

"Harry mostly. And me. Harry's napping in the front of the transport truck. He got tired of waiting for the big media turnout. He was already taking care of them at the old facility. He's got a camper back pickup, so he can stay with them as long as he thinks it's necessary," he told her.

48

"Would you like to have dinner at my place? Maybe we can sit and figure out a way to stop those two. You can even stay the night if you'd like. That way you can check on the birds in the morning."

He cocked an eyebrow and gave her a quizzical look at the last part of her invitation.

" I mean it's a big house and I have several guest rooms," she said by way of clarification, wondering herself exactly what she meant.

"Sure. Dinner would be nice. And I'd like the opportunity to check the birds in the morning. Thanks," he replied. "You're not one of those vegetarian animal rights people are you?"

"Don't worry. I'm not vegan. I eat dairy, eggs and fish. I'm sure I can come up with something you'll like," she told him.

William left the Lincoln at the aviary and they walked the half block to her house. There were two large bouquets of flowers at the door.

"Don't look back. Florio's probably standing naked in his front window waiting to see what I do with his flowers," she whispered.

"Doesn't it bother you always being pursued like that?" William asked.

"Yes. But men have been chasing me and trying to impress me for a long time. And Florio's never tried anything."

"I'll be right back." William picked up the flowers and trotted quickly across the street. Lindsey heard him knock on the door and saw it open. She couldn't hear their exchange. Then she saw William trotting back.

"I don't think he'll bother you any more," William told her.

She opened her door and turned on the lights. William stepped in and scanned the living room. It had a 20-foot vaulted ceiling with exposed wood beams. The south wall had two large picture windows with views of the Keys, separated by a native coquina stone fireplace. It appeared to be functional, for those one or two days of winter each year, where, it would actually be necessary to heat the house. The furniture was all done in heavy, pebbly white cotton fabric and the floor was covered in off-white carpeting. The walls and curtains were white as well. The tables were patinaed brass with heavy glass tops. The lamps and accessories all had marine or nautical themes.

William looked at the sea of whites, and then looked down at his jeans and well-worn work boots.

Lindsey Lee read his mind. "Don't worry, we're not going to sit in there. I never use the room myself. It's too clean. It was done by an interior decorator because Rogelio used this house as a model when he was selling the development."

What a waste of space, William thought to himself.

"It's a waste of space. In fact this whole house is a lot more than a single woman living alone really needs," Lindsey remarked, seeming to read his thoughts again.

Unseen by Lindsey, William gave her a quizzical glance. She was a very perceptive young woman and her fame didn't seem to have spoiled her.

"Follow me," she said.

Passing through the living room and a formal dining room, they made their way to the kitchen. It had polished stone floors, teak and tile cabinets and counters, and all the latest appliances.

"Want some wine or beer?"

"Beer's fine," he replied.

She reached into the stainless steel fridge and pulled out a couple of Hatueys. She liked the local beer. It was produced by the Bacardi family, the rum distillers who'd fled Cuba when Castro seized power. They used the original island recipe that they obtained from a ninety- year-old brew master who'd also escaped from the country. She popped the caps off and handed one to William, clinking her bottle against his.

"Here's to stopping the R & R boys," she said using the nickname her little group had given Rex and Rogelio. "Omelets okay for dinner?"

"Sounds good."

She sautéed some chopped scallions, yellow pepper and diced shrimp in butter and set the mixture aside. Then she grated some white jack cheese and whipped some eggs and milk together with a whisk. William watched quietly, sipping on his beer.

"You seem pretty handy in the kitchen," he commented on her domesticity.

"This is simple," she replied, "But I can cook fancier. I like cooking. It relaxes me as long as I'm not out to impress anyone. I'd almost call it therapeutic."

"Anything I can do to help?"

Lindsey told him which cabinet and drawer to get plates and forks from.

"How're you so sure Florio won't be bothering me anymore?" she inquired while she was cooking their omelets.

"I was wondering if you'd ask."

"It's simple really. Whoever made up the last two arrangements he left at your door didn't bother to trim the thorns off the roses. Like you predicted, he was naked when he answered the door. I'm sure he was disappointed when it was me and not you. Anyway, I just slapped the flowers against him. Below the belt to put it discretely. And I told him you weren't interested in any more bouquets. Said I'd be glad to return any further ones that turned up on your doorstep. He seemed to get the message."

She let out a little giggle then smiled. "I hope you didn't hurt him too much. I think he's probably harmless."

"He'll recover. Probably never look at roses the same way again though," he smiled back.

"Grab a couple more beers. I'll bring the eggs and we can eat in my favorite part of the house."

"The patio," he guessed.

"No, come with me."

He popped the tops and followed.

She led him up a staircase and pointed to the guest bedroom on her left. The room straight ahead was a study.

Turning right toward the southeast corner of the house, she opened a door. "And this is my bedroom," she announced.

William wasn't quite sure what to make of the situation. He hesitated to enter, thinking maybe things were moving a little too fast.

She looked back at him waiting, again picked up on his train of thought, and blushed a lovely shade of crimson.

"I'm sorry. I'm not inviting you into my bedroom. I'm just inviting you to pass through it," she said as she was recovering her normal coloring. " Don't mind the mess. I wasn't expecting guests."

William stepped in. She had posters on the walls from her movies and from her coaching Buns Bowl II. Clothes were strewn over the furniture and the bed wasn't made. It looked more like a college kid's dorm room.

"Follow me," she called out as she led the way to a black wrought iron spiral staircase in a corner of the room.

"I'm sorry, I didn't mean to imply…" he started.

"It's okay. Sexy posters. B-movie 'T &A' starlet. I understand. It's the image. But it's not the real me at all."

William figured the real Lindsey might just be a whole lot deeper. As he followed her up the steep steps, he couldn't help but check out her legs right there in front of him. Long, toned calves and thighs, obviously athletic, but not over-developed. And she filled out the back of her white khaki shorts nicely. His thoughts jumped back to the bed below for an instant.

At that moment she'd reached the top, pulled a long levered handle, and popped open a hatch above her head. A draft of crisp salt air swirled down to the Miccosukee and shifted his mind back to where he was headed.

Coming through the hatch, he saw that they were on a ten-by-ten widow's walk platform surrounded by an ornate carved wooden railing painted white. There was a small wicker table and a couple of cushioned wicker armchairs on each side of it. She set the plates and silver on the table and he placed the beers at each setting.

"Yes. On an evening like this it's easy to tell why this is my favorite part of the house," she stretched her arms out doing a 360-degree pirouette.

Indeed it was. The moon was an impossibly large, yellow half disc, the eyes of its man peeking over the Atlantic horizon between Fowey light and Soldier Key. The city of Miami was just a little tangerine cloud of sodium vapor lighting ten miles to the north. To the south, Card Sound and upper Key Largo were dark since these areas were essentially undeveloped. Further south the lights of the twinkling necklace that was the Overseas Highway connecting to the lower keys were just beginning to be visible. Finally, to the west, the lights of Homestead and Florida City were flickering on close by. Beyond them the greens and browns of the vast river of grass were shadowed to grays and blacks as the sun westered over the Glades.

They sat and ate watching in silence as the sun started to pass below the horizon. Both of them knew that any word spoken aloud would only detract from the magic of the moment. Just before it disappeared, there was an orange flash from the last direct rays. For an instant the Everglades appeared to be on fire. Then they were dark.

They sat in silence for a couple more minutes. They were comfortable that way, each appreciating that the other didn't try to fill the quiet with superfluous chatter.

"Impressive," William finally uttered.

"I like it better than the green flash you get watching the sun set in the Keys."

"Much better. And the show's not over," he said turning east, noting the moon was now completely above the ocean's edge.

"Yes, there's much more if you want to sit up here for awhile."

"Sure. By the way, the omelet was excellent," he complimented.

"Thanks. What are we going to do about the R&R boys?"

"I don't know." He looked down at Biscayne Bay, dark now, illuminated only by the full moon. Powerboats, with their running lights on, scooted through the channels like manic water bugs. Beneath the surface of even these heavily traveled waters there was still life. The sea grass beds of the south bay were just as important marine nurseries as the mangrove tree roots along the shoreline. Dredging for a marina and tearing out the trees to make a resort beach would be devastating. The dredging alone would silt over and kill acres of surrounding grass beds.

"They don't understand what's at stake. I could never get Rex to see the value of preserving the natural environment," he said.

"Rogelio's the same way. He told me—Look around, there's very little shoreline in all of southeast Florida left to develop. What's a few gnarly little trees and some muddy bay bottom near an old dump compared to a beautiful waterside resort that will offer pleasure to so many people?"

"Rex always uses the excuse he's looking out for the good of the tribe. But he'd be manipulating and working the angles on something even if he weren't chief."

"Rogelio's only happy when he's working on some big project that's going to make him a lot of money and boost his reputation. I've known him for years. He's always had to be the big man."

"Between the two of us we ought to be able to come up with something to stop them," he said, sounding more hopeful than he actually felt.

"We'll think of a plan," she replied.

For the next couple of hours they compared their experiences growing up in South Florida. Not surprisingly, they shared a love of nature and the outdoors. Though William's experiences growing up in the Everglades and attending tribal schools were a lot less conventional than Lindsey Lee's. Lindsey told William about her father exposing her to various athletic activities, even teaching her to scuba dive. William professed to have little knowledge of the reef system that was just a few miles offshore from where they sat. She promised to take him out and show it to him.

There was a lull in the conversation. They watched the dip netters working the bay to catch shrimp. This usually occurred during the full moon. Families would take out their pleasure boats and use fine seine nets extended from outriggers on the sides to troll for the shrimp that came up to the surface. Part of the catch would be used for fish bait, part frozen for future meals, and part sold for a little extra income. From their vantage point, the powerboats looked like slow-moving, overweight, underpowered dragonflies until they dropped their nets in the water.

"It's getting late," Lindsey said, though she wasn't really in a hurry for night to end. She'd been able to just be herself and it was the most pleasant time she'd spent with a man in a long time.

"Guess it's time to head in," William replied.

They started to clear the table. A fork fell to the platform floor and they both bent over to retrieve it. William grabbed the tines and Lindsey the handle. As they picked it up their faces came close. Their eyes met and they paused. Though they were easily within kissing distance, neither was sure just how far to take this impromptu date.

After a few seconds William stammered, "You take it."

The moment was lost.

They took the dishes to the kitchen. Then Lindsey took William to the guest room at the opposite end of the second floor hall. She gave him towels and a spare toothbrush for the guest bath.

"Sorry I don't have a change of clothes to offer you."

"That's ok," he replied, thinking to himself that it's a pretty good indicator that she doesn't have a steady guy around. "I'll pick up a change of clothes at the gaming hall in the morning. Maybe you'd like to come along."

"I've never been there. I'd like to see it."

They went to their rooms, pleased with the prospect they'd be spending more time together.

But both of them had trouble falling asleep. They'd share the same thought-that if they'd just done something a little differently, they wouldn't be sleeping alone. They dreamt of one another.

 **Chapter VIII**

The next morning, after a breakfast of French toast and orange juice, they headed back to the bird rehab facility.

Going out her front door, Lindsey noticed Florio Flores looking out the picture window of his house across the street. At least he was clothed now, wearing a white polo shirt and white linen shorts.

"Look. You've helped beautify the neighborhood a little," Lindsey whispered.

William gazed across the street and smiled.

"I've got an idea," she said. "Take my hand and we can walk holding hands. Give him the idea we're girlfriend and boyfriend."

William was happy to comply.

As they strolled down the front walk, Lindsey gave Florio a little wave with her free hand.

He frowned and returned a slight, despondent wave.

"I think you broke his heart," William observed.

He liked the feel of her soft, smooth delicate yet firm hand in his.

She could feel the strength in his brown, lightly calloused hand that gripped hers gently.

Enjoying their first physical contact, they didn't let go even after they were well out of Florio's sight. They held hands in silence all the way back to the raptors.

They checked in with Harry. Everything was fine. The big birds were adapting well to their new situation. Several would be ready for some unrestricted free flights in a short time.

Lindsey Lee and William got into the big black Lincoln SUV and headed for the gaming hall. To save time he took the turnpike north, exiting at the Tamiami Trail exit just west of the main campus of Florida International University. From there it was a straight shot west. The Miccosukee casino was just north of where the trail intersected with Krome Avenue.

As they rode, Lindsey perused the interior of the big truck. What a showy piece of equipment, she thought to herself. Six CD changer, controls for the spotlight array on the roof and the power winch on the front of the bumper guard. Looking at the burled walnut trim and the light gray upholstery with the Miccosukee logo embossed into the seat backs, she knew this vehicle could be used for utility purposes about the same time icebergs started forming in Biscayne Bay. Men, they were just larger boys with more expensive toys.

Watching her, William could pick up her train of thought.

"The farthest it's ever been off road is the driveway," he smiled. "The lights and the winch are just so tribe members will think that Rex is the kind of guy who still hunts and fishes. Of course he couldn't resist the dark tint on the windows, like you see on the limos that transport celebrities."

Having ridden in more than a few of those limos, where no one could see in, and co-stars and directors no longer felt compelled to keep their hands to themselves, Lindsey was momentarily uncomfortable. But for some reason, perhaps because he'd been the perfect gentleman last night, she trusted William. The discomfort quickly passed.

"I'm familiar with the limo thing," she responded.

"Oh, right. I forgot," he stammered, slightly embarrassed he'd forgotten her movie and TV star status.

"That's ok. I always found the big car thing a bit pretentious. No offense to your brother." She liked that he treated her like an ordinary person.

"None taken," he grinned.

Lindsey had never been out to the Indian casino, so she was surprised by what she saw when they reached their destination. After driving the last couple of miles on a road surrounded by little more than drainage canals, scrub vegetation and saw grass, they came to the intersection with Krome. On the northwest corner, literally in the middle of nowhere, stood the Miccosukee money machine. In the center of an enormous asphalt parking lot, with a big neon marquee sign just like the ones in Vegas, was the combination exhibition hall, hotel and gaming center. To her surprise, even though it was 9:30 in the morning, the parking lot was three quarters full. There were even two long rows of parked tour buses.

"Wow. I never knew your operation was so big," she commented.

"Yeah, impressive. Really in tune with nature," William replied sarcastically.

"You really don't approve of this do you?" she asked, stating the obvious.

"Admittedly, it's lifted our small tribe out of poverty. But the cultural losses have been staggering, I don't know if it's been worth the grief."

He was interrupted by the parking valet who'd rushed up to open his door.

"Good morning, Mr. Panther."

William hated the way the poor hard working valets always fawned over him when he pulled up in Rex's truck. His brother loved the little people sucking up to him, but he hated it.

"Better have it detailed," he told the young man. Not missing a financial opportunity, the hotel offered a washing and detailing service for its valet customers.

"Yes sir, as soon as I let your companion out," he replied.

"How'd he know who it was in the truck?" Lindsey asked as she stepped down from the front seat. "There's a lot of black navigators in this town. I saw that poor guy in my side mirror. He came running from the parking lot behind us. There's no way he could see through the tinting to know who's in here."

She was pretty observant. William liked that. But she'd missed one important detail. Instead of answering her, he just pointed to the back of the Lincoln as the valet drove off.

She read the vanity plate, BIG CAT.

"Oh. Knowing the egos we're dealing with, I should have guessed."

"Yeah. Subtlety is not their strong suit."

There was another obsequious "Good morning Mr. Panther" as the doorman held the door open for the two to enter the gaming hall.

William muttered "Good morning," in reply.

Lindsey's senses were assaulted as soon as the door closed behind them. In the large room directly ahead there were lights blinking and flashing on the video electronic games-poker, Keno and the slots. There were the clinking and bell sounds emanating from the machines as they were played. And also the chink, chink, chink, chink of the coin machines as they occasionally paid off. To her left she could hear a caller reading out numbers in quick succession from something called Lightning Lotto where there seemed to be a line of people waiting to play. In fact, she could see one of those take-a-number things, like they have at the deli, at the entrance to the lotto area. The walls and carpeting were done in various combinations of yellow, green, blue and orange. Everything was brightly lit. Lindsey liked the way the place looked. It was friendly and inviting.

But, overriding the whole impression was the heavy odor of tobacco smoke. William saw her wrinkle her nose.

"You can't believe how noxious this place can get," he said.

"Worse than this?" she replied, thinking it was plenty bad right now.

"Yeah, late at night when it's really packed, or if there's a special event at the convention hall, it gets even worse. You feel like you need a regulator and a scuba tank just to walk through the bingo hall. We've bought high tech air scrubbers and we change filters twice as often as recommended, but we just can't beat it. However, for the health-conscious, we have two "no-smoking" floors in the hotel. I have a room on one of them."

On her extreme left, Lindsey noticed the hotel registration desk. It appeared to be manned by two Latino women and a young black man. Lindsey had expected that she would see Miccosukees behind the counter.

"How many tribe members work at the gaming hall?" she asked.

"Did you think the staff would be all Native American?" he replied, following her gaze.

"Well, yes. I guess I did. I thought it would be a way for members to have a job where they had a say in how things were run."

"I see your point. But actually very few Miccosukees work here. Many are content to live on their share of the profits. So like a lot of American big business we contract out our labor. In fact, since no tribe members want to learn the traditional skills, we've just hired our first non-native alligator wrestler."

Lindsey remembered visiting the Indian village tourist attraction as a kid. It was five miles further west on Tamiami. She'd thought how brave those men had been to get in the pit and wrestle the eight-foot lizards. Now she knew that the secret was to hold the gator's jaw shut. They had very weak muscles for opening their mouths, and as long as you avoided their tails they couldn't do much to hurt you.

"You're kidding. Contract alligator wrestlers?"

"Yup. The guy is a blonde Anglo from Fort Lauderdale. 'The times they are a changin','" he replied.

"That's for sure," she agreed. "And now they want to bring all this to the south bay. Lucky us."

"This is only part of what you're in for. Let me show you around."

William gave her the grand tour. Lindsey was both amazed and appalled. There turned out to be two more video gaming rooms both with much darker lighting than the big room at the main entrance. Not being a gambler, she had little familiarity with advances in electronic games of chance.

To play poker, one no longer needed a live dealer, just plug your money into the slot and the computer inside the machine would deal you a hand that you turned up by pushing buttons. However, for those who still wanted a little human interaction, there was a poker room offering higher stakes. Here a dealer at each table dealt the cards for up to six players.

As far as slots went, the limited exercise factor that used to be involved was long gone. No longer was there a lever arm to pull to spin the drums in the one-armed bandit. Now you just punched a key and the electronic tumblers flashed and jangled on the pushbutton-pickpocket. The cherries, bells and lucky sevens were now video images.

There were several bars strategically stationed near the assortment of playing areas. That way it wasn't too much work for the players to keep themselves lubricated and their inhibitions loose.

For those who required solid sustenance, dining areas were located on the second level. There was the obligatory all-you-can-eat buffet room with a $4.99 breakfast, $7.99 lunch and $9.99 dinner. For those with more to spend there was an upscale dining room, sound proofed to muffle the noise from the gaming below. Along with the wine list and haute cuisine, there was the opportunity to sample more native foods such as wild boar, venison and alligator. And following the latest high end dining trends there was even an after dinner cigar room.

Strolling through the complex with William, Lindsey observed all kinds of players. Some were there to have a few drinks, a few laughs and kill some time with friends doing something different.

In the poker room and lightning lotto areas, a person got to pit himself and his luck against other live players. At least there was the pretense of human challenge. The scary ones were the people who sat on their stools in front of the video machines putting in money, pushing the buttons, putting in money, pushing the buttons, repeatedly. Some of them barely watched the results before feeding the machine again, performing mechanically almost as if in a hypnotic trance. They certainly didn't seem to be getting enjoyment out of the experience.

"What do they get out of it?" she asked William, pointing out some of the video zombies.

"Beats me. Eyestrain, finger fatigue and empty pockets. But there's no shortage of them," William responded, shaking his head. He sure didn't understand them. And though his brother didn't, William felt guilty about taking their money. It sort of felt like they were robbing people too incompetent to care for themselves.

"Finally, here is our crowning glory. What got us started into gaming in the first place," William pointed to his right.

The bingo hall. They had passed the lines of people, dressed in all kinds of South Florida garb. Many had come off the tour buses and were waiting to buy their bingo slips and colored markers before they entered the hall.

Lindsey was both fascinated and disgusted. The hall was immense, a three story, glassed-in area, separate from the rest of the gaming rooms. There were at least thirty long rows of tables with an aisle running down the middle. She figured seating capacity to be at least twelve hundred, maybe more. At the front was a raised platform where the caller stood. It reminded Lindsey Lee of a perverse version of a fundamentalist church, with the caller acting as the preacher, and the players his rapt flock. Only this church had waitresses offering bar service and spotters looking for those in the congregation who called out "Bingo" instead of "Hallelujah."

Over the whole scene hung a real cloud of tobacco smoke, from about 10 feet off the ground to the ceiling. What a toxic replacement for ceremonial incense, Lindsey thought.

"That cloud is one of the grossest things I've ever seen," she told William.

"I know. I keep telling Rex that if any of our people who work in there come down with lung cancer, we're wide open to being the loser of a major successful second hand smoke lawsuit. But he doesn't want to lose the income stream."

"What do you mean?"

"We sell most of the cigarettes that are polluting the air. Since this is reservation land, we sell tobacco products without state or federal taxes added on. Some of our customers come here just to stock up on tobacco."

"You'll never go broke helping people feed their addiction," she admitted.

"Addictions are what this empire is based on. Alcohol, tobacco, gambling. You need any of these, we provide them. One stop shopping. Rex says, if we didn't satisfy cravings someone else would. Seems like a pretty lame excuse for feeding off people's weaknesses."

Lindsey liked William's character, his moral compass, and the fact that he was uncomfortable taking advantage of people. Sometimes she felt the same type of discomfort about her career. Tits and ass movies with juvenile plots, how did they enrich society or advance civilization?

But she told him what she often told herself. "Well for a lot of people it really is just an enjoyable form of entertainment. And at least it's not illegal."

"Yeah," he replied sullenly, "But do you want to see it down the hill from where you live?"

"No. Hell no. No for any number of reasons," Lindsey was surprised by the vehemence of her own response.

"I don't blame you. I agree with you," he paused. "Speaking of the project, I need to go up to Rex's penthouse and see what his plans for the day are. Can you amuse yourself here for about an hour? I'll get you some tokens for the video machines," he said, walking over to one of the cashier counters.

"Sure. Maybe I'll figure out what these people get out of it."

Lindsey headed out to feed the machines, while William headed up to visit his brother.

*   *   *

At least the elevator wasn't as tobacco laden as the gaming level. William used his special key, required to access his brother's floor. The car glided to a stop, the doors whispered open and William stepped out.

To the left was the cypress-paneled hallway that led to his brother's penthouse. William went to the right, toward the tribal council's suite of offices. He stepped through the glass doors etched with images of sawgrass and wading great blue herons, into the reception area. Sitting behind a desk faced with native oolite stone and topped by a large plank of local mahogany was an older woman wearing the traditional patchwork jacket.

"I've gotta change my clothes. Is El Gran Queso in his office yet?" He asked with a smirk on his face.

"You should show your brother a little more respect. He works hard for our people."

"Yeah, an eighteen story chickee in the middle of the glades. We've come a long way, Mom," he replied.

"Your father didn't like it either. But at least we don't live on government handouts any more."

" No. We used to live off the land. Now the council provides handouts instead. But let's not rehash this now. Let him know I'll be back in about five minutes."

"Okay. He's meeting with that Rogelio Black fellow. I'll tell him you're coming," she said turning to the intercom phone.

William frowned as he headed for his office. The fact that the developer was here early in the morning couldn't be good news.

Compared to the planned "native décor" of the reception lobby, William's office was Spartan. It had light blue walls with a steel desk, a couple of steel filing cabinets and a cheap desk chair that he'd assembled himself. All the stuff was straight out of one of those warehouse office supply stores. His window overlooked the bus parking so he usually kept the curtains closed.

His one indulgence was the collection of Clyde Butcher photographs decorating all four walls. The black and white photographs by the Everglades' equivalent of Ansel Adams allowed William to escape mentally to some of his favorite spots while he spent time doing tribal paperwork. Although it was one of his least favorite activities, he took his responsibility seriously, and besides, it was a good idea to keep track of what his brother was up to.

William changed to a clean pair of jeans and another denim shirt. He kept several changes in his office for convenience. He was a practical man and didn't much like to shop for clothes. He usually bought socks, underwear, shirts and pants, half a dozen at a time, same style and same color. It made for minimal work when he did his laundry.

His mother buzzed him on the phone, "Your brother's expecting you."

"Thanks," he was always surprised when his office phone rang because it happened so rarely. Everybody wanted to do business with Rex. That was all right with William.

He walked down a short hall to his brother's office. The entrance had mahogany double doors, each with a large alligator hide mounted on it. Instead of regular doorknobs, there were levers fashioned from deer antlers. The decorator had convinced Rex that it was important to impress visitors with a strong Native American statement. To William it just said "tacky."

William entered without knocking. Rex and Rogelio were looking out the window, drinking what appeared to be mimosas. The office picture window faced east, overlooking the county's western suburbs with the Miami skyline in the distance. To William it was telling that his brother had picked the office with this view rather than one that looked towards the Glades.

William sat in one of the overstuffed chairs covered in gator hide and rested his work boots on the polished surface of his brother's desk. It was a larger, more opulent version of what his mother sat behind in the reception room. He knew it aggravated Rex when he put his feet up, but he liked to bring his brother down a notch.

"So, what's up for today?"

Rex walked over and brushed William's feet off.

"Actually we're going to meet with some landscapers, architects and contractors to discuss the Bayside Casino Marina project. You're welcome to come along."

"Moving pretty fast aren't you?"

"Time is money," Rogelio chipped in.

"Yeah, we're moving this thing along. They're setting up a couple of trailers on the site this morning. One for the landscapers who are going to start clearing the property and one for the construction people," added Rex.

"Really. This all seems pretty quick."

"The quicker the better. The more we get done before the media gets wind of it the better off we are. Fewer problems with environmentalists," said Rogelio.

"Yeah, we clear the property and get some building started and it'll be too late for them to make any real trouble," said Rex.

William was so surprised by how fast they were moving he didn't really know what to say. He was trying to think of a way to slow them down and wasn't coming up with much.

"How're the birds doing?" Rex asked.

"Are we going to get the seagull crap thing under control soon?" Rogelio inquired.

"Well we could let some of the healthier birds fly free soon. And that'll probably chase the gulls off. But..." William suddenly switched gears and then paused. There was something the two hotshots didn't realize about the big raptors. Maybe it was something he could use to his advantage.

"But what?" Rogelio asked.

"Nothing. I think I'll skip the meetings with your development people and go back and see if we can get some of the birds launched." He really wanted to get back to Lindsey Lee to let her know how fast things were moving. He also wanted to let her know how they might turn the rehabbing big birds to their advantage.

"Good idea. Give a hand to my buddy here, Rogelio, 'cause he's helping the whole tribe. He doesn't need the distraction of a bunch of pissed off homeowners on his back."

"Sure. And you two let me see whatever plans you have. Keep me up to date on what's going on." And I'll keep my plans for your project to myself he thought, as he got up and left the office.

"See you later, Mom," he waved as he passed through the reception area. "I've got a nice girl waiting for me downstairs."

He stepped through the glass doors before she had a chance to interrogate him.

It didn't take him long to find Lindsey on the gaming floor. He could sense the testosterone aura emanating from the jostling knot of young men surrounding her as she fed quarters to the electronic Keno machine. Fortunately, William didn't have to wade through the throng to reach her. She had also seen him and immediately got up and headed his way.

"I guess you always attract a crowd," he commented as she reached him.

"Price of fame. At least for the kind of movies I make," she responded. "Take my hand and get me out of here. If they see I've got a date most of them give up and leave me alone."

He didn't have to be asked twice. It was a situation he wouldn't mind turning into a steady habit.

"How'd you like the casino?" he inquired.

"The electronic games can be mesmerizing. The sounds and flashing lights are almost hypnotic. But there isn't much exercise in just pushing buttons. And some of the machines just pay out with a ticket you take to a cashier. I miss the plinking and the tactile sensation you get in a machine that pays out coins."

"Efficiency experts figured that you can play more coins per hour into a machine if you don't have to waste time collecting a coin payout. It's just one more edge for the house," he explained. "Another way to separate you from your money a little faster and make room for the next player."

"Well that may be true. But the machines got me to concentrate on them so much I almost didn't notice the smoke. I guess the designers did a good job."

They stepped out into the fresh air and William handed the claim check to one of the valets. While they were waiting, he pulled out his cell phone.

Lindsey gave him a questioning look.

"Never seen a corporate Indian at work?" he smiled.

"Everyone has one these days. But I carry mine only for emergencies. Too intrusive otherwise."

"I agree. But right now it might help us."

He dialed.

"Hello...Do me a favor and give the birds an extra feeding this morning," he said into the phone.

There was a pause as he listened.

Then he said, "I know. But we don't want them to fly far on their first free flights. So give them the extra food."

Another slight pause.

"Okay. Thanks."

"What was that about?" she asked.

He explained to her what his idea was. He even gave her the details from the Florida Power and Light study on the effects the birds' activities had on power transmission lines.

She was impressed. "Well my car's in the garage," she smiled.

The valet pulled up in the "Big Cat." They got into the big truck.

As she was buckling up he said, "Whatta you say we take the scenic route back?"

"Which way?" she asked.

"Down Krome. Along the edge of the Glades and through farm country."

"I'm not in a hurry. Skipping the expressway sounds great. We might even find a roadside stand to pick up some fresh fruit and vegetables."

It sounded like an invite to another meal to William. "Down Krome we go then," He enjoyed her cooking and her company.

William put the SUV in gear and drove out of the parking lot. At the traffic light he turned right, southbound. They passed the Tamiami Trail without turning, heading down through one of the last undeveloped parts of the county.

They did stop at a "u-pick-em" roadside stand. In the field they selected their own tomatoes, peppers and zucchini. From the display on the stand Lindsey also picked up some fresh corn and sweet onions.

"How's burgers, corn on the cob and ratatouille sound for lunch?" she asked.

"Great, but burgers?" he replied as they loaded their purchases in the back.

"I have veggie burgers for me and real beef burgers for friends who are so inclined. I'm pretty open minded."

Another mile down the road, William saw something in the sky ahead just west of the street. "What's that?"

"It looks like a blimp. I think I read in The Herald that the religious groups are using the Ark to keep vigil over the immigration detention center," Lindsey answered.

"Well, that means we'll be going right by it, since it's on Krome."

"I think Reuben is holding a news conference out there this morning, around eleven. He wants it in time to make the noon news."

"Should we turn back and avoid the show?"

"No, let's stop and take a look if it's not too crowded. It's kind of fun to see Reuben in action."

As they got closer, they could see there was a crowd, but not a large one. They pulled off the road and parked behind a black Ford van.

Looking up, they saw that the airship Ark had a programmable light display that was flashing while scrolling lines of scripture. There appeared to be large speakers at either end of the light board, though they were silent at present.

There was an access road just ahead of the Ford that led into the Immigration and Naturalization Service Detention Center. About a hundred yards down the road, just in front of the main gate, a media tent had been set up. All the local TV stations were represented, their cameras and reporters clustered in front of an interview table. A mix of anti-Castro and religious protesters stood behind them.

Through her window Lindsey could see Reuben dressed in white linen robes, his hair parted down the middle and his beard neatly trimmed. His clients were outfitted in a similar fashion, though their hair was much longer and less gray.

"Leave it to Reuben to work all the angles. He's dressed like he's the prophet ready to lead the second coming," said Lindsey opening the passenger side door.

William came around the front of the sport ute and joined her. The day was starting to warm up, the humidity rising, and breezes out on the edge of the Glades. It was going to be another sticky South Florida day.

As they walked toward the news conference, they couldn't hear what was being said. The blimp was hovering directly over the media tent. The steady thrum of its propellers drowned out whatever was coming out of the press conference.

"How did Reuben ever get them to let him have the interview outside the security fence?" William asked.

"Well, there've been a couple embarrassing investigations of INS treatment of detainees recently. Whoever runs the place probably would rather keep the media on this side of the fence. It limits their access. Prevents them from interviewing other prisoners and guards."

They were halfway down the road to the tent when the media board on the Ark changed its display. Instead of scrolling lines of scripture in white lights, it was now flashing "Let my people go" in red letters.

Behind them, the side door on the Ford van in front of the Navigator slid open. The sounds of the blimp's motors were obliterated by three loud thunderclaps. This was followed immediately by the sound of machine gun fire coming from several directions.

Later, of course, people would realize that there really weren't any guns. The thunder and gunfire came from the surround sound system on the Ark. Barry Gold had taken the same system usually used in large movie theaters and installed it on the blimp. Two speakers and the subwoofer were in the van. The system was normally used to make a big impression at open-air stadium revival meetings.

The impression at the detention center was certainly big as well. In South Florida, where anything from a parking space dispute to a New Year's Eve celebration often involves guns, everyone knows what to do when they hear shots. Duck and cover.

Everybody, including the INS guards, hit the deck. As many people as possible were trying to squeeze under the interview tables. William and Lindsey sprinted for the Navigator.

There was no let up in the sounds of flying bullets. The scene was one of chaos. So far everything was going just as Barry had planned.

He grabbed Jesus and motioned for Pedro and Pablo to follow.

"Head for the black truck," he told them.

They all started running. About thirty yards down the road Barry was tackled from behind. One guard, who had been brave enough to look up, figured out what was happening, and made an attempt to stop it.

"Keep going!" Barry yelled as he fell.

The three refugees didn't really need any encouragement. They knew they had to seize their opportunity. But, without Barry to lead them, there was no way to be sure which was the right black truck.

So, just as William put the key in the ignition and started the engine and Lindsey was strapping her seat belt, the back door of the Navigator opened and the holy trinity piled inside.

Left to choose on their own, they had decided to opt for the big luxury vehicle over the plain black van with the blaring speakers. Might as well hope for the best.

"What the...?" was Lindsey's surprised reaction.

William looked over his shoulder at his unexpected passengers. Then he looked back toward the detention center. Barry was still tangled on the ground with the guard, waving and trying to get the refugees' attention. So far no one else was in pursuit. In fact, no one on the site would be able to identify whose Navigator the men had escaped to. Even Barry, who'd planned the escape, really didn't know.

William slapped the transmission into drive and gunned the big truck back onto Krome, kicking up a cloud of dust and gravel as he left the shoulder.

Lindsey and William might not have been able to articulate right at the moment why they chose to drive off with the exiles instead of throwing them out of the SUV. They discussed it later and realized that, besides the inherent tendency in the American character to root for the underdog, it came down to a matter of simple fairness. To have one's fate decided by such an arbitrary determinant, as whether one's foot actually touched dry land, wasn't right. To have the government grab you up and make an example of you was just plain cruel, an abuse of power. And William, especially in the tribe's dealings with the Feds, was well aware of how bureaucrats loved to use their power.

They made the only decision they could.

"You know what you're doing?" Lindsey whispered in a low voice. "This is aiding and abetting escape from a federal detention facility."

"Listen. Nobody there knows it's us. They were all focused on the news conference till the shooting started and then diving to cover their asses afterwards. They can't identify us. This could work to our advantage," he replied as he sped south, his plan clear in his mind.

"What do you mean?" Lindsey asked.

"Sanctuary. We've got to get back to your place." Over his shoulder he ordered, "Buckle up, amigos."

"Please explain. And try not to leave me questioning your sanity."

As he turned onto the southbound turnpike, merging with the heavy traffic, William began his explanation.

The unexpected passengers were whispering to one another in Spanish, high-fiving each other. Riding in a fancy air-conditioned truck with leather upholstery was more like it. And they recognized the beautiful American starlet in the front seat, also. They'd seen her on bootleg tapes that had been smuggled into Cuba. This was the America they'd expected, what they'd come looking for. All three of them were smiling.

By the time William had explained his plan to Lindsey, she was smiling, too.

*   *   *

They got back to Lindsey's without incident. By the time any pursuit was organized, the big SUV was mixed in with thousands of others on the turnpike. No one had gotten a look at the "Big Cat" plate. They were home free.

To be safe, they pulled the truck into Lindsey's garage to keep it out of view.

"We're going to have to kinda make this up as we go," William said to Lindsey.

Looking over her shoulder at the expectant occupants in the back seat, she replied, "I know. First off. What do we tell them?"

"Let's get them into the house. Then I've got to do a little scouting and we'll take it from there."

Other than whispering quietly in Spanish to each other during the drive south, the refugees hadn't made any effort at communication.

So Lindsey and William were surprised when Jesus spoke up. Having noticed all the big ornate houses that they had driven past on top of the pyramid, he asked, "Excuse me señorita, where are we?"

"You speak English. Why didn't you say something before?" she replied.

"Oh, si. Many of us learn English in school in Cuba. I didn't speak before because no one spoke to me. Besides we were enjoying the sights during the ride."

"Well, we're at my house. Come inside," she said opening her door.

Smiling, they got out and followed her. Pedro and Pablo carried the purchases from the vegetable stand. From the garage they went into the kitchen. The unexpected guests placed their packages on the counter, and then stood waiting to find out what was next.

Lindsey and William looked at one another, then at their visitors standing there in their white linen robes and religious coifs.

"This is creeping me out," Lindsey said. "I feel like I'm in the middle of an old Heston robe and sandal flick. We gotta get you guys some other clothes."

Just to be sure, William asked, "You three aren't deeply religious or anything? Do you want to dress like that and keep those clothes?"

"No, no. Our mother liked to read the Bible, but we grew up in a Cuba without any church. So we are named after holy men but really don't have much religion. This appearance was our lawyer's idea to help get more people on our side," replied Jesus.

Eying William, Pablo said, "Blue jeans are fine. Gap, Levis or Tommy will do. T-shirts or Polo shirts are good. Again Gap or Tommy, or even Ralph Lauren would be acceptable."

"Quite the knowledgeable consumers," Lindsey remarked.

Pedro interjected, "At the detention center we have nothing to do all day but watch television. These are the things we see. Are they not good clothes?"

Considering their viewpoint, Lindsey replied, "No, they're good. Some of the best actually. Some pretty expensive."

"Oh, señorita, we don't wish to be trouble. We don't need expensive clothes. I'm sure whatever you pick will be good. We would like to go to a big American store and shop for them."

"That's not going to work for awhile, not 'til your INS problems are straightened out. But we've got some ideas on that," said William.

Changing the subject, mainly because she and William really hadn't had time to work out much of a plan yet, Lindsey said, "Let's have lunch. Then we can discuss what we'll do next."

She turned on a small television that was on the counter. They all watched raptly as the local news covered the "daring midday escape of the three most notorious refugees to arrive in years", a statement used almost verbatim by all four of the local stations. There were several shaky, out-of-focus shots of the three running away down the access road. But the staccato of a close sounding burst of gunfire was picked up by several cameras and the reflexive, protective reaction of the cameramen showed nothing on the screen except pictures of the ground. No one had even photographed them getting into the Lincoln.

The three refugees laughed seeing themselves on screen. William and Lindsey breathed silent sighs of relief that they couldn't be identified.

Lindsey took some packages of ground beef out of her freezer and put them in the microwave to defrost. She took out a couple of cutting boards and knives and put her new guests to work prepping the produce for lunch.

"Cervezas, gentlemen?" she asked.

"That would be excellent," Pedro replied.

The three were surprised and impressed to see the Hatuey label on the beer. A good cold beer was a decadent pleasure after the fare served in the detention center.

"I want to check the birds and do some quick scouting. You'll be ok 'til I get back?" William looked at Lindsey.

"Sure, we'll save you a plate," Lindsey replied.

William had watched the young men checking Lindsey out when she wasn't looking. Heck, he'd done the same thing himself. He felt protective of her and didn't like seeing guys looking at her like hungry dogs eying a steak.

She saw him hesitate as he was heading for the back door. She guessed what he was thinking, liking him all the more for the consideration. But she had long ago gotten over being an object. She gave him a little smile and a slight dismissive wave.

"Get going."

He headed out the door and down the side of Mount Basura. In half an hour he was back, perspiring from having covered a good deal of ground in a short time. Lindsey and the Cubans were just finishing their lunch when he walked in. Lindsey put his plate in the microwave and warmed his food.

She handed him a beer. "What did you find out?"

"I'll start with the last thing first. The birds are doing great. Rogelio will be glad to know that they nailed and ate a couple of gulls. Unfortunately they also bagged a few of his ferrets. We'll see how things come out," he smiled.

"I'm keeping my car in the garage for sure," Lindsey said. "What about the arrangements for our new buddies here?"

"We're in about as good a shape as we could hope for considering none of this is planned. The construction trailer is air-conditioned and has a kitchen. There's even a couple of bunks for guys stuck working late who wouldn't want to make the long drive home. Power and phone lines are already connected. That would give the guys Internet access for entertainment."

"Rex and Rogelio don't waste time do they? They probably put in a DSL line for sending plans and blueprints," Lindsey observed. "That means our friends here can probably get cable, too."

"Excuse me. What are you talking about? Aren't we staying here?" Jesus asked.

"As much as I'd like to have you as my guests, you're not safe here. Anyone sees you here and you could be arrested and returned to the detention center. And considering that you're now fugitives, it could even increase your chances of being deported," she explained.

"So what are you talking about? Have we gotten ourselves in more trouble coming with you? How are you going to help us?" Jesus was becoming more agitated as he realized the predicament.

"Calm down. I'll explain," William replied. "As strange as it sounds, you'll be safe and the government won't be able to touch you if you just come with me down the hill."

"What difference would that make?" Pablo asked angrily.

"Listen. It'll be okay. Here's the deal. The land down there belongs to the Miccosukee tribe. I'm a chief of that tribe and as such I'm offering you sanctuary. I can allow anyone I want to come and go as they please. But the U.S. government has no legal jurisdiction there. Their law officers have no arrest powers on our land and have to ask our permission to even set foot there. And we won't give it to them."

"So you're going to put us in the trailer?"

"Just 'til a solution to your problems can be worked out. We can supply you with whatever you want and you can have whatever visitors you want. Speaking of which, as I was coming back from the raptor compound, I saw your lawyer pull into his driveway next door."

"What? Mr. Reuben lives next door?" Now Jesus was totally confused.

Lindsey explained the serendipitous coincidence.

As she finished, there was a knock at the front door. Lindsey checked the security camera that monitored the door and there was Reuben Elias.

"Speak of the devil."

Apparently, Reuben had also seen William and he was coming over to protect his imagined turf. Also he probably figured Lindsey would give him a sympathetic ear over the sudden loss of his famous clients.

"This ought to be fun," William commented, as he accompanied Lindsey to meet the lawyer.

"Come in, Reuben," she invited as she opened the door.

He burst into the house dramatically. "Have you seen the news? Did you hear what happened with my holy men?"

"Yes, Reuben, we know all about it. Come into the kitchen. Have something to drink," Lindsey smiled.

"You don't understand. I've lost them. I can't help them when I don't even know where they are."

The wiry little man was agitated and appeared truly worried about his clients as he followed them through the house.

"It'll be O.K., Mr. Elias," William replied sympathetically barely suppressing a grin.

As he stepped into the kitchen, the bantam barrister, who had wowed juries while outraging prosecutors and judges with his outlandish courtroom statements, was struck almost speechless. All he could do was stutter out a "H-h-how...?"

"Sit down Reuben. I'll get you a beer," Lindsey directed.

Elias sat at the table with the three grinning refugees. They were happy to see their advocate again. He just stared at them incredulously.

"Let me tell you what happened," Lindsey began.

Reuben just sat quietly as Lindsey spoke and William filled in an occasional detail.

"This is an amazing turn of luck. Sanctuary. What a great idea," he commented after they finished their tale.

"Reuben, did you have any hand in the escape plan?" Lindsey asked.

"Although it had the flair and audacity that I have somehow become famous for," Reuben smiled," I didn't have anything to do with it. I take my obligation as an officer of the court seriously. So I really in good conscience could not be part of an escape attempt."

"Unfortunately that brilliant piece of theater also adds to our friends' problems," he continued. "If they had just snuck off and gotten lost in the exile community things would have eventually died down. But, getting away in front of the cameras from the major networks and CNN, well...it gives the INS a big black eye as far as control and security go. They're going to want to get these guys back bad."

"How soon should we move these guys down to the trailers?" William asked.

"As soon as possible," Reuben replied. "They'll probably come here pretty soon to interview me as to what I did and didn't know. It wouldn't be good for our friends to be caught off the reservation. So to speak."

William just smiled.

"Mr. Reuben, we would like to stay here in the pretty lady's house. She cooks good for us and promised to get us better clothes," Jesus made the three refugees' wishes known.

"She can bring food down for you. And we'll get new clothes to you, too. It's just that if you stay here your safety can't be ..."

As if to prove his point, his last sentence was cut short by the sound of sirens approaching from the front of the house. In the front door security monitor Lindsey watched as an INS car and two county police cars pulled up on her front lawn.

"Get them out the back now," she hissed. "I'll stall them at the door as long as I can."

There was a flurry of white linen as the four robed men all rose from the table at once and sprinted for the back door. As Lindsey watched she noticed William hesitate.

"You've got to go with them. Show them the trailers. Make sure nobody violates the sanctuary," she decided for him.

He got up to follow the others.

"Just a second," she halted him again.

There was a loud hammering on her front door.

Reaching into her pantry, she pulled out a small canvas bag and threw it to him.

"Take this. It's my video camera. The battery's charged. Reuben will know what to do with it."

As William ran out the back, she spoke into the door intercom, "This is Lindsey Lee Olson, I'm coming."

She had calculated, correctly, that the name recognition factor would at least temporarily calm the law enforcement people. The pounding stopped immediately. When she opened the door, there stood a man in a dark blue suit, with four uniformed police officers trying to peer around him to get a look at her.

"Excuse me, Ms. Olson," he smiled. "I'm INS special agent Busch. We've had a report of a man who fits the description of one of the fugitive refugees entering this house."

"Whoever could have reported such a thing?" she vamped in her best demure southern belle voice.

"I'm not at liberty to say," he replied, taken by her charm.

He didn't have to. She could see the little prick Florio standing naked in his picture window watching the goings on. He wasn't going to take his rejection easily.

"Well, that was just my neighbor and their lawyer, Reuben Elias. He was dressed the same way at the press conference. He'd just come over to tell me what happened."

"Could we speak to him then, please?"

"He went home. He lives in the house to my right," she replied pointing toward Reuben's house.

The five men turned to go, disappointed they weren't going to get into her house and spend more time with the starlet.

The delaying tactic would have bought more time, if the policemen hadn't followed proper procedure. Unfortunately two men who hadn't come to the door had been sent around to cover the back. They had rounded the corner to the rear of the house just in time to see four men in white robes jump over the hedge that bordered the top of the garbage mesa. A few seconds later they saw an Indian carrying a canvas bag follow.

One of the two ran back to the front to report while the other stayed to watch where the fugitives went. Soon all seven lawmen were staring over the hedge watching the fluttering white robes of the men heading for the trailers. Somehow the Indian had gotten ahead and was unlocking the gate surrounding the fenced construction site.

"Stop," yelled one of the policemen, starting to unholster his Glock.

"Put that away you fool," Busch commanded. "Shoot one of them and you won't even be allowed to do poop scoop patrol at the pound. Get in the cars and we'll drive down there and pick them up."

By the time the lawmen loaded up, drove across the development and down the exit road, William and Reuben were ready.

Reuben had videotaped the signs that proclaimed "Miccosukee Tribal Reservation Land" that were wired to the fence at 50 yard intervals along the border of the future resort and casino. They had hidden Jesus, Pedro, and Pablo in the trailer with the computer in it and given them access to Reuben's online account for entertainment.

When the three cars pulled up to the gate at the entrance to the reservation, Reuben started the camera rolling again. As Busch got out of the car, he could see the red record light blinking at him. He had a sinking feeling in his gut.

"Shut that thing off," he blustered. "Let's just work this out before anyone gets hurt."

"Can't do that. I'm here to protect the rights and interests of my clients," Reuben almost crowed. He was in his element and enjoying himself immensely. The tape would look great when he released it to the media.

Two of the policemen started to push the gate open.

"Stop," William ordered. "I am Chief William Panther of the Miccosukee tribe. This is reservation land. You have no authority here and may not enter without permission. The three refugees have sanctuary here as long as they need it." William's confidence fed off of Reuben's and besides he actually felt good knowing he was doing the right thing.

They stopped momentarily. Then one of them muttered, "What bullshit," and started to push the gate again.

Once more William commanded, "Stop. You do not have permission to enter."

Busch watched as Reuben Elias swung the camera back and forth eagerly focused on all the action. Then he realized the camera was aimed directly at him.

As if taking his cue he said, "He's right, men. We can't enter without permission. We'll have to consult with the higher ups. Two of you stay here to keep an eye on things."

 **Chapter IX**

The three-ring circus of media, refugee supporters, and true believers started migrating south that evening. By eleven o'clock it was the lead story on all the local news shows.

Reuben, media savvy from his many high profile trials, knew how to milk the most out of the situation. "Don't give them what they want right away," he told William. "Make 'em wait a little. Besides, if we do this right away we can make the news portion of the network morning shows."

This was the reasoning behind not allowing the three refugees to appear before the cameras that night. Reuben of course was not shy at all.

"Let me just say that I will continue to fight for freedom for my clients. These holy men arrived on our shores looking for sanctuary and so far only the Miccosukee tribe has offered it to them. To the tribe we are grateful. To the INS, shame on you."

"The Miccosukee tribe is proud to offer these men our protection on the site of our future casino and marina," William, standing next to Reuben, slipped in.

"We'll have more to say in the morning after conferring further with my clients," Reuben announced.

"Well that's it for now from this mangrove lined building site," said one of the reporters, signing off.

"We couldn't have asked for a better finish if we wrote it ourselves," William remarked. "That mention of the mangroves ought to add some environmentalists to the mix," he said looking through the gate at the diverse crowd.

"We'll need to get some more food down to these guys," Reuben remarked, thinking out loud. "Supplies, clothes and maybe some added security. I've got some calls to make. Some things to arrange. I'll send the basketball kid, Hamilton, down with enough eats to get you through breakfast. You'll have to stay here chief, you know, official tribal presence. You and the boys be up by 6:30 in the morning ready to face the cameras. Gimme a phone number for the trailer, so I can call to check in with you."

William gave him his cell phone number.

"See you in the morning chief."

"Right," replied a bemused William.

Reuben slipped out the gate, waved good night to the officers waiting in the patrol car and headed up the hill. One of the policemen gave him a one-fingered wave in response.

William went back into the trailer where the refugees were. They hardly noticed his entry. All three were raptly engrossed with something on the computer monitor. William looked over Pedro's shoulder to see what had their attention. Great, William thought to himself. How much support would the so-called holy men get from the religious groups if they found out that the trinity used the internet to surf porn websites. Well, since it was all on Reuben's account, nobody could make a direct connection anyway.

"Listen, I've got some things to tell you," he said, reaching in and switching off the monitor. He explained to them what their present situation was and that they would have to be ready for the television people early in the morning.

"What's going to happen then?" Jesus asked.

"Mr. Elias is going to say something and then have you guys say something."

"What do we say?"

"Whatever you want. The reasons you came here."

"We want to get good jobs and get rich."

"If that's why you came, say so. Mr. Elias may have a few things he'll think you should add."

"We listen to Mr. Reuben. He says he'll take care of us."

William's cell phone rang. "Ok," was all he said.

Three minutes later he met Hamilton Patrick at the gate and let him in. The basketball player brought a couple of grocery bags of food into the construction trailer.

The refugees got excited again. They were having some day. First, rescued from the detention center by a beautiful movie star. Now, food brought to them by a famous sports star. They'd seen him on television at the Krome refugee camp. This was sure some country they'd come to.

Hamilton shook hands around and told them what an honor it was to meet them. Knowing they had to be up early, he told them he'd see them again soon, and slipped back out the trailer door. Hamilton relocked the gate after he went out.

He was stopped immediately by the two officers from the patrol car.

They each requested an autograph.

Hamilton happily obliged, requesting, "You be nice to my friends in there, ok?"

"Sure," they mumbled in reply, going back to the car.

*   *   *

Agent Neil Busch had forgotten about the two men and never sent them any relief. By six the next morning, they were sound asleep in the car and didn't hear the network remote trucks arrive and start setting up. Nor did they know that several of the cameramen took shots of them sleeping to test their video feeds to the networks. Unfortunately, Fox and NBC later started their coverage of the refugee situation using that footage. The officer who was sleeping with his mouth open, drool dripping on his badge, was severely reprimanded.

What finally woke them was the sound of a heavy truck, moving close by, booming rap music. They opened their eyes to see a large garbage truck at the gate. And this was no regular garbage truck. The whole vehicle seemed to be completely covered in chrome. At the wheel was a large smiling black man and in the passenger seat was Reuben Elias.

They knew immediately who the driver was. It was, after Wayne Huizenga owner of the Miami Dolphins, Miami's second most famous garbage man. It was Seedy Player, most notorious proponent of the latest Miami music fusion style, grunge rap. As the man himself liked to say, "I ain't a Seattle garage band, I'm a Miami garbage man." His music, while not ignoring the classic rap subjects of sex and violence, emphasized the plight of the underpaid who labored at minimum wage or undesirable jobs.

Reuben represented him on some First Amendment issues after the surprise runaway success of his first CD, I Wanna BJ. Though the music video had a chorus of very scantily clad hookers singing the refrain:

I wanna BJ
Give it to me today
Don't tell me no way
Jus' say it's ok
Do it for more pay
Gimme a good BJ
I want a Better Job

The problem was really with the opening scene. It showed a voluptuous woman in a very brief uniform, with a skirt that extended only two inches below the crotch and plenty of cleavage out the top, knocking on a hotel door. Next, the door is opened by a leering older man. The following shot is close in from behind the uniformed woman who is apparently kneeling beside the bed. Her head is bobbing up and down. With the vocal refrain playing over the movements, the scene was considered too suggestive to be aired on the music channels. Even though the next shot pans backs and shows the woman's head is bobbing up and down as she pushes a vacuum cleaner back and forth under the bed while the old man is reading a newspaper in a corner chair.

Reuben Elias successfully argued that the video, which also showed gardeners, day laborers, and fast food employees, was nothing more than a plaintive cry for better working conditions and compensation. Within three weeks of the court victory, I Wanna BJ, was the number one most requested video on the air.

The success of the CD and video soon spawned the "Seedy Rags" Collection of Clothing and Accessories. These included acid washed oversized shorts, authentic garbage man coveralls, hand torn extra large T-shirts with custom placed holes to reveal tattoos or body piercings-designed and ordered online, and finally doo rags made from real rags. Instead of Ralph Lauren's polo pony, Seedy's logo was the chrome trash truck.

This allowed him to purchase and customize a brand new garbage truck as a business expense. Besides chrome plating the exterior, the compactor at the back was replaced with a lift gate elevator to bring passengers inside.

A panel was cut out of each side of the collection area and replaced with thick one-way tempered and mirrored glass, so guests could see out, but the curious couldn't see in. There was a large flat screen monitor on the front wall to watch videos with a full service bar beneath it. Adjustable two-tier seating lined both walls. There was a 1,000-watt sound system and a powerful air conditioning system. An intercom was used for communication with the chauffeur. In fact, his driver was a friend from work who used to pick up the same route with Seedy. Although, like today, Seedy occasionally drove the truck himself just to keep in touch with his roots.

William and the three Cubans came out of the trailer to see what the commotion was about and were incredulous to see the apparition at the gate. Then Reuben stepped out of the cab and approached.

William walked up from the other side. "What the hell is that?" he barked at the spotlight-seeking barrister.

"It belongs to a client. It makes for great visuals on the tube and it'll give him some free publicity."

"It's a freakin' circus," William replied.

"Absolutely, and as long as we're the ring masters and control the spotlight, we're right where we want to be. Open the gate."

William undid the lock and swung the gate doors wide to allow the big shiny monster through.

Seedy jumped down from the cab, resplendent in a set of fluorescent purple coveralls from his own clothing line with a small chrome truck embroidered on the pocket and a large one covering the back.

To the crowd outside he yelled, " I'm here to help my oppressed brothers, like me, all they want is a better life and a better job."

There was only a small smattering of clapping from the crowd outside. The Christians, Cubans, and mainstream media were not really his fan base. The few environmentalists who'd seen the news last night and also watched music videos were the only ones to recognize him.

Reuben went into the trailer, had a brief conversation with his clients and then led them out. At his request they were still wearing the white robes, though he himself was now wearing a black suit and a shirt with what appeared to be a clerical collar. He stood them where he wanted them, so that the rising sun reflected off the chrome of the truck casting them in a beautiful aura. Then he invited the press through the gate. The broadcast network coverage was similar on all the major outlets. There was a thirty-second explanation of the refugee's location, the reservation land that was now pristine mangrove lined bayfront, soon-to-be a casino and marina. William was quoted, "they may have sanctuary here as long as necessary." There was a brief shot of the two police officers, first sleeping, and now alert guarding the gate. Finally, there were the refugees standing in the heavenly light.

Jesus made a brief statement, " Pedro, Pablo, and I came here seeking freedom, a better life, better jobs and the right to practice our religious beliefs." The part about religion was added at Reuben's suggestion, "We came to escape oppression. Please help us."

Reuben piped in, "Please contact your state and federal representatives and let them know you want these men freed."

Fox closed its coverage with a shot of Seedy yelling, "Let my brothers go."

After the three men returned to the trailer, several of the reporters were asking Reuben when his clients would be available for more extensive interviews. The one's that knew him, knew it would be difficult for him to resist the national exposure.

But Reuben was shrewd enough to see that there would be several problems. There was the questionable legality of their arrival, not to mention that minimal investigation would lead to the fact that they were dropped on the beach by smugglers. There was also their escape from a federal detention facility. And though he really had nothing to do with its planning or execution, the fact that they ended up just down the hill from where he lived certainly raised suspicions. Finally, in spite of their names, there was the problem that they really held no religious beliefs. Reuben could concoct reasonable and satisfactory answers for these things, but it would take a little time.

For now, his response to requests for longer interviews would have to be, "We prefer to see how our government agencies react to the present situation first. We will take your requests under advisement and get back to you."

When they had no success with Reuben, like a pack of hyenas, they switched to a secondary prey. "Chief Panther, would you be available for either a sit down or live network interview with one of our New York anchors?" asked the NBC reporter.

Not used to publicity, and uncomfortable receiving it, not to mention surprised by the question, William blurted out a terse "No."

He liked the perky young woman on the Today Show and enjoyed watching her interviews. Her questions were intelligent and got right to the point, often making her subjects squirm. He didn't feel like being the target in her sights. Of course, he didn't say any of this out loud when the reporter asked him, "Why not?"

At this point Reuben stepped in to help out, "What Chief Panther means is that he is not available at this time. As we are all in this together, it behooves us to discuss our strategy amongst ourselves first. Isn't that what you mean, William?"

"Yes." Despite his innate distrust of lawyers, especially outlandishly behaved ones like Reuben, William found himself developing an appreciation of the smooth way the little bantam handled changing situations.

"When we're ready to talk, you'll be the first to know," Elias told her.

After the reporters took a few more opening and closing shots to be edited in later, they left.

Reuben then offered William this advice, "Don't ever just cut them off with a no. Always leave your options available. You might want to talk to them later to make a point of your own. For instance, bringing up the destruction of the mangroves and bay bottom to build the resort could just come up casually in passing. On a national broadcast you'll have the Sierra Club and the like down here in no time."

"Point taken. Thanks for the help. How come your friend didn't leave with the news people?" William asked pointing towards Seedy.

"He really wants to help. He's not just here for the publicity," said Reuben giving Seedy a thumbs up sign.

Seedy, actually Charles Deveraux a Haitian immigrant who really was living the American dream, knocked on the window of the compartment, then went around to the back of the truck. William heard the hydraulic motion of the elevator as it started to descend. When it stopped, William saw three very attractive, provocatively dressed young women step out, each carrying a couple of purple plastic bags with Seedy's logo.

"What the?" William exclaimed.

"Listen, those are young men. Unless we provide them with diversions, they're going to get stir crazy. Mr. Player has simply brought along some friends of his who expressed a strong desire to meet the boys," Reuben explained.

William, fairly conservative in his outlook, asked, "Don't you kind of feel like a pimp?"

"Every one here is an adult, all free to do whatever they're comfortable with. I don't know what's going to happen or particularly want to know," he replied. "Good show Mr. Player, don't you think?" he asked as Seedy and the girls walked over to him.

"Excellent my friend. You have an eye for staging. Perhaps you'd give me some input on my next music video."

"Absolutely. It would be my pleasure," Reuben replied. He meant it. Another shot at showbiz.

They all stepped into the trailer.

Reuben introduced Seedy Player to the three young men. They were vaguely aware of who he was, having heard some of his music while detained at Krome. They couldn't keep their eyes off his companions.

Seedy introduced the young ladies, "This is Maria, Magdalena, and Maria," he smiled. "They've brought you some of the latest samples of my clothing line. Ladies, why don't you take the boys into the bedroom back there and help them try the stuff on."

The six young people hurried down the narrow hallway to the sleeping quarters area of the trailer. They closed the door quickly behind them.

The trailer was not particularly sound proofed and the noises from the back soon made it apparent what was happening behind the door.

"Oh man," William moaned. First aiding and abetting fugitives, now I'm an assistant procurer, he thought. Reuben and Seedy looked at the distress on his face and broke out laughing.

"They could stand a little tension release," Reuben told him.

"Give the immigrants a break," Seedy chuckled.

Forty-five minutes later the refugees came out wearing matching purple silk coveralls, patterned on trash collectors uniforms with the silver garbage truck logo over the breast pocket. If they'd look somewhat strange in their biblical robes, now they looked ridiculous, sort of like young ZZ Top goes hip-hop. They did seem much less tense. All of them were smiling.

"Thank you Mr. Seedy," Jesus said, "for the clothes and everything." His brothers smiled appreciatively behind him, with the ladies grinning behind them.

"What now Reuben?" William asked, almost afraid of what the answer might be.

"I'll leave the ladies and the truck here for a while if you want," Seedy offered.

The refugees gave Reuben hopeful looks. But he didn't need that kind of distraction right now. "No, I think you'd better take everything for now," and added, in an effort to not disappoint the boys too badly, "But we'll have you back real soon."

"Ok. Let's go then girls," Seedy commanded.

Magdalena kissed Jesus and the Marias kissed Pablo and Pedro goodbye.

"We'll be back," the girls chimed in unison. The refugees walked the girls back to the truck.

"Hey Seedy, I may still get with you on the security thing. You know, if it's starting to look too out of control here," William said as the rapper stood in the trailer door. He knew his tribe wouldn't hire help to guard the refugees and that Rex, preferring to keep a low profile at the development, wouldn't hire security to guard the property. Seedy's experience on the club and performing scenes gave him lots of contacts with the security profession.

"Sure thing. Some of my Cuban brothers in trash will probably be glad to watch your gate for free. Solidarity with the boys. Jus' let me know," he replied and closed the door.

"That might not be a bad idea," Reuben mused, "We're spread kind of thin here. The situation could get hard to control. We have to be able to limit access. We don't need a hundred militant environmentalists like those Nature Pax types breaking in and chaining themselves to the mangroves. If we can control the perimeter, we can just let a few in."

"A confrontation with security people also might make the feds think twice. Just in case they don't think our sanctuary offer has enough standing to keep them from coming in and grabbing the boys as fugitives," William added.

"You're beginning to think like me," Reuben replied.

"That's a scary thought," William said quickly.

"Makes me a decent living," the bantam barrister was just as quick in his rejoinder.

"Damn if it doesn't. And you really do meet some of the most interesting people," William smiled looking over Reuben's shoulder at the hirsute fugitives in their shiny purple silks.

"My life's not boring," Elias laughed.

"There's an understatement. Listen, Reuben you watch the guys for a while, I want to go back up to Lindsey's and arrange for some fresh clothes and check on the birds."

"Sure. I'm their lawyer. With a video camera and a computer link I can hold the hordes at bay for a while."

"You live for this stuff, don't you?"

"Keeps me young. If I need anything I'll call you at Lindsey's. In the mean time, I think I'll get hold of Seedy and have him set us up with some protection," he answered as he reached for his cell phone.

William left the lawyer to work his connections. As he went through the gate, he gave a little wave to the small crowd gathered outside. A few waved back.

It was the couple of shouts of "way to go chief" that lightened his climb up the hill. The approach was certainly unorthodox and the method ostentatious for a reserved, quiet man like William Panther. But down deep he felt good because he knew he was on the right side. The voiced approval helped reinforce that feeling.

 **Chapter X**

All over the country the feces was figuratively, and in one case literally, hitting the blades. The news coverage had kick started the day for the exile community, Rex and Rogelio, Barry Silver and Agent Busch.

There were mixed feelings among the Cuban exiles. There was happiness over the fact that the three men were out of reach of the INS for the present. At the same time there was uncertainty over how long their sanctuary could last and the fact that it left them in a kind of legal limbo. Finally, there was some distress amongst the political power brokers because they continued to have no direct access to the refugees. At present, Reuben Elias wouldn't even return their calls. This limited their ability to offer any help directly and for the more cynical, their ability to exploit the situation for their own benefit.

Rex Panther and Rogelio Negro both had phones ringing off the hook. They each had individual problems, as well as problems common to the suddenly well-publicized resort development. There were so many calls that they had trouble reaching one another for more than an hour.

Rex, though the designated leader of the tribe, still answered to a Tribal Council. Several members had called to find out why they weren't consulted before the three refugees were offered sanctuary. None was really mad. This wasn't the first time the Miccosukees had tweaked the nose of local and federal law enforcement. In fact, the general opinion was that by sticking up for the little guys, the tribe was going to get good P.R. The main thing was that the Council felt it should have been consulted on a decision of such political import. Rex had to explain that William had made the decision without even consulting him.

They also questioned housing the refugees at the small development site. It would have been much easier to care for them and keep an eye on them at the reservation in the Everglades. Again, because Rex hadn't talked to William since the whole incident started, he made excuses for him. He told them that the men would have to stay in the bayside trailers now, because if they transported them off the reservation, the feds would capture them.

The Council told him they must be consulted on any further decisions concerning the Cubans. He promised to keep them apprised of any significant changes in the situation.

He needed to talk to William, but first he'd try Rogelio Negro again. Rogelio was at least there, on top of Mount Basura, and would give him a more practical, less emotional, evaluation of the situation.

The phone was still busy. He couldn't even get through to Rogelio's secretary.

Rogelio was swamped with calls from the residents of Mount Basura. Half of them were upset with the access road being clogged by protesters, supporters, and media vehicles. People in two-million dollar plus residences didn't expect to have to battle their way into the entrance of their exclusive development. They also didn't appreciate the early morning cacophony from the crowd watching the trailers or heavy bass thumping that announced the arrival of Seedy's truck.

The other half of the complaints involved an escalation of an already existent problem. And it wouldn't help that William had already checked on the raptors that morning to make sure they had a large early feeding, then got out to fly for exercise. The seagulls and other previous avian occupants of the dump had been bad enough. The fact was that the birds of prey had actually been fairly successful chasing them off. However, neither Rex nor Rogelio had considered the obvious. If small birds leave two-inch droppings, what could a large bird like an osprey leave? The fact was, according to Florida Power and Light, that they could leave six-foot long strings of scat, enough to short out power lines. Residents who'd found their cars and patios thusly decorated were impressed by, though not appreciative of, the birds' output. They demanded to know what

Rogelio was going to do about it. He told them he'd consult with his environmental advisors and get back to them. He had no freaking idea how to stop the birds.

His phone rang again. It was Rex.

"Have you seen the news this morning?" he asked the chief.

"Yes. Hell yes. Have you seen my brother? He's not answering his cell phone," came Rex's reply.

"Only on the tube. We need this kind of publicity like a bleeding swimmer needs a shark. Did you know he was going to do this?"

"No, he did this all on his own. First time he's taken initiative in tribal proceedings and he brings us the spotlight where we don't want it," Rex lamented.

"We got a lot of spin work to do. Emphasize the plight of the refugees. How we're the only ones to step in to try to protect them. Hell, if we work it right, maybe even name the resort The Sanctuary. A permanent reminder of the good we did."

"You got a gift for the bullshit," Rex complimented. "But you really think it'll shut the environmentalists up?"

"No. But maybe it'll keep them in the background. Speaking of environmental problems, you gotta help me with the birds."

"Whatta you mean? The birds of prey not working out?"

"Oh just great. The gulls and the other little birds that used to hang out here are almost all gone."

"So, that's good," Rex interjected.

"Let me finish. Apparently the large birds take dumps big enough to cover the whole hood of a Range Rover. My residents are pissed. You didn't know about this?" Rogelio asked.

"What the heck do I know about bird shit? I'm a businessman. I leave nature stuff to my brother."

There was a silent pause on both ends of the line. The idea that William was maybe not such an innocent naïf began to dawn on both of them.

Rex broke the silence, "Worst comes to worst and we'll move the birds out to the Glades reservation. Right now I need to talk to my brother."

"Yeah. You do. Let me know what you find out from him. We need to know what he's thinking."

"Right. I'll get back to you," Rex replied.

"OK. Meantime I'll get hold of some of my P.R. guys and start to get the situation slanted our way. Good bye."

*   *   *

Barry Gold was livid and not sure what to do. He had been glad when the refugees were liberated from government detention, but surprised when he'd found out they'd escaped with someone else. He had in fact planned to offer them religious sanctuary in the Church of the Kosher Redeemer.

When he'd heard that instead they'd been given sanctuary by the Miccosukees he had regained hope of at least being able to connect with his holy men. However, he had been unable to reach Reuben Elias or any member of the Miccosukee tribe to put him in touch with the refugees. So he had gone down to the resort development site to see if he could talk his way in. He arrived just in time to see Seedy's chrome waste hauler pull in and unload its cargo. The sight of the three Jezebels going into the trailer made his blood run cold. When they'd come out later holding hands with the holy men, no longer in their robes, but instead wearing hideous purple jumpsuits, he knew his faith was being put to the test. At least the women had left.

He knew he had to do whatever he could do to save them, to keep their purity from being further besmirched. He had to get them away from the secular and carnal temptations that would be flung in their path. He had to help them refocus on their holy mission.

He just didn't know how. He couldn't take other Semites for the Son and storm the gates. There were police and media watching and they would be apprehended before they could make it back to their church.

He could and would call for the Ark. An aerial assault was of course out of the question. It would be greater than a miracle to escape in something as large and slow as a blimp. But at least the Ark would be a good platform to keep an eye on what was happening in the trailer compound. And the light board could be used to flash messages of hope and salvation to remind the holy men of their purpose. Until Barry could connect with them himself, the Ark would have to do.

*   *   *

Livid would be a polite description of Agent Neil Busch's demeanor. Royally pissed and ready to rip someone's head off would be more accurate.

Losing the refugees from Krome due to an admittedly clever sound effects assault had been a terrible embarrassment. Finding them ensconced out of reach on an Indian reservation showed how the INS had been outsmarted. The last straw had been the TV shots of the two police officers outside the reservation gate asleep and drooling on each other. It made law enforcement look like a bunch of bozos.

Shit rolls down hill. As the agent in charge, Neil Busch was getting dumped on by everyone above him. He was buried up to his eyes. He didn't like the feeling and the refugees were going to pay. They had repeatedly thumbed their noses at authority and he was not going to cut them any slack. He no longer cared what the political implications were and what the higher ups wanted. As far as he was concerned, the men were fugitive escapees and any compromise in their case would set bad precedent. He was tired of people not respecting the law and law enforcement. He would recapture those sons of bitches if it was the last thing he did.

He had a few phone calls to make. The first was to set up a schedule of rotating patrols to watch both the front gate and any possible water access to the reservation refuge.

The second call he made on his own personal cell phone. It was to an old Marine Corps buddy who was commander of the county's S.W.A.T. team. He knew it was his friend's day off and phoned him at home. They had an interesting fifteen-minute conversation discussing assorted hostage night rescue scenarios and techniques. There was special emphasis on removing unconscious hostages especially those who might not wish to be saved.

*   *   *

Blissfully ignorant of all the activity that the morning's news coverage had precipitated, William trotted back up the refuse pyramid. He couldn't wait to see Lindsey again. It wasn't just that she was a beautiful young woman. In fact, though the aquamarine green eyes, sandy blonde hair, and trim body made a tremendous package, it wasn't her physical beauty that he found most attractive. He liked her character, her willingness to take chances helping the refugees and injured birds. He liked the fact that she was an honest critic of her own work. She knew her movies were nothing more than escapist entertainment and that there was nothing wrong with that. He liked that she hadn't tried to cover her physical imperfections. When her nose was broken by an errant elbow during her Tushball League career, it had healed with the middle meandering a tad to the right. She'd left it that way. And the crow's feet at the corners of her eyes from years spent in the sun remained untouched by Botox. To William these characteristics just made her more interesting, enhancing her personality.

His reverie was interrupted by unexpected movement at the edge of his field of vision. To his right, about three quarters of the way up the side of the trash mesa he thought he saw a piece of the sod cover rise in a large bubble then settle back into place. He stopped and turned to inspect the area more closely. He observed the suspect piece of turf. The grass just lay there clinging to the slope like it was supposed to. Wispy clouds scudding in front of the morning sun cast light shadows and patterns on the side of the pyramid. After a few minutes of observation with no perceptible change in the turf, William chalked it up as trick of changing light. He started on his way up again. A few steps above the suspect area he thought he caught a faint whiff of methane, but the sea breeze quickly carried it away.

As he climbed over the hedge around Lindsey's yard, he saw that she had been standing watching him come up.

"What'd you stop for," she kidded, "Catch your breath? Don't have many chances to do mountain climbing around here." She could see that actually he hadn't even broken a sweat.

"No," he played it straight, "I thought I saw the earth move, but it was probably just a change of light."

96

"What'd you see?"

He explained the percolating sod vision he'd caught out of the corner of his eye.

"You know, sometimes on a quiet night, when I'm catching the view from the widow's walk, I'd swear I could hear rumbling noises coming from down inside the Mont."

"Well there's a lot of garbage decomposing under here," he replied.

"Yeah, but Rogelio has a state of the art gas collection system built underneath the surface. It provides part of the energy supply to the development."

"But how good is state of the art? Isn't this essentially a new concept techno-...?" He stopped mid-sentence. This was not at all how he had intended for his reunion with Lindsey to go, discussing the merits of methane scavenging technology. "Let's drop the subject," he finished then added, "It sure is great to see you again." He shut up and drank her in from head to toe. She was barefoot, wearing a simple white shell top, with a white linen over blouse and a matching midi-length skirt. The contrast against her lightly tanned freckled skin was stunning. He momentarily just stood and stared.

Lindsey too had intended his return to be a lot friendlier than a discussion of gas collection. She'd understood when the five of them fled to avoid the police. But this morning watching them all on television with the additional appearance of the local rap star and his entourage, she'd felt left out. Still as she was watching William work his way up the side of the pyramid, she realized that she wasn't just happy to see him, she'd actually been longing for his return.

She stood watching him staring at her. It wasn't the first time she'd had this effect on a man. But it was the first time she'd had the "deer in the headlights" effect on a man she was interested in.

"Get over it," she told him. "It's not like you haven't seen me before."

William blinked, "Sorry, it's just that you look so good. And the boys had some pretty girl visitors. And well you look so good," he stammered. The man of few words wasn't doing too well with the ones he knew.

"Oh stop," she stepped close and put two fingers on his lips.

Looking down into her eyes he embraced her, gently pushing her fingers out of the way. They kissed.

And kissed.

And kissed.

God she smelled good, tasted good, too.

William took a half step back. He realized that he was still wearing the same clothes from the morning before and that he'd slept in them.

"You know I could really use a shower. Then maybe we could continue our discussion on methane collection," he smiled.

"Fine," she took his hand and led him into the house. At the bottom of the stairs she let go.

"You know where everything is. There's a bathrobe in the guestroom closet. Since you don't have a change of clothes just take your stuff off and throw it down. I'll put it in the wash. You can wear the robe 'til your clothes are done."

"Okay," he headed up the staircase. A couple minutes later there was a soft whump as a wad of blue denim and cotton landed at the bottom of the steps.

Lindsey picked them up. The masculine musk was slightly intoxicating. She quickly took them and put them in the washer.

Then she headed up the stairs. She did not intend to be a virgin much longer.

She tossed her clothes onto a chair by the bed in the guest room and padded quietly into the bathroom. William was inside the glassed shower enclosure. He was rinsing his hair, his back to her.

She quietly opened the door. Nice ass. There was an eight-inch lighter tan streak running down the back of his calf.

"How'd you get that scar?"

"Hunting gators with my dad. I was a kid and didn't know how fast they could whip their tails," he said as he turned around. He had obviously been thinking about her and looked like he was expecting her.

Their lovemaking was not long and langorous, more like quick and satisfying. It was lust with little control.

As they lay together afterward, she whispered, "Thanks, it was my first time."

Maybe her first time with a Native American, he mused in his head. But then he thought for a second. Though their coupling had finished well. (Was there such a thing as a bad orgasm?) There were times during the frenzy when things had seemed awkward. He was glad he hadn't blurted out his first thought. She really was something a whole lot different from her public image. He believed her.

"Really, I didn't hurt you did I?" he replied instead, taking her at her word.

"Oh no. I'm just not very experienced. Was it okay for you?" He could see in her eyes that she hoped he wasn't disappointed.

His smile let her know it was just fine.

She smiled back, "We could work on my experience."

"Excellent idea," he grinned.

His clothes didn't get tossed into the dryer until several hours later.

 **Chapter XI**

Things weren't just heating up in Lindsey's guest room.

They had worked on several lessons for Lindsey's benefit and worked up quite an appetite in the process. So they broke for lunch.

Lindsey was putting the makings for a couple of sub sandwiches on the counter, when she noticed the flashing light on her answering machine. There was no phone in the guest room and they'd been too busy to hear it ringing in the more distant reaches of the house. Not that they'd have answered it anyway.

There were several calls from Reuben over the last two hours. They had progressed from the first polite "Please call me back as soon as you can," to the last "Where the hell are you and where's that damned chief? We need to talk right away."

Lindsey motioned to William who came over and started assembling the lunch while she dialed Reuben's cell.

"What's the problem?" she asked when Reuben answered.

After listening, she tapped William and pointed to the TV, holding up the number of fingers to indicate the local tabloid news station. William switched the channel. There was a live aerial shot from a news chopper. It showed the reservation land with three police cruisers and a plain black federal sedan at the gate. Panning the camera back he could see the two government boats patrolling the shoreline. All of a sudden a large silver bulbous mass passed close beneath the news helicopter.

"What the...?" William blurted. Then he looked out the back kitchen window. He saw the outline of the Ark as it hovered at a height little higher than the top of Mont Basura.

"Well, looks like you got their attention," Lindsey was saying to Reuben. She listened for a few more seconds and her smile disappeared.

"He wants to talk to you," she said, handing William the handset and muttering to herself, "I sure hope Ham is home," as she rummaged in her purse for her cell phone.

William, a puzzled look on his face as he watched Lindsey, said "Yeah, Reuben."

"Listen chief. The phone in the trailer here has been buzzing off the hook. Your brother keeps calling, wondering where you are and he has some bug up his ass about you not consulting him and the tribal council about the sanctuary deal. We aren't going to have a problem are we? Would he kick us out?"

"Not a chance. He wouldn't risk offending all those future resort and casino customers."

While talking to Reuben, he was trying to hear what Lindsey was saying and heard, "Hamilton could you do us a big favor? Right now!"

"---From the tribe with security here?" was all William heard of Reuben's last statement.

"What?"

"I said will your brother help provide us with security?" Reuben reiterated.

"I doubt it. He isn't going to want to risk direct confrontation with law enforcement while trying to set up a casino. They could make getting the gaming thing a nightmare."

"I was afraid you'd say that. I'll see what Seedy can do. He has some interesting contacts."

"You really think we need protection?"

"Well, we don't want some of the nuts on the other side of the fence sneaking in here. And don't forget Elian."

"Yeah," William replied. The Elian Gonzalez incident several years before had torn the community apart. The early morning raid that snatched the little boy away form his Miami relatives so he could be returned to his father in Cuba was still having repercussions. Several top

Miami police officers had resigned after being made scapegoats even though they were helping carry out legal Justice Department orders. And there were still pending legal actions against both Immigration and Justice.

"And remember the relatives were still negotiating on the phone at almost the same time the police were breaking down the door. We can't risk leaving our asses uncovered," Reuben added.

"You're right. See what Seedy can do. Gotta go," Lindsey was waving at him frantically to get off the phone.

"Right. You got more pressing problems right now," Reuben replied as he hung up.

Though extremely relaxed ten minutes ago, Lindsey seemed quite anxious now.

"What's going on? Why do we need the basketball player?" he asked.

She explained to William what Reuben had overheard. Agent Busch had arrived at the gate about half an hour before. He had told two cars that they would cover the gate and to check any vehicle coming out, to be sure the fugitives weren't escaping. Then he'd told the third car it would accompany him as soon as he received the search warrant he was waiting for.

Reuben quickly put two and two together. Since they couldn't come on reservation land, the only place left they could legally search would be Lindsey's house. Now everyone knew that the refugees had been at Lindsey's at least briefly. But the question was, how did they get there? Aiding the escape and flight of federal detainees was something they didn't want to be charged with. Though there was no eyewitness identification of the Miccosukee Navigator from the Krome detention center, the big, black SUV was sitting in Lindsey's garage with a back seat full of refugee fingerprints.

"Get your clothes on," she commanded coming out of the laundry room and throwing him his stuff. "And move the truck over to Hamilton's garage. Now."

He dropped his robe and dressed right in front of her. She stopped chewing her bite of sandwich to enjoy the view of his tan, lithe body.

He saw her checking him out and winked, "Another time."

"I'll hold you to it. Get going."

He headed to the garage. The keys were in the ignition where he'd left them.

She watched from the front window as he backed out and headed around the corner to Hamilton's where she could see the basketball player waiting with his garage door open. Luckily, for once, Florio Flores was not watching her house out his front window. Two minutes later the door was closed and William was talking to Hamilton out on the front walk.

Suddenly there were flashing lights heading towards Lindsey's house from the opposite direction down the street. Though not unexpected, Lindsey still found the arrival of Agent Busch and the police unnerving. But she put on her best front. After all she was a professional actress.

"Agent Busch, what a surprise," she said opening the door and smiling before he had the chance to knock.

"I have a warrant to search your house," he said stepping into the foyer, his voice icy cold, his steel gray eyes scanning the room behind her. Two agents in matching dark suits came in behind him.

"May I see it?" she said, opening her hand to receive the order that would allow them to tear her place apart if they felt like it.

"You familiar with this process?" he smirked as he handed her the paper.

"I know I have rights," she replied trying to sound as forceful as she could. She was intimidated by the three Feds in suits but was determined not to let them see it. She perused the document. It had her name and address on it but otherwise might as well have been hieroglyphics for all the sense she could make of it.

"Seems in order," she handed it back.

"It is. Search the place. Start with the garage," Busch ordered the other two.

Lindsey breathed an audible sigh of relief.

Agent Busch who'd been on his way toward the kitchen turned back, "Did you say something?"

"Nothing," she smiled.

During the search, Hamilton and William had walked to Lindsey's, but were denied entry by the two uniformed officers at the front door. They waited patiently outside, discussing the rehabbing raptors, the weather and the upcoming basketball season to kill time.

The search didn't last long, maybe half an hour. There was little to find since the refugees had arrived with no possessions, and left not long after their arrival. About the only evidence might be a few fingerprints in the kitchen. But the agents had come without a fingerprint kit. And the only car in the garage was Lindsey's white Grand Cherokee.

"Were you expecting company? There's a couple of unfinished sandwiches on the kitchen table," Busch commented.

"Yes. The guys at the front door were coming for lunch as soon as they finished checking the bird rehab center," she replied loud enough for Hamilton and William to hear. "Unfortunately you interrupted."

"Sorry. We'll be leaving soon," the head agent replied.

"I could have told you that you wouldn't find anything. That you'd be leaving empty-handed," she smiled.

"You're wrong, Ms. Olson. When I say 'we', you're included. Lindsey Lee Olson, you are under arrest. For knowingly harboring federal fugitives," he'd been waiting to drop the hammer on her.

"What? I---" She was incredulous.

"---Anything you may say may be used against you in a court of law," he was continuing with the law enforcement arrest mantra. He finished Mirandizing her.

"I don't think the cuffs will be necessary," Busch said to his two agents. "Make sure those two don't interfere with our exit," he directed the two police officers.

They both reached for their holsters. William and Ham backed out of the way.

"You rich fuckers all think the law doesn't apply to you," Busch muttered as he passed the two astonished men. "Well it does."

"William, call Reuben," Lindsey pleaded as she was pulled into the car. "He's programmed into my cell." The car door was slammed shut.

As the Feds were backing out, an osprey returning to the rehab center dropped a big load of raptor guano on their hood. A little poetic justice, William and Hamilton agreed. A Santero priest of the local Afro-Cuban religion reading the feathers and bone fragments in the droppings splattered across the dark blue hood would have told Neil Busch the signs were not good. Trouble was coming soon.

The Miccosukee and the pro hoops player went into Lindsey's house.

Hamilton noticed how familiarly William moved through the residence. How he knew right where to go to find her purse and the cell. He'd also heard her tone when she asked William to call Reuben. He could tell that somehow the two had gotten closer and that she knew she could rely on his looking out for her.

"You two together now?" he asked, knowing the answer already.

There was a momentary pause, then an affirmative nod from the Miccosukee who was scrolling through the cell phone's directory looking for Reuben's number.

Hamilton was disappointed. He'd lost his chance with Lindsey Lee. However, he didn't hold it against William. He liked the Indian himself. Thought he was a straight up guy. At least he'd lost her to a guy with some integrity and not some sycophant looking to share the glow of her spotlight.

William was talking to Reuben, "That Busch just arrested Lindsey."

All Hamilton heard was William's side of the conversation.

"For knowingly harboring federal fugitives. Possibly for obstructing their arrest."

"You're going where?"

"The federal court house downtown. Who's going to watch the guys?"

"We'll be right down," William finished, looking over at Hamilton as he snapped the phone shut.

"What's up?"

The Heat player was getting that pumped up feeling like at the start of a game. It felt good, invigorating, to be in on the action.

"I gotta go back down and baby-sit the boys while Reuben goes up to Miami to arrange Lindsey's bail and release. I was hoping you'd come along. I'm not much of a talker and you're closer to their age, more wired into pop culture than I am."

"No problem. I'd like to talk to them about how things really are in Cuba. I met some Cuban players once at the Pan Am games. But they couldn't talk politics-had watchers hanging over their shoulder all the time."

"Great," William was relieved he wouldn't have to entertain them by himself.

He fished around in Lindsey's purse some more until he came up with a set of keys. He and Ham went around locking up the back of the house since they weren't sure when anyone would be back.

As William was locking the front door, a big black Mercedes sedan pulled into Lindsey's driveway. Rogelio emerged from the driver's side and his brother, Rex, from the passenger's.

"Where the hell you been all day?" was the somewhat less than loving filial greeting his brother bellowed at him.

Making love to a wonderful women and hiding evidence didn't seem like the right thing to say so William just answered, "Around."

"Why don't you answer your goddamned phone?" Rex barked. He was pissed off. He didn't like being out of the loop and out of control.

William's cell phone was in a compartment in the center console of the "Big Cat." That reminded him about the truck and gave him an idea.

"I left it in the Navigator. By the way, maybe you could drive it back to the casino. I've got some things to take care of down the hill."

By now Rex and Rogelio were standing right in William's face. But they weren't getting too belligerent. There was just something naturally intimidating about the seven- foot plus Hamilton standing quietly behind him. The fact that he was there with his arms crossed, clenching and unclenching his fists probably helped slow them down.

"What do you mean take care of something? What's going on?" Rex asked in a frustrated but more civil tone.

"Lindsey's been arrested."

"What?" It was Rogelio's turn to chime in. He really did care about her. After all she'd been instrumental in the success of both the National Tushball League and Mont Basura.

William detailed Lindsey's arrest for them.

"How'd those guys end up in her house?" Rex was getting suspicious.

William had left out some of the major details.

"Better you don't know. I believe the politicians call it plausible deniability. You wouldn't want to be brought in as accessories," William replied.

"Okay. Forget I asked. What are we gonna do about the refugees?" Rex responded.

"Yeah. The noise, the media attention, the traffic. My people up here paying seven figures for these places don't like all that shit. And speaking of shit, what're you going to do about the birds?" Rogelio added.

"I thought we had the seagull thing under pretty good control," William was disingenuous.

"Don't screw with us. Why didn't you say something about what the big birds would do?" Rex was starting to get heated again.

Hamilton cleared his throat.

Rex glanced at him and forced himself to calm down. He hadn't done physical confrontations in years. He had people that did it for him, sometimes including his brother.

"Hey, you just told me you wanted to be rid of the seagulls and wanted some good press. I gave you that," William smiled.

"All right. Okay. Forget the birds for now. We'll deal with them later. What're we going to do about the refugee thing?"

"What'ya mean forget the birds. One of these naturists (i.e. nudists) got dipped in shit sunbathing on his patio yesterday. He's threatening to sue. I don't need this headache."

"Act of God. Shit won't fly," Rex grinned at his own pun. "We've got to control this problem with the so-called holy men. Ratchet down the media interest. Keep the environmental people from getting too stirred up."

"Maybe we can control the media access. And do something about that damned blimp. That sign flashing repent ye sinners and return to the fold is bugging a lot of the residents up here," Rogelio added.

Sinning probably paid for a lot of these million dollar houses, William thought to himself. The owners didn't like being called on it.

"What'ya think William?" Rex pleaded. "Can't we just try to keep this under wraps? Let the legal system handle it."

"Well," William let the syllable hang for a moment relishing what he would say next. "Reuben Elias, he's the Cubans' lawyer. You've probably heard of him. Since I don't have any experience dealing with the press, I'm letting him handle it."

Rogelio groaned. He knew it would be easier to snatch a steak bone out of a pit bull's mouth than it would to separate Elias from the media.

"Listen. Hamilton and I are heading down to Reuben now. We've got to stay with the Cubans while he goes up to Miami to bail Lindsey out. You want to say something to him, why don't you come along. Here's the keys to your truck," William said handing them to Rex.

Hamilton pushed the button on his remote system and his garage door opened.

"What's it doing over there?" Rex asked curiously.

"You know on second thought maybe you should just drive it over to Rogelio's and have him bring you back to it later. And I'd have the inside well detailed when you get it back to the reservation," William replied.

Rex didn't ask any more. He'd heard the news reports about the refugees escaping in a black SUV.

"Ride with me," he invited William.

"No, thanks. Hamilton and I are taking the shortcut," William had no desire to be alone with his brother who would undoubtedly take the opportunity to chew him out.

Hamilton stepped forward and handed Rex the garage door control. "Bring it to me down on the reservation after you get your truck out."

"Sure thing," Rex replied, taking it out of the giant's big paw.

"See you down there," said William to Rex and Rogelio as he and Ham turned and trotted around the side of Lindsey's house, heading for the side of the pyramid.

 **Chapter XII**

Reuben was waiting for them when William and Hamilton reached the reservation gate.

"What happened? Tell me everything you can about the search and arrest," Reuben demanded as they entered the compound.

"Nice to see you too," Hamilton returned expecting a little civility.

"Listen kid. I don't have time for niceties. It's twenty miles north to get to the federal courthouse and it's getting late. I don't want her spending the night in jail. So give me what you know," Reuben was getting anxious. He wasn't without a conscience. He didn't want his friends to get in trouble for helping his clients.

Hamilton and William told him what little they knew considering that they'd been kept outside the whole time. William finished, "But they didn't seem to have found anything. The only thing they took out of the house is Lindsey. And they didn't bother to seal the house with tape as a crime scene when they left."

"That son of a bitch, Busch. He's just trying to redeem himself. Maybe drop the charges in exchange for the holy men surrendering. That ain't gonna to happen," the lawyer was talking to himself.

Reuben was starting for the gate when Rex and Rogelio pulled up in Rogelio's Mercedes. Rogelio popped out heading right for the bantam attorney. "Reuben, we gotta talk. I don't need all the publicity you're bringing down here."

"Don't have time to talk now. Gotta get Lindsey bailed out," Reuben responded.

"Listen Reuben, we go way back. I know you."

Reuben cut him off, "You want to talk to me. Give me a ride up to Miami. We'll talk on the way." Reuben opened the back door and got into the car.

Rogelio was just getting back into the driver's seat when he heard the deep thumping bass heading toward him. Looking west down the access road, he wasn't quite sure what to make of the convoy coming his direction.

Approaching the gate was a large silver garbage truck followed by five sport utilities, three Hummers and two Excursions. And these were not the plain, basic models. They all had custom paint jobs, with extra lighting, boosted audio systems and special rims sprinkled amongst them.

Rogelio just shook his head. Things were definitely not quieting down. He wanted to strangle Reuben. Inside the car Rex glared at the little lawyer. "What the fuck is that?"

In response, Reuben rolled down his window and yelled to William over the loud music, "The security we talked about is here. Let them in." To Rogelio he said, "Let's get moving."

Realizing there was nothing he could do to stop the show now, Rogelio reluctantly pulled around the last two SUVs and headed up to Miami. William opened the gate and the convoy pulled in, parking in a semi-circle around the construction trailers. They strategically covered the trailer doors. The sight of the wildly decorated vehicles forming a protective barrier was pushing the limit of William's credulity.

Hamilton was checking out the rides and commenting to himself, "Awesome. Phat. Cool."

Then the occupants got out and William really couldn't believe what he saw. The holy men, hearing the booming rap music, had come out to check the source of the vibe and stood frozen and utterly confused.

Seedy got out of the garbage truck accompanied by the two Marias and Magdalena. This of course made Jesus and the two disciples quite happy. It was the men from the support vehicles that had William and the trinity more than a little nervous.

There were ten of them, two from each one, each decked out in the most current "Seedy Stuff." No surprise there. It was the fact that each was wearing a shoulder holster or two. All contained large caliber handguns, .45s, Glock 9 millimeters, maybe a 44 magnum or two, nicely finished in either shiny nickel plating or brushed stainless.

Seedy walked over to William and Ham who noticed the gold plated .44 stuck in his waistband. "Yo chief. Security's here!"

"Tell me those aren't real guns and you're filming some kind of music video," William almost begged. He felt what little control he had over the situation slipping away.

" Course they're real. Got to make any intruders think twice."

"Cool," Hamilton chipped in.

William didn't find this particularly helpful.

"Tell me they're at least licensed to carry them," William pleaded.

"Right to bear arms my man. Second amendment. I studied for my citizenship exam. Who needs a license?" Seedy smiled.

"Oh Jesus," William muttered.

"Relax. I was just was having fun with you. They all got permits. Man this is Florida. Permits no big thing. God bless the NRA."

It was true. It wasn't difficult to get a concealed weapons carry permit in Florida. Make a claim that you need personal protection for some reason---carry a lot of cash, wear expensive jewelry, been physically threatened, need the extra weight as part of an individualized fitness program---pass a cursory background check and next thing you know you got a permit.

"Good. At least it's one less headache. Who are these guys?" William motioned, waving at the men who by now had gathered around the Heat's new center to check him out.

"You don't know?" Seedy replied, sincere disappointment in his voice.

"He doesn't get out much. Spends a lot of time out in the Glades, no MTV," Hamilton defended William. To the Miccosukee he explained, "This is Seedy's posse, the Refuse G's and their friends."

William looked bewildered.

Seedy took a shot at it, "You might call them my sidemen. You know, like my band. We all worked together picking up trash back in the day.

The owners of these trucks make up my group, the Refuse G's. And each one brought a friend. We're all either Haitian or Hispanic immigrants, thus the name."

William at least understood the explanation, though the old line about inmates taking over the asylum was beginning to gnaw at his mind.

"I see. And what exactly is your security plan?" William inquired.

"We just hang here. We brought plenty of food and drinks. The girls even want to cook some for the guys. You got indoor plumbing. We can take turns sleeping in your trailers or on the couches in the big rig. Got a separate generator on it just to run the A.C. and electronics for the living space."

William gave him credit for at least a small modicum of planning but asked, "Any of your guys have any security experience?"

"Listen my friend, we drove through some pretty bad places during our garbage gig and played some rough, tough joints when we started with our music thing. We been watchin' our own backs for a long time. Plus some of my Central American amigos here got military experience, too. Couple with their countries' armies. Couple as guerillas. We can cover this. No problem."

No problem? I'm surrounded with nothing but problems William observed, as he saw Hamilton taking a silver-plated Glock out of one of the Refuse G's holster.

"Put that back. Now!" William barked. "All we need is for some TV camera to show us here pulling out weapons."

"Sorry." Ham hadn't meant to cause any problem. And fortunately the news cameramen hadn't picked up on the drawn gun, their view partially obstructed by the trailers. However, Seedy and his armed sidemen had still provided plenty of colorful visuals and would be the lead story on all the local news casts as well as receive mention on all the major networks. Reuben would be happy that his boys were still centered hot under the media spotlight.

William, however, was not happy. And in reality had no idea of what to do next. A man used to spending days alone in the River of Grass, he was about as culturally removed from the inmates he was nominally in charge of as any one could be. It seemed a lot wilder here than it did in the

Glades. There was, of course, security at the Miccosukee casino, but he'd never been involved with it. Best to ask the expert.

"Seedy what's your plan?" He queried hoping to God he would understand the answer and that it would make sense.

The rapper didn't let him down.

"Girls," he addressed the holy groupies, "Get into the trailer and make us up some dinner, enough for everybody here. Take your new friends with you to help." As an afterthought he admonished, "And none of that other kind of cookin' until everyone's been fed and the place is cleaned up."

"Chief, we're going to take turns keeping guard. We'll divide into three-man, three-hour shifts. It would help if you or the hoopster would pitch in," he continued.

Hamilton jumped right on it. "I'll be glad to. Maybe somebody could loan me a gun."

"Okay, I'll make you an honorary Refuse G." Seedy paused, "We'll see about arming you." In spite of all the right to bear arms stuff he had spouted, he really didn't think that everybody was competent to carry a gun.

"Cool," the big kid was ecstatic to be a member of the posse.

"I'll be the reserve," William was more cautious. He wasn't afraid of guns. He'd hunted in the Glades for years. Some of the nuts carrying guns, that was the scary part. And these guys were all carrying small cannons.

Seedy picked his first three sentries. He told them to hang out between the trucks and the trailers and keep their eyes open. He'd send them some food when it was ready.

Everyone else stepped into the trailer that had the kitchen.

*　　　*　　　*

Overhead the observer in the Ark was down on his knees seeking guidance. The forces of Satan appeared to be surrounding Jesus and the disciples. The strangely dressed men in their gaudy vehicles, carrying guns and playing blasphemous savage music, had brought the whores back. What could he do? How could he protect the refugees?

Since God was unavailable with an immediate answer, the observer got on the radio and called Barry Gold for direction.

"Judah, tell the pilot to head back to base. He should refuel soon anyway. I'll fly back with you to assess the situation myself. One thing before you leave," Barry ordered as he reeled off exactly what he wanted done to help protect the holy trio.

As requested, Judah cranked up the sound system to full volume. Before it left the air space over the reservation, the ark circled several times, first playing "What a Friend We Have in Jesus" and then "Amazing Grace."

On the ground, the sentries turned off their sound system and listened. Two of them started to sing along. After all, like many performers who had been dirt poor at the beginning of their careers, they had first started to hone their musical skills in their churches. Several of the occupants of the trailer, including the three Cubans, came out to see what was going on. Looking up to the source of the music in the sky, Jesus remarked, "Hey, they're singing about me."

William had a weary smile on his face. Hamilton gave him a knowing nod. They both had the same thought. Where would the naïve young man ever have had a chance to hear any religious music? Certainly not in the oppressive country from which he'd escaped.

William considered the bizarre situation he was in. Only in America he thought. Thank God for America.

In a way at least, Barry Gold had gotten his message through.

*   *   *

Inside the northbound Mercedes, things weren't nearly so peaceful.

"Dammit Reuben. You saved my ass when I needed it saved. And I know I owe you. But you've got to tone this thing down. My millionaire residents don't appreciate all the noise and the media circus," Rogelio complained as he drove.

"In a minute," Reuben waved his hand dismissively, "Gotta take care of things for Lindsey Lee first."

The lawyer took his cell phone out of his briefcase and made a call. He arranged to have a bondsman meet him at the courthouse in case he needed bail to get Lindsey out.

"Okay. That's all I can do 'til I get to the courthouse. She's not spending the night in jail."

Although it wasn't the subject Rogelio wanted to cover, his curiosity got the better of him, "You have something going on with her?" he asked. Rogelio had taken her to dinner a couple of times, but she'd kept things strictly business. He'd always wondered about her love life. Either she was really discreet or she didn't have one.

"Yeah. She's helping me with my treatment of the nymphomaniac case."

"What?" Rogelio replied in a confused voice.

Reuben looked at him. "Ok, you mean dating. No, nothing like that. She's helping me with my screenplay. She said she might even star in it if she likes it. I've got a tentative title, For Love, Not Money. Even got a promotional logo."

He whipped a yellow legal pad out of his briefcase and did a quick sketch. 4♥⑤ First he held it in front of Rogelio so he could see it without taking his eyes off the road. Then he flashed it to Rex in the back seat.

"Like it?" He asked, expecting positive approval.

"Not bad," Rogelio admitted.

Rex had been watching the interplay from behind the two in the front seat. What was with his so-called business partner? How'd they gotten so far off track? He'd had enough and exploded. "What the hell has all that got to do with our present problem?"

"What problem? You couldn't buy all the good coverage I'm getting for your resort casino. You should be paying me," Reuben replied, his opinion of himself being anything but modest.

"We don't need a lot of publicity right now. There's nothing up and running yet," Rex said.

"So, you got lots of goodwill building with the immigrant community. They love what you're doing for my clients. Giving 'em refuge. Standing up to the government," Reuben replied.

"You're not getting it," Rex growled, believing that maybe the little smart ass was getting it more than he let on." There's no ground broken and we can't break any now with the news coverage and police surveillance."

"Why not?" Reuben did his best at feigning confusion.

"Because, we go in there now to clear mangroves or dredge a marina and we'll have the environmental groups all over us," Rex explained.

"So. It's reservation land. You can pretty much do what you want."

"And all the goodwill goes right out the window. We'll have the Sierra Club laying down in front of our bulldozers and Green Peace circling our dredge barge in their chase boats. That kind of free publicity we don't need," Rex continued.

"And now that the government is pissed off at us," Rogelio added, speaking from experience, " they could tie us up in court for years. With EPA impact statements and Corp of Engineers dredging permits we could be old men before we get anything up."

"That could happen anyway," Reuben pointed out.

"Cut the crap," Rex was mad. He knew that Reuben knew a lot more about how things worked in South Florida. After all, Reuben had gotten Rogelio's fat out of the fire after Hurricane Andrew. "You know damn well how things go down here. Lots more gets done if nobody's watching."

Reuben knew very well what he meant. Just recently a new island had been discovered in South Biscayne Bay. Apparently someone had hacked a path through mangroves on state land, carted in fill and built a footpath causeway and island in the bay. On the island they built a nice gazebo. On shore, they'd also cleared out mangroves and built storage facilities. None of this was discovered by any government authority. It was found by a news helicopter covering another story in the area.

Rogelio laid it on the table. "Come on Reuben. You know the score. Nobody's watching. We go in and clear the building site and do our dredging, fast as possible. Dig our footings and start getting the buildings up. Then if we get caught, well it's too late. We pay a fine, plant some mangroves in a new place as mitigation. Just the cost of doing business."

For once Reuben bit his tongue. Every bit of remaining natural resource in South Florida was precious. Once you tore it out, you couldn't replace it. Planting a few new plants in a different place wasn't, couldn't be, equivalent. But since his clients were a big imposition for Rex and Rogelio right now, he didn't disagree. Diplomacy was what was required at present.

"Well there's no safe place or way to move my boys right now. I guess the faster we get the situation settled and get out of there, the better for you."

"Reuben, be reasonable. Try to cut down the media attention. Play it quieter," Rogelio pleaded.

"Don't know if that's what I want to do."

"Didn't you hear anything we just said?" Rex barked.

"Strategy. I'll have to think about it. High profile equals high pressure. Maybe a quicker resolution. Yeah, I'll have to think about it," Elias reiterated, knowing damn well that the arrival of Seedy and the Refuse Gs would keep things cranked up for awhile anyway.

"Think hard," Rex commanded.

They rode the rest of the way in silence until they reached the courthouse.

"Reached any decision yet?" Rex inquired as Reuben opened his car door in front of the Federal Court Building.

"My clients' freedom is my primary concern. And Lindsey's arrest has just elevated the stakes. I'll see how it goes with her. I'll let you know later."

"Reuben, you want me to wait or come back later?" Rogelio was still loyal to his friends.

"No. Get Rex back to Mont Basura and get his SUV out of there. Joey'll get us back," he replied, referring to the bail bondsman he'd called. The attorney slammed the door and trod confidently up the courthouse steps.

Reuben had managed to arrange an emergency bond hearing by calling in a few markers. He found Lindsey, surrounded by the three federal agents, sitting on a bench outside a courtroom on the fourth floor. Joey Kanzer, the bondsman, was sitting on a bench across the hall from her, talking on his cell phone. He gave Reuben a nod in recognition as the lawyer approached Lindsey.

"I'd like a moment to confer with my client, " he said to agent Busch.

"Okay. Come on," he said to his two assistants and the three of them crossed the hall and stood next to Joey. The bondsman, not wanting them to be part of his conversation, mumbled a few words into his phone and snapped it closed.

Reuben sat down next to Lindsey and asked softly, "Are you ok?"

"Yeah. It's a little scary to have the government rummaging through your house. But they didn't find anything."

"You sure?"

"I'm the only thing they took out of the house."

"Did you say anything to them?"

"I haven't said a word since they put me in their car. I didn't want to give them the satisfaction of knowing I was upset."

"Good girl," he replied and then added just loud enough for the agents to hear, "Did they say anything to you of a sexual nature or touch you inappropriately?"

Their three heads whipped around almost in unison, staring at the little attorney. They sure didn't need a sexual harassment charge from the starlet. When they saw her give a small nod, they came charging back.

Just in time to hear her ask, "Would you repeat that?"

Which Reuben was more than glad to do.

"No. I don't think so. In that regard, at least, they were gentlemen," she turned and smiled at the agents.

"Good," Reuben smiled at them, too.

"Listen you little son of a bitch," Busch was just short of hoisting the lawyer by his lapels.

He didn't get the chance to finish his statement as the door to the courtroom opened and the bailiff stepped out.

"The judge is ready for you now," he announced.

As they entered, the judge, retired federal magistrate Herbert Spahn IV, glowered down at them from the bench. It was bad enough that he'd been called out of retirement to help alleviate the backlog of cases piling up in the federal system. Drugs, government corruption and immigration problems added to the usual slate of federal crimes, were enough to keep the legal industry in South Florida booming. Unfortunately for judge Spahn, the "second coming" wet-foot, dry-foot dispute had landed on his docket, along with the ancillary problem of Indian tribal sovereignty and the sanctuary issue. So, instead of being at his weekly poker game with old cronies from the Chamber of Commerce, here he was with yet another aspect of the case to deal with.

"What now?" He glared at Reuben, making no effort to hide his displeasure at being called away from his evening's pursuits.

"Not me this time, your honor," Reuben replied. "I'm just here to defend my client. You'll have to ask agent Busch why he arrested Ms. Olson."

"Why?" The judge now had Busch in his sights. He wanted this over as quickly as possible. The poker game was played in a reserved room at an upscale steakhouse, and the judge was also missing his dinner.

"For harboring federal fugitives," Busch responded quickly.

"Are we talking about the three so-called holy men? I thought they were on the Miccosukee land down by Mount Trashmore," Judge Spahn stated.

"Yes, we are. And yes that's where they are now. But Ms. Olson was harboring them before they fled to the reservation land," Busch explained.

The magistrate looked momentarily crestfallen. He'd hoped that maybe the three had been captured when Lindsey was arrested. Then he'd only have to decide on the immigration. Apparently no such luck.

He turned back to Reuben, "Plea?"

"Not guilty. And I ask that Ms. Olson be released immediately."

The judge just nodded toward agent Busch for his response.

"Your honor, I and several other law enforcement officers observed three fugitives as well as their lawyer, Mr. Elias, fleeing from the back of Ms. Olson's property down to the Miccosukee property."

"Your honor, my house is adjacent to Ms. Olson's. When the police cars pulled up in front of her house, my clients feared for their freedom and fled. Does the agent have any other proof that Ms. Olson was harboring them other than that they were on her property?" Knowing the answer he added, "Can he connect her at all with their escape?"

The judge stared at Busch awaiting his reply.

"No," but then adding somewhat defiantly, "Can he explain how they got taken there then."

"Although I don't have to answer, your honor, I will. As to how they escaped, I had no hand in it. I would hazard a guess that the explanation belongs to Barry Gold."

"And how do you account for them being behind Ms. Olson's house?" This time the judge was asking.

"Again I don't have to answer. However again I will," Reuben didn't mind a little grandstanding, even if it was only for a small crowd. "If you were me and serendipitously found your lost clients returned, right to the very development you lived in, no less, wouldn't you be happy? Wouldn't you be proud to show them how you can make it in America if you try? Maybe show off that you were a good neighbor to a beautiful movie star? And besides the view from her corner of Mont Basura is absolutely breathtaking. Certainly worth showing three men who'd been locked up out in the Everglades for the last few weeks."

Reuben, being the good lawyer that he was, had carefully crafted his answer mostly as rhetorical questions. Never actually stating that what he was saying had happened. Obfuscation and hypotheticals, two of any defense lawyers' main tools.

"And you have no idea how they got to Mont Basura?" Judge Spahn queried.

"I know I had no part in their escape or their delivery back to me," Elias replied, not exactly answering the question.

Now Judge Herbert Spahn IV had been on the federal bench for over thirty years and he could easily recognize when he wasn't getting a straight answer. He'd also dealt with Reuben Elias on several previous cases, and was well aware that the answer he'd just received was all the clarification the lightweight lawyer with the heavyweight mind and ego was going to give him. If he questioned Reuben again and got a similarly evasive answer, he could cite him for contempt. Then the little bastard would cite attorney-client privilege and refuse to name the client. They'd end up right where they were now and the judge's stomach would be grumbling even louder.

"Okay. Fine. Does your client have any idea how the refugees got to Mont Basura?" The magistrate knew the answer before he asked, but thought he'd at least make the attempt.

"Your honor," Reuben let the words hang in the air for a few seconds while giving the judge an admonishing look. "You know I can't let her answer that."

"Yeah. I know," he responded wearily.

"But she knows Judge. She's in this up to her eyeballs," the frustrated INS man butted in.

"Agent Busch, do you have any actual physical proof for that statement?" came the question from the bench.

"No your honor," came the dejected answer.

"Then Miss Olsen you are free to go. Agent, uncuff her," commanded the judge.

As he was unlocking Lindsey's cuffs, Busch gave it one last try. "What about him, Your Honor? He knew they were fugitives and helped them flee down the side of the development."

"You honor," Reuben replied in an exasperated tone that implied why do we even have to listen to this moron. "How am I supposed to stop three healthy young men from running when they hear the sirens. You didn't really think they'd wait to be arrested and shipped back to detention out on Krome. All I did, as their lawyer, was to follow them down the side of Trashmore. Just trying to make sure they got legal representation when they needed it."

Always the master of the plausible explanation, the judge thought.

To Busch he said, "Give it up agent. Next time you appear in my courtroom you better have hard evidence. This has been a colossal waste of time."

Stung by the reprimand, Busch submissively muttered a quiet "Yes, your honor."

"A pleasure as always," Reuben said to the judge.

"Yes, I suppose I'll be seeing you again soon. This case is a long way from over."

"Looking forward to it sir."

"That makes one of us," came the judge's candid reply, as he rose and headed for his chambers.

Reuben smiled.

"We're not done," Busch threatened Reuben and Lindsey as they all headed for the exit.

"You're lucky we don't sue you for wrongful arrest."

The three government men said nothing else and headed down the hall.

"Joey, can you give us a ride back?" Reuben asked. "Sorry we didn't need your services."

"No problem. And as far as bail goes, well, this case ain't over yet."

"If it's not too big a deal, could we stop and get something to eat?" Lindsey asked. She hadn't gotten to eat her lunch. And, now that she was free of the tension of being under arrest, her appetite had come roaring back.

"Sure thing," Joey replied happily. " I can discuss a few other clients with Reuben over dinner. I'll buy. Make it a deductible business meeting."

What he didn't say, but what made him smile, was that he'd be more than glad to spend a couple of hours with the beautiful young woman. She was hands down, far and away, and whatever other superlative you wanted to use, much better looking than the clients he usually kept company with.

 **Chapter XIII**

Maybe things would have gone differently if both Neal Busch and Reuben Elias hadn't been tied up with each other in a federal courtroom twenty miles away from Mont Basura. Maybe one of them would have seen the news coverage and made some effort to alter the situation that was developing down at the reservation sanctuary. But the local 6 o'clock news was over by the time they left the courtroom. Busch went home to have a drink and lick his wounds. Reuben went out with Lindsey and Joey to celebrate their victory.

If Busch had seen the arrival of Seedy and the Refuse G's and the defensive perimeter they'd set up, maybe he'd have called off the reconnaissance mission. Instead, he sat in his apartment, in the dark, sipping his single malt scotch, plotting his next move.

If Elias had seen that the Refuse G's were all packing large handguns, maybe he'd have called Seedy and told them to stow the weapons, allowing the presence of big strong men to be deterrent enough. Instead, he was sipping champagne and cracking stone crab claws with Joey and Lindsey at Monty's in Coconut Grove. After all, the chief had everything under control on the reservation.

So instead, about 9:00 pm, the black Zodiac inflatable slipped away from the Metro-Dade police boat patrolling the bayside of the reservation. The two officers, dressed completely in black, paddled silently toward the mangrove-lined shore. They quickly broke a sweat. Long sleeves, gloves, long pants tucked into black combat boots, and black masks with only eye and mouth slits were not conducive to comfort in the South Florida humidity. They didn't complain; they were professionals with a mission to carry out. They were to land, reconnoiter the terrain and assess the feasibility of extracting the federal fugitives. The legality of the mission would be for others to worry about at a later time.

As they neared the shore they donned their night vision goggles. Their world immediately became a mixture of varying shades of green and black. The moon was hidden in a cloudbank on the horizon behind them. And as extra cover a light rain started to fall. This was almost the last good luck they would have.

As they eased up to the shoreline they could see it was completely covered by mangrove trees with no real beach for them to land their boat. They paddled in as close as possible, tethered the boat to a tree root and hopped out.

For those unfamiliar with mangrove trees, a description is in order. They tend to grow together in clumps, like bushes forming a thicket, with the emphasis on thick. Each tree is like a hundred-legged spider, the roots projecting above the water and mud into which they grow, covered by a short, convoluted canopy of gnarled branches, overlaid with oval semi-glossy leaves. The roots of each tree intimately entwine with those of the mangroves around it. This provides tremendous natural stabilization to a shoreline in the face of tides and storm surge. The roots also provide protection from predation for the infant and juvenile fishes and crustaceans incubating beneath them.

While this is good for the crabs, fishes and lobsters developing until they've grown big enough to make a foray into the larger marine environment, it is hell for the mammalian biped trying to navigate through the roots and branches. The term impenetrable soon came to both officers' minds. Yet they persevered. Despite repeatedly cracking shins, knees and elbows, having their feet stick in the muck, and catching their sweaty, soaked uniforms on branches, they pressed on. They used the lights from the homes atop Mont Basura to guide them in the right direction.

After half an hour, their efforts were rewarded. They reached the construction clearing and found their objective. They could see the two trailers, separated from them by the last few mangroves, five huge SUVs and the most outlandish garbage truck they'd ever seen.

At this point most reasonable men would have turned back. Just the fact that it had taken them thirty minutes to cover half a mile of terrain should have dissuaded them. Obviously, it would take even longer to return to the boat were they dragging uncooperative or unconscious hostages with them.

But these were professionals. They'd busted their humps to come this far and they were determined to get as close as possible to evaluate the situation. They moved up under the cover of the trees closest to the vehicles.

On the other side of the trucks, the second shift of men was walking guard duty. The group consisted of a Haitian childhood friend of Seedy, one of the Central American Refuse G's, and the Heat center Hamilton Patrick. Ham preferred to be outside because, at over seven feet tall, he felt cramped being inside the trailer.

All three were wearing royal purple ponchos with the silver trash truck logo on the back and front to keep the rain off.

Fortunately, or unfortunately, depending on your point of view, Manny, the Central American had brought out something to divert them while they stood out in the rain. When he was nearly a teenager he had been conscripted into a guerilla army that was formed to fight the leftist government ruling his country. He had learned to stand sentry duty at an early age to protect his group's hidden mountainside encampment. His American advisors had versed him well on the use of night vision equipment. Right now he and his two cohorts were using the night goggles he'd brought with him to fight off the boredom of standing out in the rain. They were having a contest to see who would spot the most opossums, or manicous as they were called in Haiti, and raccoons. If they watched closely they could discern the animals foraging for their dinner, looking amongst the mangrove roots for crabs, rats, mice and snakes to become their meals.

Imagine Manny's surprise when he happened to focus on two sets of night scopes staring back at the trailers. He quickly squatted down behind the closest Hummer, drew his gun out from under the poncho, and started circling silently to his left. His intent was to flank the two intruders and capture them.

For the two officers, the observation process was more difficult. Each trailer had a porch light by its entry stairs. Without enhancement, the 75-watt bulbs barely lit the 30 feet of ground between the trailers and the semi-circle of trucks. However, multiplied in strength through the night vision goggles, they were bright white back lighting and almost blotting out everything in front of them. They never saw Manny duck down and start to move their way. They could make out the outline of the vehicles and a tall, narrow, triangular shape standing between them. The triangle started to move.

Hamilton turned toward Manny to give him his contest animal count. But Manny was nowhere to be seen. Swiveling back to look for him the other way, Ham too picked up the two sets of goggles under the mangroves. Unfortunately his reaction was much less measured.

To make him feel like one of the posse, Seedy had loaned Hamilton his gold-plated magnum against his better judgment. But what bad could happen out there in the rain and the dark?

Under his magenta poncho, the Heat center pulled the big pistol out of his belt. He thumbed the safety off as he drew the gun outside his poncho. The two officers got a brief glimpse of shiny metal sticking out from the side of the thin triangle.

Boom!

Ham snapped off a warning shot over the intruders. The big gun sounded like a small cannon. No wimpy, popping noises like with a .22. The basketball player knew very well what he was doing. When he lived in Montana he used to hunt and was very good with guns.

Unlike when he hunted however, this prey was hot, sweaty, tense from being in a questionable legal situation and, finally, pissed off at being shot at. Also his prey had never been armed.

It was supposed to be a surreptitious observation mission, but the officers certainly weren't stupid enough to come without means to defend themselves. It was after all, South Florida, where just about anyone could be carrying a gun.

Hamilton's single shot was met by a return fusillade of automatic weapon fire, a short warning burst from each officer before they beat a retreat back toward the shore. He was so shocked to see the two muzzle flashes he didn't even duck.

"Coño, coño, coño!" Manny muttered the Cuban expletives. He had been startled by the report from the .44 and even more shocked by the flurry of rifle shots. He hadn't been able to flank the intruders but was close enough and good enough to nail them both if he wanted to.

First he looked back toward the trucks. The big man was still standing. Manny made a critical decision. Though he could have killed the two intruders, he let them go. The dead bodies would do the refugees' cause no good, not unless they were agents sent by Castro. And that wasn't likely. He trotted back toward the trailers.

Seedy's buddy, Henri Duvalier, no relation to the dictators who'd destroyed Haiti, had ducked when the police officers returned fire. He'd heard plenty of gunfire in his homeland. Now, with his gun drawn, he came running to see if Hamilton was all right.

The giant seemed to be rooted where he was standing. The huge pistol hung at his side, the safety back on.

"Hey man. You o.k. ?" Manny asked as he jogged up to him.

The big man shook his head, like he was coming out of a trance. "Yeah. I think so." He paused, "I never been shot at," he said softly, almost to himself.

"No fun. Wouldn't recommend it to anybody," Manny commented knowingly.

There had been a long enough lull in the gunfire that the occupants of the trailer came spilling out to see what the hell had happened.

Henri noticed a hole in the back of the hood of Hamilton's poncho. "You sure you're O.K., kid?" he asked again.

"Huh?" He was pivoting to see everyone pouring out of the trailer, but was distracted by a warm, sticky feeling on his left shoulder that was slowly spreading down his back and chest. He stuck the gun back in his belt then reached up to touch his shoulder. "Maybe not," came his delayed reply.

The shots the officers fired to cover their retreat weren't meant to injure and normally would have gone over the heads of any perpetrators. Indeed most of them went into the side of Mont Basura near its top. Though two bullets went through a picture window of a left-leaning documentary producer who swore the whole thing was a thinly disguised effort to assassinate him. It would become the subject of his next film.

However, Hamilton was not a normal perp. One of the bullets had whizzed through the opening in his hood, clipped off the top third of his left ear and exited through the back. It was such a clean shot he hadn't really felt it. He pulled the hood back off his head.

"You been shot," Seedy stated the obvious as he reached the three men. "Where's the top of your ear?"

The question made Ham start to wobble. He'd have turned white if it weren't for the fact he already was. Manny and Henri each took an elbow and leaned the big guy against the Hummer.

"You're going to be fine man. These days they can just take the piece and sew it back on," Manny assured him as Henri tied a couple of doo rags over the wound to staunch the bleeding.

The missing piece of skin and cartilage hadn't come out through the hood. The hole was too small. It had gently slithered down the inside of the cape and fallen between Ham's feet.

The holy men were scouring the muddy ground where he'd been standing. Pablo bent over and picked something up.

"Here it is, I think," he said, holding something out in the rain to let the drops rinse the mud off. "Ay! Mierda!"

"What's wrong?" Jesus and Pedro asked as they came over for a closer look.

"Shit," Jesus switched to the English expletive.

"Get it on ice," Henri said as he came over for a look.

"Oh. Never mind."

"What's wrong?" Hamilton asked, still feeling a bit weak.

Unfortunately, the piece of ear had gotten crushed between the player's size seventeens and an underlying piece of coral rock as he pivoted to see who was coming out of the trailer. It looked like a cheap cut of beef that had been tenderized with a meat hammer. There would be no re-attaching it. Seedy walked over, looked, then came and quietly broke the news to him.

"Oh," was all he said.

"Gives you some street 'cred'," Seedy told him. "Plastic surgeon could probably build you a new one."

But Hamilton would never have it fixed except to even up the ragged edges. What Seedy had said about credibility with the hip-hop and gangsta crowd was true. His jersey number became the biggest seller of all the Heat players and he soon got his own multi-million dollar sneaker endorsement. His insistence that Ham Slammers be manufactured in the U.S. was almost a deal breaker, but at over $200 a pair, the company found enough profit to accede to his demand. He was also a hero for the Cuban refugee cause, "El Media Oreja," ranking up there with others who'd given body parts, like the county commissioner who'd lost a toe in the Democracia Flotilla. And as his pro basketball skills developed, the sports broadcasters couldn't pass up the obvious. His artistry on the floor soon had them referring to him as the Van Gogh of the hardwood.

Of course all this came later. For now his head was starting to hurt and he needed to clean himself up. His new friends walked him into the trailer. As a precaution, Seedy posted a new set of sentries.

In a strange balancing of the karmic wheel, the identity of the intruders was left a mystery, just like the identity of those who'd helped the holy men escape. Shell casings were found under the mangroves the next morning, but they were from a common brand of ammunition with no distinguishing marks.

The only problem the two officers had was that Hamilton's single shot had carried through the mangroves and torn through two of the air chambers on their inflatable boat. They'd had to swim back to the police craft, towing the remains of the Zodiac behind them so no evidence would be left on shore.

*   *   *

In the dark, Busch's cell phone rang. He pushed the talk button.

"Busch, you sonofabitch, why'dn't you tell me they had armed guards? My guys coulda been killed. As it is you owe me a boat."

Neal recognized the angry voice as his SWAT commander buddy. He paused for a few seconds trying to figure out what happened. Finally he just asked, "What the hell are you taking about?"

"My men got shot at, you dumb fuck. That's what."

"What?" He parroted back. He was sitting literally and figuratively in the dark.

His friend dialed it down and explained the information his men had relayed to him.

"What?" Busch reiterated. "They shot back? Did they hit anybody?"

"No. I don't think so. But they popped off quite a few rounds. Some of 'em could've hit the snooty housing development on the garbage pile."

"Jesus. What the hell were they thinking? Did they get made?" the special agent had a lot of questions.

"They were thinking they wanted to get their asses out in one piece. They were protecting themselves. What kinda stupid question is that? They didn't leave anything behind that could be used to I.D. them."

"Good. Wouldn't do for us to be found out. As for your boat, I can either replace it out of my discretionary fund or give you an upgrade with one of the boats we take in a seizure. Meanwhile I gotta figure out what I'm gonna do next. Far as I'm concerned, they just upped the ante."

"Count me in," the SWAT commander was mad. He didn't take to his men being shot at. He wanted to even the score.

"I'll be in touch. Soon," Busch pushed the end button.

*   *   *

Reuben's cell phone rang at almost the same time as Busch's. He was having an enjoyable discussion about turning For Love Not Money into a movie. Both he and Lindsey thought that maybe Joey Kanzer could play himself in the movie. Joey was amenable to the idea. After all he'd bailed out the nympho subject of the story and enjoyed her resulting gratitude. As far as ability, he'd put on more than a few acts for judges and clients.

Reuben checked the caller I.D. It was Rogelio. Reuben pushed the talk button.

"This is your concept of toning it down? What the hell are you doing?" Rogelio was nearly as upset as the SWAT commander.

"What?" Reuben unknowingly mirrored Busch.

"Gunfire. Bullets hitting my development. Are you outta your mind?"

"What?" Elias was just as much in the dark as the special agent had been.

"Are you near a television?"

Reuben was at the outdoor section of the restaurant. There was a TV over the bar. As he looked up there was an interruption in the regular broadcast and a banner moved across the screen that read "Breaking News. Special Report." Reuben tapped on the table and directed Lindsey and Joey's attention to the screen.

"I'm watching. There's a breaking news thing coming on right now," He said to Rogelio.

When the rain had started, the network affiliates' satellite trucks had closed up and their crews headed back to their studios. Only the remote crew from the tabloid station remained. Liz, the hot young blonde, was going to make the most out of her shot at a real news story after doing the weather for the last year and a half. She buttoned up her blouse to cover the cleavage that had made her weather segments so popular. She wanted to be taken seriously. Then mic in hand, she'd made her cameraman follow her around while she practiced doing interviews with protesters and true believers encamped outside the sanctuary.

Her instincts, or perhaps her luck, paid off. When Hamilton had fired Seedy's cannon she'd been just outside the gate. "Gunfire from inside the refugees' compound," she'd managed to interject before the return volley from the infiltrators. The cameraman managed to frame her in front of the gate with the muzzle flashes from under the mangroves over her shoulder.

"Automatic weapons," she whispered while staring straight into the camera.

"Get your ass down," was the command that came from the video man off camera. He focused over her as she went into a crouch. But there was no more gunfire. The sound of glass breaking at a distance was picked up by the microphone. The camera swung around toward Mont Basura. The trained eye quickly picked out the blown away picture windows and zoomed in to show them close up.

"Violence has struck in the heart of the religious sanctuary and overflowed to the surrounding environs," came the commentary from the young woman. Environs was a bit highbrow for the tabloid audience, but Liz had graduated cum laude with a degree in journalism from Boston University and couldn't help it.

"What the hell?" It was Reuben's turn to invoke fire and brimstone, though he spoke it more softly and questioningly. Rogelio still heard him through the phone.

"What do you know about this? Have you talked to anyone down there?" Negro asked.

"All I know is that the music guys were mainly just there to provide a presence. To make anybody think twice about making a raid and snatching my clients. I didn't even know they'd be armed. I sure as hell didn't expect an armed intrusion so soon. And certainly not a firefight, and no I haven't talked to any of them since I got out of your car."

"You didn't know your guys would be armed? You're not that naïve," Rogelio chastised. He knew Reuben Elias, Esq. usually had all the angles covered.

"I'm sorry. I really didn't see this coming. I'll get hold of William and find out what's going on. As soon as I know what's what I'll let you know."

"You do that," came the emphatic reply.

"We gotta get back," Reuben said to his companions as he flagged the waitress for the check. They both rose from the table to join him.

*   *   *

Rex Panther had retrieved the Navigator and driven back to the casino on the edge of the Glades. He was working in his office when he started getting bombarded with phone calls from tribal council members. He turned on his plasma screen television and switched from the casino's security monitor channel to the local tabloid news. He watched the replay of Liz's report. He thought she was a pretty girl and that, in the face of live ammunition, she did a credible job.

He had to decide what to do next. The council was about evenly split. Half didn't like the public exposure. Thought it was bad for the tribe and put them in a bad light. They just wanted to sit back and quietly rake in their gambling and tobacco royalties. The other half, those who had been more involved in the fight with state and federal government to build the swamp gambling facility, wanted to send in their own security. Or at least hire their own people, like they now did with alligator wrestlers, since it was a risky job that no one in the tribe would want. They figured the incident was some type of government intrusion on to their reservation.

Before he decided, he needed to get the full story from William. He picked up his phone and punched in the number for the construction trailer on his speed dial.

*   *   *

Inside the trailer things were finally beginning to settle down a little. After the initial fear and confusion began to dissipate in the crowded and cramped space a multilingual chorus broke out, with the story of what happened being told in Creole, Spanish, and English all at the same time.

William decided to take control. He slapped his hands hard down on a counter. The clap got everyone's attention.

"Everybody just be quiet. We'll get the story in turns, starting with Ham. But first, does anybody have any medical experience?" he asked, eyeing the bloody doo rag covering the remainder of the ear.

Magdalena spoke up, "I went to nursing school for a year. I'll take care of it."

William pulled a first aid kit out from under the counter and handed it to her.

As Magdalena cleaned and dressed his wound, Hamilton recounted what had happened. Then Manny described what he'd seen, adding the observation that, whoever the intruders were, they were obviously professionals. Finally Henri told what he'd seen and, in an effort to lighten the tension, added that he'd won the contest. This drew a weak chuckle from Hamilton.

The phone rang. Seedy picked it up. It was Reuben.

"Hey man. You didn't tell me we was going to get shot at," the rapper complained.

Listening to the reply, Seedy smiled. "No big thing. None of my guys got hurt any way. Just the big man. Maybe I should get us some vests."

After Reuben's next reply, Seedy handed the phone to William. "He wants to talk to you."

William spent the next ten minutes filling Reuben in on what had transpired while he was in court. He finished with a detailed description of Hamilton's injury.

"Okay. You're on your way. We'll just wait here 'til you arrive," William hung up.

On the other end Reuben was smiling as he clicked his cell phone shut.

The phone rang again. William picked it up this time. It was his brother. Rex got pretty much the same explanation Reuben had.

When the senior Panther hung up on his younger sibling, he was reconsidering the situation and whether or not it was still best to keep a low profile. He too was smiling.

 **Chapter XIV**

Reuben was disappointed when they reached the gate. There was only one TV remote truck parked there and it wasn't from the networks. Unbeknownst to the lawyer the network trucks were on their way back, along with a flock of Cuban and religious supporters for the refugee trio. Still, Reuben had to work with what was available.

"Joey, pull up to the news truck," he requested.

The bail bondsman pulled alongside.

Reuben rolled down his window. He saw a blond young woman holding a microphone.

"How'd you like an exclusive interview inside the reservation?" he asked her.

Liz looked inside the car and saw both Reuben Elias and Lindsey Lee Olson. This story was breaking her way.

"You bet. The cameraman comes along though. Right?" She wanted this on tape.

"Absolutely. Come on," Reuben did, too.

Liz and her cameraman trotted behind the car as Joey slowly rolled up to the entrance and honked. Reuben got out of the car so the security men would recognize him. One of them unlocked the chains securing the gate and the curious quintet passed through.

"Right this way," Reuben said, leading Liz and her technician to the right trailer. Lindsey and Joey followed. Reuben knocked on the door before opening it as a courtesy warning to the occupants.

"I'm back," he announced stepping inside. "And I've brought the press."

The bright floodlight atop the video recorder signaled the arrival of Liz and the cameraman. Everyone in the trailer took turns blinking and squinting as the lens panned across the group. The cameraman turned down the intensity of the lamp.

"Reuben, am I glad to see you," William said, glad to dump some of the problems back on the man who'd help create them. He grinned when he saw Lindsey come in behind the news crew.

"Good to see you, too, chief," Reuben replied, slapping him on the shoulder. "We got work to do."

In the short time it took to exchange greetings, Liz had zeroed in on the main story in the room. Liz had a microphone in the Heat center's face and the camera was getting a good close up of the bloodstained bandage covering the remainder of his ear.

"Hamilton Patrick, rookie center for the Miami Heat, can you tell us what happened here tonight?"

Before he could reply, Reuben cut him off, "Not yet. We've got to arrange a few things."

"Mr. Elias, they may be your clients but this is my interview. I won't let you control it. I'll ask the questions and, if you want, you can advise your clients not to answer. But I won't sacrifice my journalistic integrity," Liz wanted to do the story her way and didn't want him controlling her coverage.

"You're new at this, aren't you?" he smiled. "A little naïve, too. Lots of stories are shot with only pre-approved questions that the principles allow. But don't worry. Ask whatever you want. I just want to clear some of the clutter. Reduce it to just the people involved. Gimme a second."

"Okay," she blushed faintly at his accurate assessment. But at least she was going to get the story.

Reuben whispered something to Seedy. At the rapper's behest the young ladies and all the security group except Manny and Henri stepped out.

Reuben set the stage for the interview. He had Hamilton seated at a table with Manny and Henri seated on each side. Behind them, Reuben stood with the three holy men. Presentation was important.

"Fire away young lady," he commanded.

Liz stood in front of the group, faced the camera and started her intro. "We are here inside a construction trailer on the Miccosukee Reservation in south Miami-Dade County. Earlier, gunfire was reported coming from this site of sanctuary for the three so-called Cuban holy men. In an exclusive interview we will talk to a victim of that attack."

Turning toward the group behind her, she asked, "Hamilton Patrick, can you tell us how it was that you came to be shot tonight?"

Liz, William, Seedy and Joey stood in a corner of the office, behind the news crew, and watched the proceedings.

After a minute, Seedy leaned over and whispered a question to William. "Mind if I use your computer?"

William thought the timing was a little bad, but replied, "Sure, go ahead."

The rapper sat down and logged on. William watched the interview again for a couple of minutes. But his curiosity got the better of him. He turned and looked over Seedy's shoulder.

The guy didn't miss a trick, William thought. Good thing he wasn't hooked up with Rex running the casino. The place might be ten times worse.

Seedy had logged on to his own website and clicked into the merchandise section. The Haitian entrepreneur looked over his shoulder once, grinned at the interview in progress and started to make a few changes.

It wasn't hard for William to figure out the reason for the changes. Hamilton and the other two security men were still wearing their purple "Seedy Stuff" ponchos. Large drips of blood were easily visible on the left shoulder and front of the center's raingear.

As a fascinated William watched, Seedy doubled the price of the poncho. Under the special instruction section he offered to have a realistic bullet hole blown through the hood in the exact same place as the one belonging to the Heat center. And for only an extra twenty dollars. He also added the legal disclaimer that obviously this would affect the poncho's ability to keep water out. Finally, he changed the product name from Hazardous Weather Gear to Purple Graze in honor of the big man's grazing head wound. As a finishing touch he added a music sample from

Jimmy Hendrix's Purple Haze that would play when you clicked on the poncho's site.

Seedy Devereux looked up at the Miccosukee, "You know these things have hardly moved since we introduced them, basically a loss as a product. That ought to change now."

Knowing he was right, William just shook his head.

By morning, the thousand Purple Grazes in stock had sold out, more than sixty percent with the requisite bullet hole in the hood in solidarity with the Heat's big man. Over the next week more than ten thousand units were sold.

Back at the interview, things were going as well as Reuben could hope for. Ham, then Manny, and then Henri took their turns telling their version of the story. Liz asked concise questions for clarification where necessary. Then she turned her attention to Jesus, Pedro and Pablo and asked if any of them had a comment.

Jesus spoke up, "No comprendo. I don't understand what is going on. My brothers and I just want to be free to get jobs and work. We don't understand why the government makes us hide in this sanctuary. People treat us good here. We get new clothes and ladies come and cook for us. The airship even flies over playing music about me. Then a few hours later someone is shooting at us. We love America. We want to stay here. But we're so confused."

Liz was momentarily bewildered by the allusion to the blimp music, but the camera, focused on a tight shot of Jesus, didn't pick it up. When he finished his statement, she turned full face to the camera and commented, "There you have it. Gunfire from unidentified intruders. A superstar basketball player nearly killed. Confusion, despondency and patriotism from captives in a hip-hop sanctuary."

Up until now she may have only done the weather but she'd paid attention and Liz had picked up the proper way to spin a story for a sensationalist type newscast.

Reuben had been watching his melting pot bubbling, Central American Hispanic, Haitian African-American, a couple of Anglos and the three Cuban refugees all in the South Florida sofrito. He couldn't have been more delighted with this stew. And of course he couldn't resist making a few remarks.

"May I comment?" he inquired as a courtesy, intending to talk whether he got permission or not.

"Of course," she replied, thinking to herself that they could always edit him out if he got too windy.

"I just want to point out that support for my clients extends across the racial and ethnic spectrum, a point made obvious by the three witnesses who were protecting them from the violent intrusion into their sanctuary. Speaking of which, who were these well-equipped and well-armed men who assaulted my security personnel? Just as important, how did they get by the police who are supposedly watching the perimeter?"

God he loved being in the spotlight. Reuben actually had a pretty good idea who the two intruders were. But he wasn't going to make any charges while he didn't have any evidence. Perhaps by putting the question to the public someone would come forward.

"Interesting points, Mr. Elias," Liz commented. The station would undoubtedly run his whole statement. Just as he did, her editor and news director wanted to appeal to as wide an ethnic and racial demographic as possible. Couple that with the inference of a government conspiracy or collusion in an illegal act and the storm was irresistible. That clever little bastard knew how to use the media.

Liz looked over her cameraman's shoulder and could see Lindsey and William whispering in the corner. Interesting. The starlet and the Indian chief would make a pretty good story, too.

"Chief Panther," she smiled to get his attention.

William looked over her way. The cameraman did a one-eighty, lit William with the floodlight and focused on his face through the viewfinder.

"This is your tribe's land. Would you like to comment on the incident tonight?" Liz continued.

"Keep it short and simple," Lindsey whispered to him.

"The illegal incursion and following violence here tonight were uncalled for. It only serves to heighten tensions surrounding this whole situation. But it will not weaken our resolve or change our offer of sanctuary. The refugees will stay here until their situation is decided."

"Will you be bringing in more security?"

"No comment," William had no idea what to do next. Or what either Reuben or his brother had in mind.

"Have there been any threats? Do you have any idea who might be behind this?" the reporter pressed.

"No comment." Remembering Busch's open animosity when he arrested Lindsey, William, like Reuben, had a good idea who was behind it. But he had no proof.

"Anything else you might want to say regarding the incident?" she asked, seeing that he was clamming up.

"No."

Lindsey gave William's hand an encouraging squeeze figuring the interview was over.

Liz caught the motion out of the corner of her eye.

"Are you and Ms. Olson seeing one another?" Might as well ask as many questions as possible, Liz calculated. Sweeps week started next week and a celebrity's love life was just the kind of story that made a good lead.

"Just friends," he replied quickly. Fortunately William was darkly tanned or Liz would have been able to detect him blushing. He hadn't forgotten their afternoon lovemaking and he wasn't a very good liar.

"I've been helping Chief Panther with the raptor rehabilitation facility next to my house," Lindsey spoke up to take the attention from William. The camera and microphone swung toward her.

For Lindsey, the experience was like going to work. Just another interview. Another camera and mic. No problem. And to further distract from her personal life she had the perfect response.

"What's more, I was arrested this afternoon for aiding and abetting federal fugitives, the very refugees who were shot at tonight. I was just returning with Mr. Elias who secured my release this evening." That should pique her curiosity Lindsey thought. Probably get Lindsey a little publicity at the same time.

"Is that true? Does anyone else know?" Liz thought all the stars must have aligned in her favor. A celebrity arrest was even better than a celebrity affair, especially since the guy involved was a relative unknown.

"Yes, it's true. You can have your station check the courthouse, Judge Spahn's courtroom. And you're the first media person I've talked to. It's an exclusive," That ought to change her focus Lindsey thought.

"Can you give me the details?"

"Gladly," Lindsey Lee replied and proceeded to describe her arrest and hearing. In the process she made Agent Busch look as arrogant and as abusive of his power as possible. Naturally Reuben came across as a knight in shining armor.

"Thanks," Liz responded when Lindsey finished. "That was great." With the luck she was having tonight, Liz thought, she should have bought herself a lottery ticket.

William had retreated to a corner and watched the pro handle the interview. Waiting in the shadows was just fine with him.

But Liz had one more story idea. She may have gone to college in Boston, but she'd grown up in Miami. She'd been a news junkie at an early age, devouring the local paper, The Miami Herald, and watching and analyzing the local broadcast outlets. She knew a good deal about local zoning and environmental issues.

"Chief Panther, one more question," she said returning her attention to William.

The chief had relaxed watching Lindsey handle Liz. Now he was tense again.

"What?" he asked cautiously.

"Has your tribe made an environmental study and pulled permits to remove all these mangroves? This resort doesn't seem like a very ecologically sound project. For a group that in the past has represented itself as a steward of the natural world, it surprises me that the Miccosukee tribe would be involved in this."

"It surprises me, too!" came William's completely unexpected reply.

"Would you care to elaborate?" she was almost holding her breath.

"I would." It was William's turn to use the media.

"Go ahead." She wanted to keep him talking.

"Well," he paused. He wanted to be careful, not put his brother in too bad a light.

"My tribe does very well with our resort and casino on the edge of the Everglades. It provides a good supplementary income for every member.

My brother, Rex, and Mr. Negro, the developer of Mont Basura, came up with the concept of a high-end gaming complex for this site. From my brother's viewpoint it would provide jobs and a substantial increase in tribal income. And Rogelio Negro, he's a developer. This is the kind of thing that developers do. But I look at our casino, the gaming boats that sail from Miami and Miami Beach, and the big casinos nearby in the Bahamas and think—does this area need another gambling complex? Should we really tear out one of the last pieces of native shoreline for electronic Keno, slot machines, lightning Lotto, and high stakes poker tables? Personally I don't think so."

"Do you have permits?" she asked again.

"I don't know. You'd have to ask my brother and Mr. Negro. But remember, this is reservation land. The same law that allows us to offer the holy men sanctuary without government intrusion, pretty much allows us to do whatever we want to do with the land."

"Do you care to make any other comment?" Liz wanted to give William every opportunity. A conflict within the tribe would be a good local interest piece.

"No." William kept it succinct. He wasn't into public speaking and didn't care for being in the actual spotlight. But at least he'd said his piece, and, if the station ran it, his view would be out on the table, in spite of the trouble it might cause.

"Thanks," Liz replied moving her hand in a horizontal slicing motion across her throat indicating to the cameraman to cut the taping.

She looked at her watch and turned back to the other occupants of the trailer. "Thanks, Mr. Elias. Thanks everybody."

Then she turned again and opened the door, talking over her shoulder. "If we get this up linked fast enough it can still be on the air by 10:30. We'll beat all the eleven o'clock stations."

The cameraman hurried after her. As they exited the compound gate, they could see all the network trucks coming back and setting up.

Reuben heard the commotion of their arrival. He grinned at his clients, "Well men, here we go again." What a fun night, He was pumped.

William felt like the trailer and the events were closing in on him. Lindsey picked up on the trapped look in his eyes. "Come on. Let's get out of here. I've had enough for one day. Reuben can handle this," she said.

"Yeah," his relief was audible," I need to get away from this."

"We'll go back to my place," she said taking his hand and leading him out the door.

As they trudged back up the side of the development William asked wearily, " How do you do it? Put up with the lights in your eyes and a microphone jammed in your face?"

"You really hate it don't you. I could see how uncomfortable you were."

"Yeah. It's so pushy. I don't like being crowded."

"After awhile you get used to it. They're just doing their job."

"Let someone else be their job."

She laughed, "It's not that bad. Besides it gave you the chance to express your viewpoint on developing the marsh land."

He smiled at her laughter, "True. And it'll probably piss Rex off. But I'd be fine if I never stood in front of a camera again."

"Unfortunately for you the way things are right now that's not likely to happen."

"No," he grimaced. He'd been quite happy as the quiet unseen chief.

They stepped over a low spot in her hedge and looked back down on the sights below. A small caravan of TV trucks, their antennas stretched into the sky transmitting images into space stood on one side of the gate. Reuben and his circus troupe were waiting on the other side to satisfy the hungry reporters heading their way. In the background were the five radically customized SUVs and the silver trash hauler. It looked slightly surreal.

William shook his head, "Can I borrow your jeep?"

"Why?"

"I need to get further away. Back to the Glades."

"Just come into the house. We'll close the curtains. Turn down the lights. Peace and quiet."

"Thanks. And I don't want to offend you. But it's not the same."

"Sure. Okay. You can take the jeep," she was confused and uncertain, maybe a little hurt. They'd just been lovers that afternoon. And now, unexpectedly, he was leaving her and heading out to the swamp.

William heard the trepidation in her voice. He'd been so desperate to escape the commotion he hadn't considered how it would appear. "It's not you," he blurted out tactlessly. "I just need to get away from what passes as civilization. I need some solitude. You can come along if you want."

"What kind of solitude would that be?" she replied, unimpressed with his lame invitation.

"Listen. I'm not very good at this. I just meant I need to get away from people."

She arched an eyebrow at this explanation.

"Damn. Give me a break. I screwed it up again. I'd really like you to come along. See how the uncivilized folks live."

The poor guy hadn't been able to get comfortable all night. He hadn't intended to hurt her and it was time to let him off the hook. "I'd love to go."

"Great," he sighed, relieved. "You'll need to change your clothes," he told her as she ran up the stairs.

In five minutes William was backing the Jeep out of her driveway with Lindsey in the passenger seat.

"Where're we going?"

"Feel like catching a little late night dinner?" he replied.

"Sure. Whatta you have in mind?"

"It'll be a surprise. You'll see when we get there."

 **Chapter XV**

They caught the turnpike, headed west and took the Tamiami Trail exit. They stopped at the casino on the edge of the Glades, just long enough for William to pick up a couple of changes of clothing and some supplies. As they rolled toward the wilderness, Lindsey watched him inhale the fresh clean air. In a few breaths she saw his shoulders relax and his grip on the wheel loosen. His tensions were melting away. He really did need this she smiled to herself. Come to think of it, she could feel some of her own muscles loosening up. Therapy indeed.

They rode in silence, their faces occasionally lit up by the high beams of the oncoming traffic heading east out of the dark. William, in no hurry, was doing ten miles less than the speed limit. After about twenty minutes he slowed, put on his blinker, and pulled over to the south side of the Trail.

Lindsey saw a couple of old dilapidated buildings boarded up, with no lights on anywhere.

"Where are we?" she asked.

William flicked on the high beams and pointed through the windshield.

Lindsey could see a large cut out plywood sign. It had once been a bright green. Most of the paint had long ago flaked off and what was left had faded to a pale pastel. It was in the shape of a cartoon frog and at the bottom said "Frog City-Population 24". The 24 and several following decreasing numbers had been x'd out. The last number was a faded 5.

"Not exactly a thriving community," Lindsey quipped.

"Nope," was the laconic reply as William pulled the Jeep around behind the largest building so it couldn't be seen from the road. He rolled the windows back up, grabbed his bag, jumped out and came around to open Lindsey's door for her.

"It was the idea of a few old timers who used to make a living from selling what they hunted and fished for out here," he continued. "But times changed. People no longer were interested in fresh game. Or they were zipping by here too fast to stop and check the place out. The government made it harder to hunt. In fact, though now they're so many gators that they're becoming a nuisance in places, for awhile you couldn't take them because they were considered threatened. So as the older guys passed on, no one came to replace them. Take whichever explanation sounds best. Whatever, the place just withered and died."

As he looked around the miniature ghost town, William sounded wistful, even a little melancholy.

Lindsey stood in front of him looking into his face. "You miss them, don't you?"

"Yes. Some of those old guys taught me to hunt. It was an honest simple life. Basic and pure. Except for a few members of the tribe, it's pretty much dead now. And not coming back."

"Is this what you do to make yourself feel better?" She poked her index finger into his sternum to snap him out of his depressing reverie.

"I'm sorry," he smiled. "I really do come here to feel better. Reconnect with nature. It's just that I do miss some of the old ghosts."

"That's okay," she said gently.

"Follow me. I'll guarantee you an experience you haven't had before."

He led her down a path overgrown with cattails and scrub foliage. The starry sky was clear and there was an almost full moon, plenty of light to see by once their eyes adapted. The trail led silently downward and they soon came to an embankment. There was an airboat and a smaller, twelve-foot aluminum johnboat pulled up on the shore.

William placed the bag he was carrying on the front seat in the johnboat. He reached into the airboat and pulled out what looked like three poles and a burlap sack. He put two of the poles and the sack into the smaller vessel, holding on to the longest pole.

"Get in," he motioned to Lindsey Lee.

"We aren't taking the one with the motor?"

"This one's more peaceful," he replied.

"No dugout canoe?" she teased.

"We buy them from Sears these days," he grinned gesturing toward the aluminum craft with the camouflage paint job.

Lindsey stepped in and centered herself on the middle seat. William pushed the boat off the bank, stepping onto the back seat at the last second. He began to pole them through the marsh grasses and water plants. He quickly settled into a nice steady pace.

Lindsey enjoyed the ride. The cool breeze whispered through the tall grasses. The slow moving water of the wide shallow river babbled ever so softly. Insects clicked and whirred. Frogs croaked. In the distance came the occasional hoot or screech of a hunting owl or the mating grunt of a bull gator. All in all a pastoral rhythmic quiet cacophony.

The only problem to Lindsey was that one section of grassy swamp looked the same as the next. She knew better, but couldn't help herself. "You know where we're going?"

The only response she got was a slight upturn at the corners of William's mouth and a slow affirmative nod.

She could have pressed for more information. But why break the spell. He was in his element and obviously enjoying himself. And, actually, so was she.

William pushed them along for about half an hour and finally Lindsey noticed a change of scenery. They were approaching a hammock, a raised mound like an island in the swamp where larger shrubs and trees such as mahogany and cypress grew. There was a cleared area, a watering hole on the bank of the hammock.

As they emerged from the grasses into the open pool of water, William reached into his travel bag and pulled out a flashlight. He clicked it on, playing the beam along the shore while reaching for one of the two poles in the bottom of the boat with his other hand. He sighted his target and flicked his pole toward it. There was a wet thump sound. He picked up the second pole and repeated the sequence in just a few seconds.

"Whaaa?" Lindsey barely croaked out. There was no change in the placid night sounds. But the tranquility of the moment was shattered by the silent violence.

"Get the sack," William ordered. "We're going to need more than these two to make dinner. But there's plenty here."

He pulled in the two poles. Actually they weren't just poles. They were more like spears, each tipped with a barbed trident at one end.

"Just pull 'em off and put 'em in the croaker sack," he directed, swinging the two impaled creatures over Lindsey's lap.

"You really know how to impress a girl. You could've told me what you had in mind."

"I told you I was gonna catch you dinner. Why'd you think they called the place Frog City? You want to give it a try?"

"I'll just watch you for now."

"Suit yourself."

Pulling the skewered bullfrogs off the prongs wasn't all that pleasant an experience, so in the end Lindsey decided to try gigging so William would have to pull them off the barbs. She wanted to carry her own weight. She nailed three on four attempts. She hadn't been made quarterback of the Coconuts for nothing.

"That's enough," William said, putting the last frog into the sack. He rinsed his hands in the watering hole. Lindsey followed suit.

"Now what?" she asked.

"I promised you dinner."

William poled the boat for another ten minutes until they came to another hammock. This one had a chickee, the raised open platform covered with palm thatch considered the traditional Miccosukee dwelling, with a clearing around it.

"We're home," William announced.

"Love what you've done to the place," Lindsey quipped. On the platform there were a couple of large plywood boxes for storage, topped with mattresses so they could double as beds. There were also several hammocks, the sleeping kind, suspended between the roof supports. And a large cast iron grill that could be used both as a stove and a barbecue. That was about it. The place was about as Spartan as the houses on Mont Basura were opulent.

"It serves its purpose well," he replied, sounding slightly defensive.

"I'm sure it does. What a great place to get away from it all." She hadn't meant to offend him and continued, "What about dinner?"

"You're right. It's after midnight. You've gotta be hungry."

"Actually now that you mention it I am."

William grabbed the duffel bag and stepped out of the boat. "Bring the croaker sack would you?" he asked over his shoulder.

Lindsey gingerly grabbed their fresh caught bounty and followed. William put his bag down on the edge of the platform and pulled out a soft-sided cooler. Lindsey set the bag of bullfrogs next to it.

William started a fire in the grill and took a large iron skillet out of one of the storage boxes.

"Beer?" he offered, reaching inside the cooler. Lindsey nodded yes and William pulled out two Hatueys, popping the top off hers before handing it to her.

She watched him clean their catch. She'd caught and cleaned her own fish before, so the process wasn't completely foreign. Still when he got to the part where he peeled the skin down the legs, it sort of seemed like watching a woman peel out of panty hose, suggestively sensual and slightly obscene.

By then the fire was going well. William put the big frying pan on the grill, put in some butter, chopped garlic and then threw in the frog legs. He quickly sautéed them, then put a splash of his beer and covered them to steam for a short time.

He pulled a couple of plates out and announced, "Dinner is served."

He handed Lindsey her portion. She looked down at the meaty little legs with webbed feet on the ends. Having never eaten them before she watched William for the proper etiquette. He picked up a leg and gnawed the meat off more or less like one eats a chicken wing. When he was done he tossed the remains out into the water to let nature recycle them. Lindsey followed his lead.

After she finished her first pair and threw the remnants into the slough, William gave her a questioning look.

"Never had anything quite like this before. They don't really taste like chicken. They're better. In fact they're delicious. But they are kind of hard to look at," came her response.

He laughed, "You're right. They take some getting used to. It's the main reason there was never more than a small gourmet market for them. One of the reasons Frog City never took off."

"But they really are good," she insisted.

"Thanks," he said, leaning over to give her a friendly kiss. "I'm glad you came. I got to thinking on the drive out here that this might be a big mistake. It's certainly not the kind of thing for everybody."

"I'm glad I came, too. It reminds me of good times I had fishing with my dad before my parents divorced and he moved away."

They sat with their legs dangling over the side of the chickee platform and polished off the rest of their catch. A couple of opossums tentatively waded into the water and retrieved some of the leg pieces to make a meal of their own.

"Not much goes to waste out here," Lindsey said.

"One way or another all part of the food chain," William replied.

He took Lindsey's and his dinner dishes and the skillet and washed them and put them away. She was about to remark on his orderly domesticity.

"You don't clean and store 'em and the bugs or animals will be in them in no time," he seemed to anticipate her comment.

"Makes sense," she replied.

"You want me to take you home?" he asked.

Surprised, she replied, "You weren't planning on staying here tonight?"

"Well, yeah. But it's up to you. I figured you might have had enough."

"Well I thought we were staying. Haven't camped out since I was a kid. And the weather's beautiful."

The answer he'd hoped for. And indeed the weather was perfect, cool and clear. And it was still the dry season, meaning the mosquitoes weren't out yet.

He came back and sat next to her. They took turns picking out the constellations in the black crystal sky. They cuddled against each other making small talk and discussing the bizarre events of the previous day. Finally, they were just holding one another nestled in a sleepy silence.

"We'd better get some sleep. Could be another long day tomorrow," he said, helping her up.

When she stood he kissed her. It was slow, warm, and tender, with just a hint of garlic. She loved the earthiness of it.

"You wanna?" she started to ask.

"As much as I'd like to, it's not that comfortable here and we're both too tired," he said picking her up and depositing her in one of the hammocks.

He flopped into one next to her, "Night Lindsey."

"Good night, William."

They were asleep in seconds.

*   *   *

Lindsey was slightly disoriented when she awoke. She'd been sleeping deeply and when she opened her eyes the thatched roof over her head seemed to be moving. As she came to, she realized William was swinging her hammock.

"Sleepy head," he smiled down at her, " The day's a wasting. The sun's been up for over an hour. Breakfast is ready."

She rolled out of her hammock. Her hair was mussed and there were crisscross net marks on the side of her face from the hammock's weave. She ran her fingers through her hair to try and tame it.

"I must look awful. What's for breakfast?"

"You look fine to me. Here's your plate," he said handing it to her. "There's coffee on the stove."

Lindsey looked down and saw bacon and eggs and something that looked like a cross between a small pancake and a biscuit. She picked it up and nibbled at the edge.

"Take a bite," William said watching. "It won't hurt you."

She took a mouthful. It was like a heavy, oily, doughy pancake. "That's a real sinker. What is it?"

"Indian fry bread. Thought I'd give you the whole authentic experience. Eat the whole thing and it will stick with you most of the day."

"You won't be offended if I don't finish it?"

151

"Not at all. It's awful heavy. Notice you don't see one on my plate. I'm watching my weight," he laughed.

"But it's ok to fatten me up?"

"Nah. You're just fine the way you are."

They sat and ate their breakfast as the slanting rays of the sun woke the dayshift animals of the Glades. A great blue heron from a rookery swept down and picked at the leftovers that the opossums had missed during their foraging the previous night.

An appreciative "mmm" came from Lindsey, her mouth full at the time.

"Majestic. I never get tired of seeing the animals here. Never take it for granted."

"Should I throw him some fry bread?" she asked.

"No, for a couple of reasons. We don't want him to get used to taking food from humans. Some tourists could feed him things he might not be able to digest and others might abuse him if he lets them get close."

"Yeah. I hadn't thought about that."

"It's ok. Like most people your intentions are good. Besides, there's a more important reason. Feed him that thing and he may be too heavy for lift-off."

She laughed. "What do I do with it?"

"Throw it out in the deeper water. The fish can nibble on it and it won't hurt them. Fatten 'em up for the birds and other animals to eat."

"That circle of life thing sure is a lot more up close and personal out here," Lindsey observed.

"The what?" he asked.

"It's from a Walt Disney movie, The Lion King. You know. Life. Death. A place in the food chain."

"I don't see many movies," he replied by way of explanation. "But you're right. So-called civilized society insulates you. Food appears in the store almost by magic. If you need it you just go pick it up. And the waste from its production and consumption, the things that you don't see that are mysteriously hauled away."

"Some of us see them. Live on top of them in fact."

"Touché," he smiled.

"But I get your point," she continued, "The process is generally hidden, or at least out of conscious perception. And generally underappreciated."

He nodded in agreement, "Heavy."

She smiled at his reply, straight out of the 70's. She liked that he didn't take himself too seriously.

"All right smart guy. Let me ask you something. Do you bring all your dates out here to the middle of the swamp for deep philosophical discussions?"

"Short answer. No."

"Long answer?"

"It's not the middle. It's nearer the eastern edge."

"That's evasive enough to be Reuben, or worse, a politician."

"Well I am chief number two, but let me finish. You're the only woman I've ever brought here. I haven't dated much, so there aren't that many to talk about. But even the Miccosukee girls are more interested in what goes on in the city. And as for philosophical intercourse, I believe you started it."

"You may be right. I may have started it, but it seems to be the only intercourse available out here," she played the word to remind him of what they passed on last night.

"The other's available, too," he replied leaning over to kiss her.

It was a good thing it wasn't mosquito season. For the next half hour the little biters would have had a veritable buffet from the two naked bodies. Light meat or dark. Lindsey or William.

When they were done, they lay entwined on one of the mattresses, gently tracing each other's contours with their fingers. The morning sun toasted their bodies that glistened from the heat and pleasurable exertion.

"Now what?" she whispered.

Not sure what she meant, William kissed her again.

"Well of course we could go again. But we can't do this all day," she continued.

"We could try," he gave voice to his very male fantasy.

She sat up and stepped down to the chickee's floor. He watched her stretch and yawn. She turned to face him.

The view had an immediate resuscitative effect on a part of his anatomy. He put his hands over his lap.

"I guess you mean we have to go back some time. Check on the mess we left. We just can't hide out here forever," he replied despondently. It sounded like a condemned man facing his execution.

"Right. But it's not that bad," she smiled at him. "We can still take the time to fix your little problem before we go."

"It's not that little."

"True."

This time when they finished, they took a quick dip in the pond by the hammock to rinse and cool everything off.

The boat trip back to Frog City didn't take as long. It turned out the frog pond was further from the road than William's chickee. Lindsey asked for a try at poling the boat and found out it wasn't nearly as easy as he made it look. But at least they didn't capsize.

As they beached the boat on the shore of the abandoned settlement Lindsey asked, "Promise me you'll take me out there again."

"Sure thing. There's a lot more to show you. And I'll bet you've never had fresh gator."

"No, I haven't and I can't say the hunting was my favorite part. But the whole experience was so special."

That's for sure he thought. "Just let me know when you want to go back," he replied.

In the jeep William reached under the seat and pulled out his cell phone. "I hate this damn thing. No privacy. I didn't want it to ruin our night."

As he pulled onto Tamiami Trail joining the eastbound traffic he flipped the power button on the phone. The screen indicated about a dozen voice mails, all from his brother.

He handed Lindsey the phone. "Would you listen to these and tell me what he wanted?"

She put the phone to her ear and played the messages back.

"They start out civil and get more angry as they go. The gist is where are you, where the hell are you, where the fuck are you, etc.? Also, what happened down there, what the hell happened down there, what the ...? Well you get the idea," Lindsey grinned at him.

"'Bout what I expected," William still seemed relaxed. But then he should be, Lindsey thought.

"Wonder how much of our interview made the news last night. Since we drive right by his office, think we should stop and see him?" she asked.

"Nah. Probably better to assess the situation in person first."

They continued eastward, each mentally replaying the enjoyable events of their trip. On their right the Everglades stretched beyond where the eye could see, all the way to Florida Bay. On their left were the flood control levee and the canal, sparsely populated by the occasional fisherman.

Lindsey didn't turn on the radio until they crossed Krome, her mental border between the Glades and suburban sprawl, between peace and chaos. According to the local news station the situation down at the trash reservation had certainly not settled down over night.

Lindsey could see William's shoulders start to tense up and it wasn't hard to figure out the words he mouthed silently, "What the hell have we gotten into?" Especially since she felt the same way.

 **Chapter XVI**

The access road to Mount Basura was clogged with traffic. Police were now turning back all vehicles except those that could prove they lived on or had legitimate business at the development.

"What is all this?" William was a bit incredulous.

"Power of the media my love," Lindsey said using the language's strongest four letter word for the first time in their relationship.

His only acknowledgement was to tip his head slightly toward her. And he didn't protest.

"Think about it," she continued, "Depending on your viewpoint, someone just took a shot at three of God's messengers and/or at three helpless refugees trapped by a government that obviously didn't do a very good job of protecting them. Passions are high and a lot of people feel they have a personal interest in what's going on."

After they parked the Jeep, they walked out on Lindsey's patio to the hedge. Looking down they were astounded at the change from the previous night. Inside the compound things appeared much the same, the two trailers and the rappers' outlandish vehicles all in the same place. But outside the fence there was now a police perimeter being patrolled by officers on mountain bikes and four-wheel ATVs. In the distance off shore, there were at least a half dozen marine patrol and police boats, with a small flotilla of assorted protest boats beyond them. But that was nothing compared to the number of protesters and supporters massed outside the law enforcement's no trespass zone. All the groups that had supported the refugees when they were captured by the Coast Guard were now here in force. And of course the network news trucks were back. In addition, there were a few pro law enforcement groups demanding that the refugees be recaptured and repatriated to Cuba.

"What a mess," William shook his head.

"Yep. The circus is in town. Our town. I wonder how Reuben's doing," Lindsey said.

"I suppose we should call him," William replied, his heart obviously not in it.

"Come on. He might need a break. And we've just had a nice one. Give him a call," Lindsey chided.

William turned on his phone punching in Reuben's number then holding the set so that both of them could listen.

"Chief. I was wondering when I'd hear from you again. Where's Lindsey?" The voice on the other end didn't sound tired at all. If anything, Reuben sounded excited.

"I'm right here listening, too," she spoke into the receiver. "How's it going, Reuben?"

"Great. Couldn't be better. You should see all the people out here. And the news media are all back. Where are you two?"

"We can see it. We're in Lindsey's backyard," William replied.

"Well as they say on TV, come on down," came Reuben's response.

"We're coming," said Lindsey as she motioned for William to follow her over the hedge. "How's the big guy doing?"

"Tell you when you get here. See ya' soon," Reuben clicked off.

The Miccosukee and the starlet held hands as they traversed a slanted path down the slope of the rubbish plateau.

About halfway down Lindsey paused and inhaled. "Smells like the methane collectors aren't doing the job."

"Nothing like the smell of decaying organic matter in the warm sun," William sniffed back.

They continued on their course. When they reached the bottom, they had to work their way through the crowds surrounding the reservation. The Ark airship traced a low, lazy figure eight over the area blaring religious music and adding to the surrealism of the situation.

And what diverse groups of people they passed through. The expected, such as the religious supporters sporting robes and large crucifixes, and the exile supporters, some well into their sixties and seventies, but still sporting their camouflage fatigues and ready to battle Castro at any moment. To the reactionary groups like the America for Americans bunch who wanted to send all refugees back to the land from whence they came. But whose name, in the context of the situation, seemed absurd considering that technically America or at least the Americas stretched from Argentina's Tierra Del Fuego in the south to Canada's frozen tundra above the Arctic Circle. And therefore just about everyone in the crowd was an American of one ilk or another.

The last group they passed, just outside the compound's gate, was about a dozen young men each with a doo-rag around his head and a patch over the left ear dyed red.

Lindsey could feel their eyes checking her out as William unlatched the gate. "Would you look at that? Talk about hero worship. A bunch of Hamilton wannabes," she muttered to herself.

"Whatta you think?" said Reuben who was waiting inside as they came in.

"You sure know how to calm things down. Keep a lid on the situation," William replied facetiously.

"Especially the future Hamilton Patricks of America. What a nice extra touch," Lindsey added.

"Yeah. I'm not quite sure what to do about them. A little overzealous even for my taste. Watch your step," Reuben warned.

They looked down.

"They're not---," William gasped, repulsed.

"Yup. Tributes from real fans," Reuben responded.

"Oh God," Lindsey started to retch but managed to avoid losing her breakfast.

On the ground inside the gate were scattered a dozen halves of left ears.

Reuben gently turned Lindsey away from the sight. "Even for me that's carrying solidarity too far."

"That's freakin' sick," William exclaimed.

"Where's Hamilton? What's he think of this?" Lindsey asked wanly.

"He's not here. These guys just arrived and he doesn't know anything about this. He hit it off pretty good with Liz, that young reporter from last night. She's up with him at his house doing a more in-depth interview. Might run on ESPN as well as the local station," Reuben informed them.

"How about the three stars of the show? How are they doin'?" William inquired.

"Okay. They're confused by the whole thing. They just want to be let free and get a job. Don't understand why there's such a big fuss. But right now they're resting with the three hand maidens," Reuben replied.

"Thank heaven there is some small solace for them," Lindsey smirked. "Any progress on getting them released."

"Pressure's building obviously. We've got the politicians' nuts in a vice and we're squeezing harder but we're still stalemated. The local mayors would like nothing better than to play to their Hispanic constituents but a couple have statewide aspirations, governor or state seat. And law and order granted only to those arriving legally is a big concern to the voters north of Lake Okeechobee, especially after the Elian fiasco. So these guys just sit on their hands. Same at the national level. It's an election year and Florida has 27 electoral votes. The politicians want the big contribution from South Florida's Cuban community and don't want to offend them. By the same token they have to uphold the law and not appear to show favoritism to any single immigrant group. So for now everybody's sitting around hoping someone else will do something."

"And this is how we get them to budge?" William looked apprehensively through the fence.

"Keep squeezing the vice. Hope that when something gives it gives our way. This situation with the national spotlight back on us is the best we can hope for."

"Really?" William was still skeptical.

"Sure. The one thing worse than offending one constituency is offending them all. And politicians who do nothing to remedy a volatile situation eventually lose the respect of everyone. Somebody's gonna have to make a move soon."

"But I thought the judge's decision on the wet foot-dry foot aspect would decide this," William countered.

"Ah, my innocent young friend. Perhaps it still might. But with inconclusive evidence which way will the judge go? Best to build public sympathy on our behalf."

"But he's a federal judge. He's not elected. He doesn't have to answer to voters. He's s'posed to decide the case on its legal merit."

Lindsey knowingly smiled at Reuben, "Look, William. Even judges face political pressures. After all they're appointed by politicians. They socialize with them and garner their support on the way up. And they still get their input after receiving their appointments."

"So it's all a big game. And the law isn't really equal for everyone and justice isn't really blind," William's disillusionment with the system was obvious in his voice.

"No. It's not a game. Three young lives hang in the balance here. Don't ever lose sight of that. Unfortunately the law isn't always applied equally. Some people are fortunate enough to get better representation and justice's vision is improved because of it," Reuben responded in a serious tone.

Their conversation was interrupted by a long mechanized rumble coming toward them from the access road.

"What?" the three of them said almost in unison.

"Oh shit," was the next thing out of William's mouth when he realized what was approaching.

"This is great. Did you arrange this, Chief?" Reuben asked.

"Hell no," William spat.

Approaching the gate was a procession of half a dozen swamp buggies, converted pick-up trucks with monster tractor tires and raised chassis to keep their steel bodies out of the water. Each was occupied by three or four men and several also contained large pit bull cross breeds. Rex was riding shotgun in the lead buggy. The bastard never drove himself unless he had to.

The vehicles were given a cursory inspection by the policemen manning the access road and allowed to pass since they obviously had the right to be there.

When they passed through the gate the first truck slowed and Rex hopped out.

" Hey, little brother. Thought you might need some additional security," he said to William.

William watched the buggies parking to form a second perimeter, covering the gaps in the line of the rappers' SUVs.

"When's the last time you wore one of those?" William asked referring to the loose fitting traditional Miccosukee cotton patchwork blouse that Rex and all the newly arrived tribe members were wearing. It had been so long since William had seen Rex in anything but silk or suits that he was highly suspicious.

"Come on. I'm the chief. This is our land. We deserve the free publicity. This could be almost as good for us as the Marlins winning the World Series," he replied, referring to the tribe's recent marketing coup. At the beginning of the last baseball season the tribe had placed a large billboard right under the stadium scoreboard advertising the casino. It had cost next to nothing, and, when the improbable wild card team made it to the playoffs and then won the World Series, the swamp resort had received tremendous national exposure.

William had figured that was his angle. "Okay. Fair enough. But Rex, the hog dogs? Not exactly the friendliest image you could project."

"No. But tough. I'm serious about security, too. And those dogs will make any intruder think twice before setting foot on our land."

"True enough." The pit mixes were bred to run down wild boars in the swamp. They had to have endurance for the chases as well as the tenacity and strength to withstand the ferocious assault of a cornered tusker.

A couple of the dog handlers had come over to say hi to William. They actually knew him much better than they did Rex because he'd gone hunting with them.

Several of the dogs, tethered to their handlers by heavy rope, snuffled at the ground. Finding what to them were delectable morsels, they gobbled up pieces of ears lying on the grass.

"Bear, whatcha got there?" one of the men said to his dog. There was an audible crunching of gristly cartilage.

Lindsey, realizing what was happening went, "Nooo...Aw..." This time her breakfast was gone.

Bear lapped that up, too.

"What's up with her?" the handler asked.

William gave him a brief explanation.

"They ain't dedicated. They're crazy," the man replied, looking through the gate at Ham's loyal followers. Some in the doo-rag brigade were looking a little pale as the realization hit them that, for sure, there was never going to be a way to reconnect them with their lost body parts.

"Them things aren't going to make the dogs sick, are they?" the man inquired.

"Don't think so. Dogs have pretty strong digestion," William replied.

"Can't we discuss something else?" Lindsey asked weakly.

"Sure," Reuben piped in, "Rex, what made you decide to join us?"

"I turned on the news this morning and saw the crowds gathered. Wasn't sure whose side the police are on, but saw their numbers sure had increased. Our side, even with your security people, looked potentially outmanned and under-equipped. Thought you could use some help."

"Thanks," Reuben replied. He had been wondering himself how his small crew would've been able to withstand a full assault from either police in riot gear trying to arrest the refugees or from one of the paramilitary groups trying to rescue them. After all, they weren't really gangsters and had no desire to get into a shootout with anyone. The addition of extra bodies and especially the dogs made him feel a lot better.

William had winced when he heard Rex use the term "our side". He knew his brother was co-opting the situation for his own end.

"That's all? You just came to help," William's skepticism was obvious.

"Isn't that enough? I brought my reinforcements. And I have a few other ideas that might help."

William knew the other shoe was about to drop. "Like what?"

"Well, like clearing those mangroves out of there. We remove them and we remove the cover that allowed incursions like the one last night. I can have the heavy equipment here in a couple of days."

"I should've figured," William responded knowingly.

"What?" I'm providing better protection for your guys and helping the tribe's interest at the same time. It's win-win."

"Yeah, sure," came William's surly reply.

"Look brother, I'm chief and I'm here now. I'll be looking out for our tribe's interest. You can leave if you want," Rex was now directly in William's face, reminding him who was actually in charge.

William started to clench his fists.

Reuben grabbed Rex by the shoulder and pulled him away while mentioning, "Come on. Let me take you over and introduce you to the press. You'll need to make your points with them."

It wouldn't help them to have a fistfight between the two chiefs captured on camera.

"Sure. Fine. You're right," Rex stared back over his shoulder at William. "Remember who's the boss here!"

As William's hands unclenched, Lindsey took one saying, "Let's go check on our charges."

"Right. Like Reuben said it's all about them and their lives," William agreed, following along.

"Well, we know that's not exactly true," she replied.

"Not exactly. Not hardly," William muttered so softly Lindsey barely heard him, as she watched his brother march with Reuben toward the clot of media trucks.

 **Chapter XVII**

Neil Busch was a very unhappy man. His effort to recapture the refugees had exploded in his face. They were now protected better than ever. And the damn Indians were really beginning to stick in his craw. First the younger one helping them avoid capture when he nearly had them, then giving them sanctuary, then the older sleazy one bringing in more troops and those damn dogs.

He was beginning to look at this as a military situation.

And now he needed to plan either a successful siege or an assault and extraction scenario.

The siege would take time and if the courts ruled against him he might never get to prosecute the bastards. However, if he recaptured them, he could hold them on federal fugitive warrants for the escape. Even if they were later found to have arrived in the country legally, they could still be deported for repatriation to Cuba based on the federal felony. Somebody had to make lawbreakers pay.

The assault and extraction was the way to go. His infiltrators would help. Informers, infiltrators, whatever. Modern law enforcement required these tools.

No, required was too soft a term. These tools were critical to maintaining public safety. With anarchists, or anti-Christs as he liked to call them, on the loose with bomb making instructions available to them on the Internet, any small splinter faction had the ability to create tremendous mayhem and destruction.

Infiltration and paid for information were the only ways the police had any hopes of keeping tabs on some of the nut cases. Right now, the assortment of law enforcement agencies he was in contact with gave Busch access to informers or planted members in at least five of the protest groups arrayed around the refugees' sanctuary.

Fortunately for Busch, at least in this situation, a couple of them were familiar with the use of explosives and wouldn't have any qualms about employing them. They also had some minimal practice at ground assault and rescue techniques. These capabilities were crucial to the operation he had in mind.

The aerial views from the news helicopters had shown him the weakest point in his enemy's defenses. From there he started to mentally cobble a plan together. It was time to start implementing it. Luckily he had the assets, or could contact the ones he needed to get the ball rolling.

He picked up his phone and punched the SWAT commander's number. The man was glad to hear from him. He was still pissed off about his men being shot at the previous night.

The SWAT man listened patiently to Busch's plan adding tactical suggestions to improve its chance of success.

When finished Busch asked, "Think it's doable?"

"Risky. But yeah," was the terse reply.

"Too risky?"

"Look. There's always risk trying something like this. And I wish I were sending my own guys in, but yeah, I think it can be done. And my people'll be waiting to snatch them up as soon as they're off the Indian land."

"Can we go by tonight?" Busch queried.

"Hmm. It means we'll have to get the supplies we need down to the refugee paramilitaries and our other friends quickly. That's not too big a deal. It's the coordinating of the other groups. I've gotta go through a few contacts. An extra day's planning would be better. What's the rush?"

"The rush is I want those lawbreaking bastards and I want them now."

"Like I don't?" the SWAT man replied.

"Listen, word has it that Judge Spahn is ready to hand down his decision soon, maybe as early as tomorrow. If he says they're dry foot they'll be free to go. Nobody's going to stick their neck out and prosecute on our fugitive warrant once some judge says they should've been free in the first place."

"Okay. I'll get to my people fast as I can. Consider it a go for tonight unless I call and tell you different. I'll get back to you with a start time later."

The SWAT commander clicked off.

Busch felt better. He was getting some control back.

*   *   *

As they entered the trailer, Lindsey and William saw Seedy and some of his band sitting around the kitchen table. One of the men was pounding out a Caribbean flavored rhythm on the table while Seedy worked on lyrics that included the refrain "Refugee jus' wanna be free. Getta chance to make an honest fee."

Seedy looked up as they closed the door. "Gotta go with the inspiration when it comes," he explained as the Refuse G kept up the beat.

"Plenty to get you started around here," Lindsey smiled.

The trailer smelled of spicy congri, a beans and rice concoction. Each Central American country and Caribbean Island nation had its own version of the dietary staple. The beans could be black, red, pinto, or, as in the Bahamas, pigeon peas. The spicing ranged from moderate to intense, mild not allowed. Meat enhancement was usually some form of pork, either ham, bacon or sausage.

Lindsey normally liked to try cuisine from around the Caribbean basin, but her recent encounter with the hog dogs had killed any hunger she might have had. William, being of a more tolerant constitution, found that the aroma whetted his appetite. "Any of that left?" he inquired.

"On the stove. Help yourself. The boys have already eaten," Seedy replied.

William scooped himself a large helping.

Lindsey, her stomach still protesting, didn't even want to look at food. So she sought to engage Seedy in conversation. "How's the music going? How're you boys doing?"

"The music's good. So much positive energy for those boys. It's good to be a part of that. So much conflict around them, around this sanctuary. It gets the creative flow going. If I had my studio here I could produce a whole cd in a day."

"The boys are another story. I'm not sure they're doing so good. Reuben puttin' em in front of the cameras whenever he feels like it. Getting' shot at last night. Even in Cuba nobody shot at them. Least not 'til they was leavin'. Being stuck in this trailer. Even with the handmaidens to relieve their tension, they gettin' a little stir crazy."

"Not exactly the freedom they were expecting," Lindsey said emphatically.

"Not at all. They're like animals at the zoo. Everybody wanna see 'em. But they still caged in with no say of their own."

"Some of you rappers really are poets," Lindsey replied appreciating his insights.

"You movie people. Always sucking up to us," he said deflecting the praise.

"Why don't we get 'em outside? Get 'em some exercise—fresh air," William suggested between mouthfuls.

"What're they gonna do, calisthenics? Run laps around the cars?" Lindsey wasn't being nasty. She just didn't see what kind of activity they could offer the refugees.

"I've got a couple of soccer balls in my truck," Manny contributed from the table.

"Great. A pick-up soccer game," Lindsey was enthusiastic.

"Sounds good. But don't you think you ought to ask them?" Seedy suggested.

"I'll do it," William offered.

He walked down the hall past the storage closet and bathroom and knocked on the bedroom door. There was a muffled scrambling and shuffling, the soft sounds of clothing or bedding being returned to their proper places, followed by a feminine, "Momento."

A few seconds later Jesus opened the door, "Si, Mr. Panther, what is it?"

"We were wondering if you guys might like to get some exercise. A little sunshine. Maybe play a little soccer?"

"¿Futbol?"

"Yeah. Right. Football," William responded remembering that football had a different connotation to the rest of the world, compared to the game played in the United States.

"¿Futbol?" The door opened wider as both Pedro and Pablo asked the same question.

"Yeah," William smiled.

And so it came to pass that a makeshift soccer field was staked out in the area between the trailers and the vehicles. The game was co-ed. The teams ended up being the Native Americans, the Miccosukees with Lindsey, versus the Caribbean basin, which included the Haitians, Central Americans, Cubans and the three ladies. Considering the popularity of the sport around the Caribbean, it didn't look like a very fair match up. But the Miccosukees were surprisingly good. Their relative wealth and success were recently acquired. Living on the reservation they'd grown up mostly poor, like their opponents. And soccer was the poor kid's game requiring no other equipment besides the ball and an area big enough to play.

It was a friendly game. There was as much laughter by the men and giggling by the women, as there were shouts of encouragement when someone got close to scoring. No one had shin guards so there wasn't a lot of fancy close footwork between attackers and defenders. None of the players wanted to bang their unprotected bones against anyone else's. Initially the play was pretty ragged since most of the players had never played together. There were a couple of exceptions. Several of the Miccosukees had played together as teenagers, mostly as forwards, and they soon mounted a fairly coordinated attack. Fortunately for the Caribbean contingent Pedro and Pablo had played fullback with Jesus in goal, thus offering a good defense.

As the game progressed there was still some effort at security. The Indians with the dogs still walked at least a cursory perimeter, though they were often distracted by the action on the soccer pitch. And a couple of Seedy's people still paced the sidelines, their full shoulder harnesses apparent to anyone looking.

There was a lot of activity outside the fence. A tingle of excitement had run through the crowd when people realized that the refugees had stepped out of the trailer. There had been a reflexive surge toward the hero holy men. It was quickly repelled by the police who wanted to maintain their security perimeter. Then there was curiosity as the players had started setting up the field and another press as the crowd realized it was a soccer game and tried to get a better view. Again they were repulsed.

But the protest and the support groups this time had a second choice. Those who wanted to see the game simply moved to the slope of Mont Basura. There was enough elevation to see over the tops of the trailers and get a good view of the game. Better than the cheap seats at the Dolphins games.

The rooting was one-sided, heavily favoring what appeared to be the underdogs. The Miccosukees, at Rex's request, all wore traditional tribal shirts and jeans and looked like a sponsored team. The Caribbean team, with the exception of the three refugees still in their purple jumpsuits, had no coordinated couture whatsoever. They wore shorts ranging from cut offs to baggy gangster with the girls wearing tight minis. The guys' tops ranged from expensive sports jerseys to T-shirts and wifebeaters with the girls wearing assorted floral halters knotted under their breasts. Of course the fact that the refugees were on the Caribbean side also helped make it the crowd favorite.

While the soccer game was being set up Rogelio was at home, at his house on the northeast corner of the development. He was in his backyard, the one with the fantastic view of Miami to the north and the breathtaking view of the bay and the ocean to the east. His attention, however, was focused on the traffic-clogged access artery to Mont Basura and on the surrounded Indian reservation that he was now a part of. As he watched, he could see the soccer game in full swing inside the compound. Then suddenly the crowd started moving up the side of the pyramid toward him. Shit. Why hadn't he listened to the other developers who told him never live in one of your own projects?

The crowd stopped when it reached the vantage point for viewing the game. Still, Rogelio wished he'd listened to the advice. Just the movement of the protesters up the slope would incite another cascade of calls to his office from residents on the east side of the mesa who feared for their security. It was the reason he'd come home. All the phone calls and irate residents who'd shown up at his office to complain were driving him nuts.

The final straw had been the head of maintenance who'd barged in to tell him the methane scavenging system wasn't working right. Something about the ferrets chasing all the rats underground and the rats getting into the collecting pipes and blocking them up. He'd pushed the repairman out of his office telling him to just fix the problem. And he'd followed close behind locking his office door and telling his secretary to hold his calls. Now he was looking down on his problems, most directly or indirectly of his own making.

He needed a drink. He went inside and poured himself three fingers of dark rum over ice. It was from a small private distillery in Jamaica. And smooth enough to sip straight up.

He couldn't help himself. He took his glass back outside. The sound of the commotion below was kind of like hearing a car wreck; it was impossible not to look. He pulled a chair over near the edge of the slope and sat down to watch the game and the crowd.

About an hour later he noticed his new partner, Rex, and his old pain-in-the-ass friend Reuben emerge from the circle of television trucks and head back toward the new reservation. He felt a little better. The media savvy promoter and the savvy media exploiter would put the casino resort development in the best light for the public. He wished he could hear what they were saying.

"That went quite well I'd say," Reuben said to Rex.

"I agree. Except for that young girl, nobody even bothered with any environmental questions."

"Yeah. Liz. She grew up here. Knows more about local issues. But her station is from one of the second tier networks. She shouldn't hurt us too much."

"You sure?" Rex asked looking for positive spin.

"Look. The big three all sent reporters from their national pools, no local stringers. With them you came off looking real good."

"Right. The benevolent tribe delaying development of its beautiful upscale bayside hotel and casino…"

"I was impressed with how many times you managed to insert that description," Reuben interrupted.

"So that it could protect these brave young men from the actions of a heartless, uncaring government," Rex finished.

"Thanks for making my guys out as heroes."

"Least I could do. The more sympathetic I make them, the more goodwill I build for our venture."

As they passed through the gate, the cheers from the crowd and the yells from the playing field diverted their attention from their conversation. They walked over to the sideline to watch.

"Watch this," Rex told Reuben. "My guys are pretty good."

One of the Miccosukee forwards was advancing the ball toward the goal from the left side of the field. Pablo took an angle and cut him off. The man kicked the ball to the right to a teammate who had a straight-on shot. At the last second Pedro moved in front of him. The second Indian lofted the ball to a third standing at the right corner of the goalie box. The third man headed the ball up straight toward the inside right corner of the goal. Jesus, running across the goal's mouth, leapt high into the air and grabbed the ball just before it crossed the goal line. The crowd roared.

Reuben couldn't resist, "So it's true what they say."

"What's that?" Rex was the unwitting straight man.

"Jesus saves," Reuben laughed.

So did Rex.

Jesus dribbled the ball once, and then booted it down the field to his offense.

"Who's winning?" Reuben asked Magdalena who was standing on the sideline waiting to make a substitution.

"We are."

"What's the score?" Rex asked.

"We're up a couple of goals to nothing. The Miccosukees are actually pretty good, but Jesus is just a supernatural goaltender," she replied without a trace of irony.

The game lasted a little over two hours. Substitutions were made as players got tired or thirsty. The Miccosukees finally scored when Manny replaced Jesus as goalie.

During the middle of the game intermediaries from Busch or his contacts delivered special packages and orders to different members of certain of the protest groups.

Overhead, the observer in the Ark was getting really agitated. During breaks in the game, the young harlots were draping themselves all over the holy men in a much too familiar, in the biblical sense, manner. They were sullying the sanctity of Jesus and his disciples.

Judah turned to Barry Gold, "What are we going to do? This isn't right. Those sinful women are despoiling our brothers."

"I must speak to them. Help set them on the right course. Give me strength. I'm being tested while they're being tempted," Barry replied.

"How'll you reach them? Even if the police allowed you to pass, the heathens would never allow you to enter."

"I must find a way," Barry replied, looking down at the layout of the development below him. There were the two trailers lined up about five yards from the perimeter fence with the law enforcement no man's land strip beyond. There was the open area on the other side of the trailers that had served as the soccer field. It was closed by the two half-circles of outlandish vehicles and patrolled by men and dogs.

Barry raised his eyes skyward, looking for inspiration. Approach by land was impossible.

He glanced around the inside of the ark's gondola. His eyes fell on an iconic picture of a dove descending from the clouds with an olive branch. "There is a way, a way to reach them," he announced. "We must return to base."

"We are abandoning them then?" Judah was confused.

"No. Patience. Good things come to he who waits. Presently, they are safe enough," Barry counseled. "For now I need to make a few acquisitions, rope and dark raiment. We will return in the night."

Like angels in the night, he thought to himself. He went forward to the pilot's station to direct him to head for home. Plus he had a few questions. He wasn't sure of the Ark's lift capacity. A few alterations might be needed before they returned.

As the ark departed in the slow, pompously sedate manner peculiar to blimps, the game on the ground was over. The players were too tired and hot to continue. It ended in a three-to-three tie with Lindsey sneaking the last goal by Manny.

"Well done," William complimented her, as they headed to one of the swamp buggies to grab a cold beer from the cooler.

"Thanks. This was a good idea," she returned the compliment. "Look at them," she said as she pointed toward the refugees.

The three were all sitting in the shade leaned up against one of the oversized swamp buggy tires. The girls brought them cold cervezas, the Hatueys that they'd never been able to taste back home in Cuba. There was loud friendly banter in Spanish accompanied by exaggerated demonstrative gesticulations as the participants replayed the game to one another. It was the first time the three men had looked truly relaxed. Almost normal.

"Really good idea, huh?" William fished for a little more praise.

"Yes," she replied, "I already said it was, but since you want more, how about this."

She turned toward him. Threw her arms around him and gave him a big movie style kiss.

Normally William was reserved and might have even blushed at this public display of affection. But her body still heated and damp from recent exertion felt too good against him. Her scent, a mixture of perfume and perspiration, was intoxicating. Even the holy men and their women whooping and pointing at him didn't bother him. In the spirit of the moment, he arched her backward nearly sweeping her off her feet and kissed back.

The whoops, whistles and gestures increased as the Miccosukees in the compound joined in.

When they broke their clinch, they were both breathless. And smiling. Lindsey knew someone in the surrounding crowd would have caught the moment on film and she would pay for it somewhere down the line in the tabloids. But right now she didn't care.

"Maybe I can get you a part in my next movie," Lindsey teased. "But you're going to need some more practice to do the love scenes."

"I don't know about the movie part. But I wouldn't mind continuing the practice. Perhaps we can go somewhere more private, like your place, and work on it."

"An excellent idea," she replied.

They headed for the gate.

"There's enough help here that they won't miss us for a few more hours," William rationalized.

As they worked their way back up the slope, William got a taste of what it was like to be a celebrity. Some people blocked their way in order to get their picture. Others thrust pens and paper at both Lindsey and William in attempts to get their autographs. Lindsey, the seasoned pro, graciously deflected those who she could, acquiescing with a smile or quick signature for the rest.

She could feel the tension rising in William in the hand she was holding. And she could have sworn she heard him growl at some of the people obstructing their route.

"Just smile and wave off the autograph seekers," she whispered. "We'll be through them soon enough."

Although he immediately mastered the dismissive wave, his smile looked much more like an aching grimace. It took almost half an hour to work their way through the fans. When they finally cleared the last of them, William was sweating bullets.

"Not big on crowds, " she observed.

"Not hardly," was the pained reply.

"Well we're home now," she said, pulling him through the hedge. "I'll make it worth your while."

To their surprise, Hamilton Patrick and the television reporter, Liz, were waiting on Lindsey's patio.

"Guess you weren't expecting to see us," Ham remarked.

"Well it's not exactly a surprise to see you here," Lindsey Lee replied," but with company, yes, it's a surprise. Especially a pretty young reporter."

Hamilton reddened slightly at her allusion to his intrusions onto her patio but explained, "We heard the yelling and cheering for the soccer match and came over to watch. Then you two started to make out for the crowd. So we decided to watch you come up and wait for you."

William winced at the mention of the big kiss.

"He's learning about the price of fame," Lindsey remarked to the couple. William was the only member of the group that hadn't been a media celebrity of at least some stature. Even Liz had had a fan club when she was the "hot" weather girl.

"Like the spotlight, chief?" Ham asked.

"You can have it," he replied.

"You two an item?" the young reporter inquired.

"I'll make you a deal. You leave us alone and give us our privacy, and I won't mention you and the Big Hoopster to any of my reporter contacts," Lindsey bargained. A few minutes before when she'd stepped through her hedge, she'd seen the two of them in an embrace that, in an understatement, would be described at least as friendly.

"Fair enough, " Liz replied.

"Since I can't use you as a story, what say I make you two dinner instead?" Lindsey offered.

"Deal. Though you can give me your story, too. Tell me what went on inside the compound this afternoon. The swamp buggies and the soccer games. What's going on?" Liz negotiated.

"Fair enough. No harm in that. We might even be able to give you insight in to ulterior motives for tribal support," Lindsey replied.

"What about us?" William whispered in her ear, not particularly happy about the interruption in their plans.

"I haven't forgotten. It'll just have to wait a little longer," she whispered back.

"Ham, you wanna talk about celebrity, let me tell you about some of your newest fans. Real wannabes," William said out loud to the ball player, to tweak Lindsey a little for putting him off.

"Tell me," his curiosity was piqued.

"It's a lot more than just buying a jersey with your number on it," William continued.

"Wait 'til I'm out of earshot," Lindsey commanded. William laughed out loud at her choice of words.

"What? Why?" Liz asked.

 **Chapter XVIII**

After getting Liz's word that the evening's meal and discussions would be off the record, Lindsey started dinner. At Lindsey's direction, Liz assembled a large salad of mixed greens, chopped pecans, crumbled bleu cheese and dried cranberries dressed with a raspberry vinaigrette. William diced ripe, plum tomatoes and sliced chicken breasts while Lindsey minced garlic and chopped fresh basil. These would be sautéed together in olive oil to be served over linguine. The big man was relegated to grating a chunk of Parmesan to be used as topping. Lindsey's main worry was that there would be enough to serve the two hungry men.

While the four of them shared their meal along with a couple of bottles of California zinfandel, several intertwined scenarios were developing as the sun began to set.

When the soccer game had finished, many of the different groups of demonstrators had stayed at their vantage points halfway up the side of the trash mesa. It afforded them a good view of the refugees, rappers and the Miccosukees at their leisure.

But as night started to fall and the garbage plateau began to cast its shadow on the reservation compound, most of the groups started back down the slope to assume their original positions while observing the off-limits area.

If the sentinels inside the compound had been more vigilant, perhaps they would have noticed a few of the groups making significant positional shifts and called them into question. But the truth was that they weren't professionals and the sun and heat, not to mention the beer consumption, had dulled their powers of observation.

So when a couple of the anti-refugee bunches moved to the far ends of the demonstration areas, no one inside the compound took any special notice. By the same token, when the anti-Castro forces, the old guys in camo-fatigues, took up a position directly outside the fence from the habitation trailer no suspicions were raised. However, this move was questionable because this position afforded them no view into the compound or of their three Cuban brothers.

Up northwest of the world's most expensive rubbish mound, southwest of the city of Miami, the Ark was approaching its docking site at the Tamiami Airport. Tamiami was a small private airport, lightly trafficked and now being slowly surrounded by suburban sprawl.

Unlike other aircraft, a blimp doesn't actually land. It only comes close enough to the ground so that lines hanging from its frame can be grabbed and secured to mountings strong enough to keep the giant motorized balloon from floating away.

As the tethers were secured to the docking mast, Barry Gold jumped down out of the gondola. "Pull her into the hangar," he directed his ground crew. He figured that his airship was at least as fickle and difficult to handle as any seagoing vessel, so it was proper to give it a female gender.

Barry liked the small private airport for several reasons. The rent for docking and hangar space was relatively reasonable, certainly much cheaper than Miami or Ft. Lauderdale International, or the local commercial airports. And the tenants were friendly but not nosy. Mostly they minded their own business.

If they didn't, he would divert their attention by trying to save their souls. For some reason this drove most of them away. For those few who stayed around, undeterred by the salvation track and asking too many questions, he had the hangar. He'd just have the blimp towed inside and shut the doors. He'd had the windows covered with a one-way reflective treatment that allowed the hangar occupants to see out but didn't let the curious see in.

With his recent problems, this precaution had taken on the aura of remarkable foresight. His freedom of speech and freedom of religion rights had kept him out of jail for his involvement in the refugees' escape from the detention at Krome. But he'd had to pay a fine for violating restricted federal airspace.

Now he was sure that he was being watched. And in fact he was right; the FBI was keeping tabs on his whereabouts and activities. So he waited until the Ark was inside and the doors closed before he gave the crew directions for the modifications he wanted made.

As they started to work removing everything from the gondola that wasn't necessary to keep the dirigible airworthy, Barry stepped through a side door and got into his car.

The vehicle was a '67 Caddy top-down convertible painted pearlescent ivory, with "Semites for the Son" in gold on both sides, the hood and the trunk. The "I" in Semites was dotted with a gold crown and the "t" was enlarged and made to look like a cross on Calvary Hill. The only way for the FBI tail to lose the car was to fall asleep at the wheel.

After half a mile the shadow knew where Barry was headed. Back to his church.

The woman radioed it in to headquarters and asked, "Should I maintain surveillance?"

"No. Come on in. He's most likely done for the night. Besides, there's not much he can do down at the reservation now anyway."

"Okay," she replied. She didn't necessarily agree. When he'd driven past her pulling out of the airport, his face had looked like that of a man on a mission.

But then again these religious fanatics were always on a mission. Still her intuition was that he was up to something. But headquarters had a point. What could he really do in that fenced and armed compound?

Blissfully unaware of the surveillance and whistling, "Onward Christian soldiers," Barry pulled into his reserved parking spot. He hopped out of the car, over the side, not bothering to open the door, and strode into the church. He went into the trunk in his room where he stored winter clothes that he used on ski trips to Colorado. After that he made a quick visit to the choir practice room to pick up a couple more items. In all, his stop at the church lasted less than ten minutes.

If the FBI agent had kept up her watch, she'd have seen Barry throw a nylon duffle bag into the back seat of the Cadillac and then hop over the door into the driver's seat. As he pulled out he was now whistling, "Climb Every Mountain."

His course at first would have appeared to take him back to the airport. But he drove south, past the entrance, then turned west on a perimeter road that led to a warehouse district. One more stop.

He pulled up in front of a building with a jagged line depicting a mountain painted on its side. On top of the peak was a stick figure with its arms raised in exultation. Barry yanked open the heavy steel door at the left base of the mountain and stepped inside.

"Evening, Mr. Gold," greeted the man from behind the counter. "Need a partner? It's kind of slow so I could work with you."

"Thanks Phil. Not tonight. I'm not here for a workout. Just need some supplies," Barry replied to the owner of the indoor rock-climbing center.

He helped Barry pull together what he needed. Looking at the pile on the counter, Phil asked, "You planning a climbing trip to Colorado? This looks like it's going to be a big outing."

"Colorado? No. Never gone there for climbing. Just for winter sports. Big outing? Yeah, with any luck," was the cryptic answer.

Phil was puzzled. He knew Mr. Gold well enough to know that he answered to a higher authority, and it wasn't an expedition leader on the summit.

"You need any help?" Phil ventured. A big outing to real mountains might be an interesting adventure.

"Have you been saved?" was the reply.

Thinking back to when he'd been climbing in a narrow canyon in Arizona and trapped by a flash flood he answered, "Yes."

Thank God those park rangers had come along and pulled his ass out he thought.

"Really?" Barry strung the question out while staring into Phil's eyes.

"Yeah. Really," Phil stared back. He'd had a few other close outdoor calls that he'd had help getting out of, if Mr. Gold needed a record of his bona fides.

Barry relaxed his probing gaze. The man certainly seemed sincere. Had the attitude of a true believer. But it was probably more prudent not to bring someone new on board just as the plan was near fruition.

"Thanks for the offer brother. Maybe next time. I have all the help I need for this one."

"Whatever," was Phil's casual reply. No loss. If nothing else he'd made a big equipment sale.

Later, when he found out what Barry's outing entailed, Phil was delighted to not have been included.

His new purchases stowed in the backseat next to the duffle, Barry headed back to the airport.

When he arrived he pulled the Caddy inside the hangar. The Ark had been stripped just as he had directed. He took his bag and climbing gear out of the car into the gondola compartment and started his preparations. He explained his plan to Judah and the pilot as he placed his rigging. He had them repeat the plan to him several times until he was sure they absolutely understood what was to be done. They would only have one chance at this.

His preparations complete, his plan inculcated into his assistants, Barry was ready. He ordered the hangar lights turned out and then had the hangar doors opened. The Ark was towed out into the darkness. Its tethers were released. The divine mission was underway.

*   *   *

The atmosphere in the trailer was the most relaxed it had been since the beginning of the sanctuary ordeal. The three young men were feeling more comfortable about their situation. They had female companionship and futbol, excellent forms of tension release.

They could hold out a long time under these conditions.

Dinner was over and arrangements for the rest of the evening were being discussed. It was still fairly crowded inside the trailer, even missing the two couples at Lindsey's house. The consensus was that it would be a good time to allow the refugees a little breathing space, some time to themselves.

Reuben said, "Seedy, maybe you could give Rex and me a ride up to my house. Take one of your guys and get some more supplies."

"No problem. Manny and I'll take you. We'll take the young ladies, too. Those boys can go a night without 'em. And the girls'd like to get home. Freshen up some. Get a couple changes of rags."

Pablo looked disappointed, "No ladies tonight?"

"We'll be okay, man. It's been a pretty good day," Jesus told him.

"Yeah. We haven't had a chance to just be brothers for awhile now," Pedro added.

"I'm not complaining," Pablo replied.

"Settled then," Seedy responded.

The handmaidens each kissed their man good-bye and whispered they'd be back in the morning before they went out the door.

"Look guys," Reuben addressed the refugees, "You have any problem just give me a call. I'll leave you my cell phone. Here's my number on the speed dial."

Reuben showed them how to find and call the "home" listing on the menu.

"You need immediate help, just call out the door. My men'll come running," Rex offered. His reputation was now riding with these guys and he didn't want to miss a chance to help and to enhance it.

"Same for my posse," Seedy added.

As they left the trailer both Seedy and Rex stopped to talk to their men to give orders and update them on the situation.

"Which car?" Reuben asked.

"My Hummer, closest to the gate," Manny replied.

The seven people piled into the truck and Manny started the big engine. As they drove toward the gate, one of the Miccosukees with a pit mix dog opened it and then quickly shut it after they passed.

Manny drove west on the access road 'til he reached the entrance to Mont Basura Harbor. He turned left and began the climb up the side of the trash heap to drop off Reuben and Rex. If he'd bothered to glance in his rear view mirror, he'd have seen three solid black Chevy Suburbans, all their windows tinted black, heading east on the road he'd just turned off of.

The Miccosukee at the gate noticed the three trucks pull up and disgorge their occupants. The drivers then turned around and parked facing west. The guys that got out were dressed in camouflage fatigues, similar to the old anti-Castro guys set up outside the fence near the trailer. But this bunch looked at least a generation younger and more physically fit. When they took up a position just behind the old guys, he didn't think much more about it, figuring the two groups were together.

If he'd had any reference to go by, he might have figured something wasn't right. After all it was his job to watch the road and note anything suspicious. But he wasn't a pro, just a hunter dragged out of the swamp to help the tribe put on a show of force.

If he'd been there the last two nights, he'd have known that most of the protesters went home to the comfort of their air-conditioned beds after night fell. Only a few hard cores stayed. But it was his first night and crowd behavior wasn't his specialty. As far as he knew, the fact that several of the groups got reinforced was normal.

At the same time, the number of police officers patrolling the perimeter was decreased. How or who ordered the reduction would later become the subject of an investigation. But at the ten o'clock shift change the police presence was reduced by half.

On top of the development, Reuben had called Lindsey to fill her in on the plan to let the refugees have some time to themselves. She'd passed the information along to Hamilton and William. The couples had split up shortly afterward.

William was looking forward to the start of his long delayed practice session with Lindsey Lee. Ham, being a pragmatic young man, and realizing he now had no chance with the starlet, talked Liz into coming back to his place. Perhaps he could still practice his off-court scoring moves. Liz figured spending time with a rich young athlete with enough social conscience to sacrifice half an ear wouldn't be the worst way to spend her evening.

Agent Busch received a phone call from his buddy the SWAT commander, "We're on."

"How's it look? What're our chances?"

"From what my sources on the ground tell me, very good. Your people are in place. Have been for more than an hour. Conditions are actually better than anticipated."

"How? Give me the details," was Busch's eager reply.

"The targets appear to be alone."

"How'd you pull that off?"

"Not our doing. Appears to be just really good luck," the commander responded.

"I'll be damned. I hope that's a good omen."

"Me, too."

"When do we go?"

"After 11:30."

Busch knew why, "when the evening news is over and the satellite trucks are gone."

"Right. Not the kind of thing the public needs to know. The fewer witnesses the better."

"Let me know when things get started."

"Right."

They clicked off the cell phones simultaneously.

The agents and infiltrators within the protest groups bided their time. The experienced pros rested, some napping, using the slope of the rubbish mount as a bed. The first-timers and amateurs fidgeted, sweating in the heat, talking too fast, their pulses racing. The leaders warned them to stop checking their watches every few minutes.

Bucking a ten-knot wind, the prevailing southeasterly that occurred this time of year, the lightened Ark plodded quietly along. The message boards weren't lighted; they'd been removed. The airship beat a slow, steady, determined course back toward Mont Basura.

 **Chapter XIX**

By 11:15 all the news trucks were lowering their satellite antennas, having finished their live feeds from outside the compound. Liz had come down from Ham's house and covered the latest in the story along with the other reporters. They were all similar in content, showing the reporter standing live outside the compound gate, then cutting to footage of the soccer game shot earlier along with the reactions of the groups arrayed on the Mont Basura hillside. Then it was back to the live reporter for a brief closing comment. Neither Liz nor her fellow members of the fourth estate understood the logic of reporting live from a place where essentially nothing newsworthy was happening just so that the home studio could show tape of something that had occurred there hours before. But it seemed to be standard ops for the industry and it was a paycheck.

When her bit was done, Liz wrapped up with the crew, wished them a good night and headed back to Ham. He'd walked her down to do her shot and waited quietly in the shadows until she finished.

"You want to stay the night?" he asked hopefully.

"Well, my remote truck's leaving without me. So you'll either have to give me a ride up to the city or put me up for the night. It's late and the round trip would be a long drive. It's up to you," she replied coyly.

"If you'd like to go home, driving you would be no problem," he responded and he meant it. He'd been raised in a part of the country where manners and morals still had value. In the upper west, out on the farm, chivalry was alive and well and he would do whatever the young lady wanted.

"But I'd be glad if you stayed," he meant that, too. He really liked her company.

She smiled. "Let's go back to your place. I don't have to work 'til tomorrow evening. So you can drive me back in the morning."

She really liked the big guy. He'd been a perfect gentleman all evening. He was a pleasant change of pace from the hip urban testosterone pumps that hit on her so frequently.

As they walked up the incline, Liz noted, "Seems to be more people here tonight."

"Couldn't go by me," Hamilton replied.

"Well you haven't spent the last couple of nights outside the compound here waiting for something to happen. You were inside last night."

"Don't I know," His hand was halfway up to his head, but he resisted the impulse to feel for the missing ear. Even though he knew the top half was gone, he had the constant urge to touch to verify it. But he had to keep trying not to because he didn't want it to become a nervous habit.

"Sorry. That wasn't very considerate," she apologized.

"Don't worry about it. Besides, Seedy says it'll make me famous, give me some opportunities outside of basketball."

"You want to be famous, in the spotlight? Off the record," she added. "Just between us?"

"Not really. I like pro ball. The money's great. You get to meet interesting people. I just wanna play as long as I can and as well as I can. Take the money and buy myself a ranch back in Montana and keep my place here by the water. Pretty simple."

"Yeah. Simple. You don't have any cause you'd really like to promote?" she pressed.

"I'm not that political. Like with the guys here, or the injured birds up top, I help. I feel like it's the right thing to do. But I don't have my own specific agenda."

"You wouldn't like to..." Liz was interrupted as they were passing through the group of protesters wearing fatigues. Several of the younger men came up to talk to the basketball player and shake his hand. A few got an autograph. None of the older guys even gave him a look.

"Fame, huh?" she commented as they left the group. Generations shift, she thought to herself. The old exiles still had their hearts in Cuba, the young born here, already becoming Americanized.

"Yeah. I could live without any of that. I don't mind it. But I don't need it. Some people do."

"Like Reuben," she answered.

"He thrives on it. But at least he tries to do good with it," Ham replied.

"Most of the time anyway," she rejoined.

The young men in camouflage followed the couple's progress up the side of the hill, watching until they disappeared over the top.

One of them called the SWAT commander. "The last of the media has cleared the area," he reported.

"Wait twenty minutes. Then commence," came the command.

Soon, via cell phone, the message was passed to the appropriate people in the different groups about when to start.

The Ark had almost reached the reservation.

The three young refugees, after a hard day of interviews, soccer and entertaining their lady friends, were sound asleep in their beds.

Just before midnight, as planned, things began to heat up. It was a volatile situation and easy to stir up.

At the south end of the reservation perimeter, the America for Americans cadre began to taunt the refugee group next to them, a group of Central American immigrants there to show solidarity with the Cubans.

"We're the homeboys. Get out of our home."

"Get back on your boats and go back."

Even resurrecting the old "Don't tread on me."

It wasn't anything the immigrants hadn't heard or seen before. Though, when they'd seen it on placards before, most of the time not all the words were spelled correctly. So they did what they always did, ignored the fools.

Next came the epithets and expletives. Harshly hurled invectives in both English and Spanish. At least there was some effort to communicate with the Hispanic newcomers by attempting to learn some of their native expressions. Still even these efforts to bridge the cultural gap were also ignored.

An escalation of instigative effort was required to start producing results.

Many of the hermanos in solidarity had brought the flags of their home countries with them to wave in support of the Cubans. Proof that many countries disapproved of the conditions Castro had forced on his people. The worse the harassment became from the U.S. isolationists, the more vigorously the flags were waved.

The homeboys took the provocations to the next level by spitting on the Caribbean basin flags and in some cases ripping the flags out of the owners' hands and trampling on them.

Enough was enough.

The Central Americans, some of them new U.S. citizens, some studying for citizenship, knew more than most how precious was the value of free speech. Several among them had been imprisoned practicing this first amendment right in their homelands under oppressive regimes. This American right to protest was the reason they'd put up with the bullshit from the bunch next to them. It included the right to be complete assholes.

However, it did not include the right for the one group to stop or desecrate the other's demonstration. That crossed the line. And it called for self-defense.

The new Americans fought back against the old, at first just spitting, cursing and shredding their misspelled signs. Soon though fists were being thrown and a full-fledged brawl had broken out.

It was more than loud enough to attract the attention of those in charge of security. The first police officers arrived in less than a minute. Seeing twenty-five to thirty people actively engaged in the fighting, they quickly called for back up. At least half of the officers at the reservation site were soon involved.

The battling was intense, punching, kicking, gouging and biting. Broken noses and limbs and a multitude of lacerations would have to be repaired later.

The officers took their time subduing the participants. They picked them off one at a time from the periphery of brawl, cuffing them face down on he ground with the heavy plastic snap ties. Care was taken to divide their combatants into their two original groups to keep the problem from flaring again.

The police weren't the only ones drawn to the melee. The rappers and Miccosukees patrolling inside the fence came running when they heard the yelling and screaming. Now they watched like an audience at a pro wrestling match. They clapped and whistled for a good police takedown or shot with a nightstick. But also cheered for a last second escape before the cops could get the plastic cuffs on. It was great live entertainment and beat the heck out of shooting the bull while patrolling in the dark, a wonderful distraction from the boredom of sentry duty.

Meanwhile, past the entrance gate, on the northern edge of the perimeter, a different confrontation was starting.

Barry had requested that members of Semites for the Son create some type of distraction for him starting around midnight. They were somewhat at a loss for what to do. Being morally upright they couldn't start a violent confrontation for they really had no desire to hurt anyone. They'd considered rushing the fence, trying to break into the compound. But, on the one hand, it was against the law, and most of them had no desire to be arrested. And on the other there were big, possibly vicious, dogs and strange, armed, men on the other side that they really had no desire to confront.

They fell back on their rather weak alternative; they started singing hymns at the top of their lungs. "Jesus is Just All Right with Me," "Go Tell it on the Mountain," "Love, Peace, and Happiness," "He's Got the Whole World in His Hands, and "People Get Ready," a mix of popular and classic standards. To further attract attention, a couple of the bolder members set off some fireworks- firecrackers, M-80s, and smoke bombs.

The music didn't do much, but the pyrotechnics were enough to attract law enforcement. At least five officers showed up to evaluate the situation. The sergeant in command picked out a couple of likely leaders, dressed in robes, from the group and motioned for them to come parlay with him.

Three men came forward. As the slightly noxious, sulphurous haze from the smoke bombs wafted over them, the police informed the trio that they had to cease and desist. They were violating noise ordinances, keeping the people up on Mont Basura awake, and that anyone caught setting off illegal fireworks would be arrested. While this was going on the choir managed to crank up another few decibels.

The three spokesmen promised to discuss it with the group and try to reach a peaceable compromise. They turned to walk back to their people.

The sergeant took a quick step to follow. He wanted to impress on them that there was no real compromise. They had to pipe down or be arrested. His eyes were watering from the smoke, his vision a little blurred. As he reached out to tap the center protester on the shoulder he didn't watch his feet and stepped on the man's trailing robe.

Unfortunately, the man started to fall and as he reached out to steady himself, took down one of his companions with him. The last man standing whipped around and seeing his fallen brethren shouted out that religious standard, "What the fuck?"

To members of the other religious groups there to support the holy men, now watching the confrontation, it looked like the police had, in a sneak attack, used excessive force to subdue their religious cohorts.

It didn't help that when the sergeant reached out to help them up both men cowered with their hands clasped in prayer, unsure of what had happened and what would happen.

The five officers were quickly surrounded by the religious protesters yelling in their faces, telling them to repent their evil ways. These were supposedly holy people, but sometimes even the pious get out of hand. The officers felt threatened and radioed for back up.

Help again came quickly. And like the southern melee, the northern one pulled in spectators from the security force inside the compound. However the entertainment value wasn't nearly as good. There were no great takedowns or blows with nightsticks and none of the protesters attempted to escape.

In this situation the arriving reinforcement moved with judicious restraint. They again worked from the perimeter, separating the protesters in groups of two and three, moving them away from the clot of humanity surrounding their fellow officers. Three or four policemen would separate off a lesser number of protesters and gently herd them a safe distance away. No guns were drawn and there was no use of batons. These particular protests didn't warrant a heavy show of force. The police department didn't need the bad press for violating the first amendment rights of religion and free speech of a bunch of true believers. Besides these types of protesters made excellent credible witnesses in lawsuits charging excessive force. The officers handled the situation smartly and patiently, gradually working their way toward their stranded brothers.

The only disconcerting element was that whoever had the firecrackers and smoke bombs would still periodically set off a new bunch. The rapid-fire reports made everyone jumpy and the colored fumes irritated everyone's eyes. But they only added a minor distraction. And nobody overreacted.

Still the net effect is exactly what was hoped for by several interested parties. The security forces inside and outside the fence were more or less evenly divided at the far ends of the compound. No one was guarding the center. And the refugees, blissfully sleeping in their trailer were unaware that they were unprotected.

The Ark, flying at low altitude, had to angle up to pass over Mont Basura. The pilot climbed to an altitude of 250 feet, enough to easily clear the tallest houses atop the rubbish mesa. He was flying the airship completely blacked out. Violating FAA regulations, even the nighttime running lights were extinguished. Once he was east of the development he angled back down, toward the target Barry Gold was directing him to.

Unlighted, they knew they would be harder to see. However, there was no way to mask the sounds of the blimp's motors. What they were counting on was the fact that the Ark had become a fairly regular presence over the reservation. The people on the ground would relegate the engine's drone to just a background white noise. Their calculations were correct. No one even looked up as they descended toward the compound.

Barry was thrilled as he viewed the scene from the Ark's vantage point. The situation was even better than he had hoped for. There was no law enforcement or site security anywhere near his target. The only anomaly on scene was a group of exiles congregated near the fence outside the holy men's trailer. As long as they stayed in their place they wouldn't be a problem.

And heaven must have been watching out for him. There was an access hatch on the roof of the trailer. Probably to make it easier to reach the cargo racks on the front half of the mobile construction office. Whatever the earthly explanation, the Lord had provided.

Barry donned his black robe and ski mask. Somehow he managed to put on his safety harness, pulling the billows of his robe through the leg holes. He put the spare harness over his shoulders. Then he put on his black climbing gloves. Finally, he checked to see that his lines were properly secured inside the blimp's gondola.

He directed the pilot toward the operational objective. Frankly, the pilot thought Barry was nuts. He looked like some little kid playing at superhero who didn't have enough money to buy the costume. But it was the tropics and in the tropics nuts and fruits, in this case more like a nutty fruit bat, grew well here. Besides, Barry paid him very well. Who's to say whether his plan would work? Right now things seemed to be going his way.

They reached the hover point. Barry dropped his black ropes out the doorless hatch into the darkness of the night. The tips of the lines hit the trailer's roof. Barry attached his carabiner to the rope, gave the pilot an OK sign and disappeared out the door.

*   *   *

 **Chapter XX**

The old men in camos had been training for a long time, some as much as forty years. Starting not long after Castro came to power. Initially they had received clandestine instruction in the Everglades from the CIA and Army Rangers. They were to be secretly reinserted into Cuba to start a counterrevolution. It never happened.

A select few had continued doing extra training with unnamed intelligence groups. Their assignment was as an assassination team to be introduced into Havana to take out the bearded one. Officially that never happened either. Though some members of the special group seemed to have disappeared.

Finally the government support and training had stopped. They were on their own. They kept training.

Their youth gradually slipped away. They kept training.

They were ridiculed by their progeny; the American born generation called them swamp locos. They kept training.

They still had maneuvers in the Glades and in a secret warehouse. Now it was probably more for the camaraderie and pork barbeques after their exercises. Still, they kept training.

And finally their training was paying off. They wouldn't be going back to their homeland to free their people. But at least they could free their brothers here.

After quickly scanning to see that the approach was clear, the first unit moved up to the fence. Out came two sets of bolt cutters. A four-foot wide section of the chain link was cut and removed in less than a minute. Not bad for old guys with arthritic hands. They motioned for the second unit, the specialists, to come through.

Now came the tricky part. The second group actually had very little practice performing their assignment. But they moved in and placed what they considered to be the proper charges in what they guessed were the proper locations.

In reality they couldn't have told the difference between Semtex and C-4 or which of the two was more powerful. They didn't know how old the plastic explosive was that was given to them or how much of its potency it retained. Not wanting to fail at their mission, they erred on the side of placing a little excess.

The younger men in camouflage dress initially kept lookout and softly called out words of encouragement to the sappers. After watching the explosive placement they still kept watch, but judiciously moved their vantage point about twenty yards up the side of the dump hill.

The detonating caps were placed and everyone cleared the area, back to the other side of the fence. The plan was to open the hole in the side of the trailer and get the refugees out before the security forces could react. Once away from the reservation they would be hidden in a series of safehouses, with their own people, until their situation could be resolved satisfactorily.

The old commandant of the brigade gave the go signal. The demolition specialist pushed the button on the radio detonator. The blast was spectacular.

The concussion knocked every one of the old men flat to the ground. It sent tremors greater than four on the Richter scale pulsing through the garbage mountain. Everyone and everything was momentarily stunned. There was complete silence for at least fifteen seconds following the explosion.

The old guerillas were the first to recover. They still had a mission to accomplish. They got up and started through the gap in the fence toward their objective.

The blast had been wildly successful. Half the side of the trailer was blown away. The refugees' sleeping quarters were completely exposed.

The group of younger men moved back down the hillside, stopping outside the hole in the fence.

Lights were coming on all over in the houses atop Mont Basura. Earthquakes didn't occur in that part of Florida. Several irate homeowners staggered out in their pajamas heading for the eastern side of the plateau to look down and see what the hell was going on now. They correctly figured that the fiasco at the reservation below was the most likely the source of this new problem.

*   *   *

Barry Gold was certain Providence was on his side now. His feet had almost touched the roof of the trailer when the blast ripped through it. The shockwave lifted the blimp skyward carrying Barry back into the air. With cat-like reflexes he unclipped from his line and dropped back down to the trailer roof. He knew his pilot would regain control and come back for him, the blessing was that the blast had also blown the access hatch clean off.

Barry headed for the opening and dropped through, not bothering to use the ladder built into the wall below. He landed in the central hallway. The air was full of dislodged dust and pulverized insulation created by the explosion. The particulate fog made it difficult, especially with the ski mask on, to make out much inside the enclosed space. The problem was further exacerbated when, due to a short in the electrical system caused by the blast, the lights winked out. The only illumination now was from the doorway exit signs powered by backup batteries.

Still Barry's luck held. Out of the dark haze, a dazed figure staggered right into him. It was harder to say who was more surprised.

The stumbling man could barely hear anything for the ringing in his ears. He was shaking his head trying to clear the cobwebs, blinking his tearing eyes trying to find his way through the trailer's interior cloud. It didn't help his confusion to run into the apparition, what looked like a giant black bat, before him. He was wondering if he'd suffered some type of brain injury.

To Barry it was a miracle, a pre-ordained salvation. The figure tripped on his own shuffling feet and fell forward. Barry opened his arms, like a blackbird spreading its wings and caught the falling Jesus. Barry looked skyward, through the open hatch, and whispered a silent thanks.

When the plastique was detonated, the three refuges had been asleep in their room. Fortunately the bunks were not against the wall that was blown out. Still the inside of the room became instant chaos.

The three men had granted themselves the almost sinful luxury of turning the air conditioning to high. It was a pleasure not available to them in Cuba, where any electrical power at all was at best an only part time proposition. Consequently, due to the cool conditions they all slept in their purple coveralls. So, at least when their world exploded, they weren't naked.

Jesus, closest to the door and against the wall opposite the blast, fell to the floor then staggered into the hallway. Pablo and Pedro were in a bunk that was against the end of the trailer. The explosion ricocheted them both off the wall then onto the floor. As they rose to their feet they looked for the nearest exit. Both stumbled out the hole where the side of the trailer had been.

The old commandoes rushed back to help them. Two of the old timers in the camouflage took each man under the arm for support as they stepped out into the night.

Pablo and Pedro could see the men mouthing words at them but had no idea what they were saying. At least temporarily, the explosion had cost them their hearing.

If they could have heard, what they would have heard was, "Vamonos. ¿ Dondé esta Jesus?" We go. Where is Jesus?

Instead all they had to go on was what they could see. There were old men in military uniforms apparently yelling at them. They were being led toward the hole in the fence toward more men in uniforms. This did not give them succor. Quite the opposite, they were very scared.

The commandant stepped in front of Pedro, held up his chin and looked him directly in the face. He realized the young man was probably stunned from the blast. So very slowly he asked, "¿ Donde esta su hermano? ¿Donde esta Jesus?"

Pedro read his lips. He wasn't sure he should tell the man. But he didn't know what else to do. He waved vaguely over his shoulder, " Esta allí." He's there.

The commandant motioned for a couple of his men to go into the trailer and look for Jesus. He hoped the blast hadn't injured or killed him. It would be a terrible outcome for the mission.

The men returned quickly. It didn't take long to search something as small as a trailer for something as large as a human body. The report was, "No esta allí."

It was then that the group noticed the Ark. The ringing in their ears was beginning to subside and the sound of the blimp's motors became more pronounced as it hovered down toward the trailer's roof.

They watched in amazement as a dark clad figure attached itself and Jesus to ropes and began to hoist the two of them towards the gondola. As they neared the open hatch, the blimp began to lift away.

When Barry had broken Jesus's fall, he'd caught him so that they ended up staring each other in the face. Barry saw the blank look in Jesus's eyes. Rapture. No doubt.

In fact, Jesus seemed in such an otherworldly place that he hung limp in Barry's arms. Give me strength Barry thought. He picked up the young man over his shoulder and climbed the ladder to the roof opening. Once through, he set the passive figure down and put the safety harness on him. When the Ark arrived back on site he clipped them both to the ropes and started to haul Jesus and himself up.

Of course it wasn't exactly rapture. More like stunned incomprehension. Jesus wasn't sure what was happening. It had to be a horrible dream. He kept waiting, willing himself to wake up.

It was only after Barry had set him down on the gondola's floor and the sea breezes blowing through the doorway hit his face that he realized he might already be awake. His hearing was starting to come back and the sound of the blimp's engines was familiar though louder since they were closer. As he snapped back to reality, he figured out where he was. But still wasn't exactly sure how he got there.

Back on the ground, the commandant quickly realized that, for now, Jesus was beyond his reach. At least the young man was escaping.

"¡ Rapido, Vamos, Rapido!" He shouted to his men directing them back to the hole in the fence.

They had wasted several minutes searching the trailer and watching the aerial getaway. They didn't have much time left. The police and reservation security forces had to be wondering what happened and would be coming back to check.

As the old guerillas and their two refugees stepped through the chain link opening and off the reservation, the younger generation warriors stepped forward and blocked their path.

"Thanks old man. Immigration. We'll take them from here," said one of the men in the center of the group. "Back to Krome then back to Cuba for them."

The commandant and several of his comrades drew .45s out from under their camouflage jackets.

"¡ Gusanos, Hijos de Puta!" Literally worms, sons of a whore. "I don't think so," the old man replied.

"You don't want to do that," the wide-eyed young man warned.

"The hell I don't. Get out of our way," the commandant ordered.

"No," came the quavering reply. They had obviously underestimated the commitment of the old freedom fighters.

The old man didn't say any more. Just shot the impudent fool through the thigh. All those years of target practice paid off. It was through and through, a non-vital wound.

"What the...!" The young man was probably going into shock.

"What kind of idiots did you takes us for? Didn't you think we'd check you out? We have sources in this community you'll never know. D'ya think we'd believe you were helping us out of the goodness of your hearts? Didn't you figure we'd know you were using us?" The old man scoffed.

The young agent slumped to the ground. One of his men, while never taking his eyes off the commandant, knelt down and put a tourniquet around the leg.

This was more than Pedro and Pablo could comprehend. They weren't sure who was good and who wasn't. Their hearing was starting to improve and they'd picked up on the curse, Gusanos. It was the same term Castro used for those that fled his island prison. Were the men who'd helped them out of the trailer his agents? What about the younger ones threatening to return them to Cuba? The duo were so confused, who could they trust?

They didn't know and they didn't want to stick around to decide. They nodded to one another. The men supporting them had loosened their grips watching the interplay between the young and old leaders.

Simultaneously the two refugees snatched their arms free and took off running. Not back to the Miccosukee land. Obviously they weren't safe there.

Nope they scrambled up the slope towards Lindsey's house. If only briefly, it was the one place they'd felt safe without being overwhelmed. It was there they'd just been treated as people with no demands or expectations placed on them.

The young man on the ground stared down at his leg. As far as he could tell the bleeding had stopped. He was regaining his composure and wanted to take control of the situation. Leaning on one of his men, he pulled himself back to standing.

Defiantly staring the older man in the eye, he gave the order, "Go get them. What are you waiting for? Don't let them get away."

The old commandante just shook his head from side to side. Then he shot the agent through the other thigh. To emphasize the point his compatriots fired a volley into the ground at the feet of the other Feds. They froze in their tracks.

"Are you fucking crazy!?" The twice-wounded man cried in disbelief as his second tourniquet was applied.

"No, but what kind of morons is the government putting in charge these days? What'd you think, the first shot was just a mistake? If I have to shoot one more time, you'll never walk again," the commandante warned.

This time the wounded man stayed down. He believed the old guy. He and his men stayed huddled in a knot. Defeated for now.

The old warriors watched the pair of refugees fleeing up the hillside. The youngest of them was sixty-four. There was no chance any of them would be able to overtake their two youthful fellow exiles and explain that they were just trying to help.

"Vaya con dios," the commandante whispered as the young men disappeared in the darkness.

He wasn't far off the mark.

 **Chapter XXI**

The two disturbances at the ends of the compound came to an abrupt halt as soon as the plastique detonated. The noise and tremors stopped all participants in mid-motion.

At the north end the religious protesters separated and allowed the two groups of police officers to unite. They held a quick huddle about what their response should be.

At the south end there was also discussion about proper response. Not all the officers could go back to investigate. Some would have to stay to guard the arrestees and keep the combatants separated. The ranking officer in charge divided her command accordingly then turned back toward the site of the explosion.

The amateur security personnel inside the compound also turned to look back at the blast area. They quickly realized that they'd been diverted from their assignments. Probably deliberately decoyed.

"Oh man. We fucked up," was the succinct analysis by one of Seedy's posse.

"Or we were fucked on purpose," replied one of the swampers.

"Most likely," the rapper rejoined.

Although everyone was facing the source of the explosion, no one made any move toward it. Delay, hesitation, in South Florida these would be considered wise moves toward self-preservation in a situation like this. Radical protest groups in the area had a history of using bombs to carry their messages. And some times they used more than one. Trepidation in the face of the volatile unknown was an intelligent reaction.

Finally, after a couple minute's wait, and radio discussion between the north and south police groups, the officers from both ends started to converge on the scene. They were trailed at respectful, and cautious distances by the protest groups they'd been trying to control. They were also shadowed on the other side of the fence by the Miccosukees and the posse.

Some members of the Semites for the Son smiled when they saw the Ark swoop down and stop briefly over the center of the compound.

The two knots of people hadn't gone very far when they heard the first gunshot, the firing of the commandant's .45. There was a sudden collective halt of all involved in the pursuit. The police adjusted their body armor and unholstered their weapons. The musicians inside the compound also unholstered theirs. The Indians brought their rifles up and the distinctive sound of some of them racking rounds into firing chambers broke the quiet.

It also caused a good deal of consternation amongst the law enforcement personnel. They didn't relish the idea of possibly being caught in a crossfire between the reservation people and whoever was ahead in the dark.

The lieutenant in charge went to the fence and motioned for one of the Miccosukees to come over. She told him she knew she couldn't enforce the request, but asked that the reservation guards secure their arms. She radioed to have the message passed to the northern group.

The rap posse and the Indians reluctantly drew down. After all, they had promised to protect the young men. At the same time none of them had a bulletproof vest or, consequently, any great desire to be caught in a firefight. They dropped back a few yards when the police started to move again.

The pincering groups had just come into where they had the trailers in sight when they heard the second gunshot. This time they also saw the muzzle flash. Again they all halted.

This time the only ones who moved forward again were the police officers. Finally they arrived on the scene to find the two groups of fatigues and camouflage clad warriors. One man lay on the ground bleeding from both legs. Several men from each group were looking southward up the hill. To the east the gaping hole in the blasted trailer was still spitting out fine pieces of shredded paper and insulation.

Only in Miami, the lieutenant in charge thought to herself. She and her officers would be filling out reports for a freaking week.

"Put those weapons down," she ordered. "Then someone tell me what the hell just happened here."

"Not so fast," the commandant replied. He and his men still had their guns trained on the immigration agents.

"That wasn't a request. Damn it Miguel. Drop'em or I'll have my men shoot you. I'm in no mood for more bullshit." She'd recognized the commandant from his appearances on TV news over the years. Plus he had a local reputation as certain of his training sessions had resulted in brushes with law enforcement.

They dropped their weapons.

As soon as the guns were picked up by the police, the wounded INS man found his courage, "Arrest that motherfucker. He shot me. His men too. Arrest all those assholes."

"And who the heck are you?" she demanded.

"Immigration. Those men interfered with our apprehension of three men wanted for escape. We have federal fugitive warrants for their arrest."

"I'll bet you do," she replied sarcastically. "And I know you want to explain to me why you're dressed just like these bozos. I saw you arrive. I Know you've been here a couple of hours. So I'm sure you're just aching to explain to me how the fence got cut and who blew up the trailer. You all appear to have been witnesses to the whole thing."

She actually had a pretty good idea of what happened. The old guys were smiling when she came up on them. And cutting the chain link then setting off the blast was just the kind of thing they'd go for.

The federal agents were silent. She had a point. If they had watched a crime being committed and made no move to stop it they'd be considered complicit. Even more interesting was the matter of who'd delivered the C-4 (not Semtex) to the old freedom fighters. Two of the agents certainly did not want their hands swabbed for chemical residue at the present time.

"Resounding silence. I'm shocked," she rubbed it in.

"Ok then. How 'bout somebody tells me where the three holy men got to?" she continued.

Again no answer. But she noticed some members of the camouflage group looked up toward the sky while others looked up the hill.

By now the cautious stragglers, both the protesters and reservation security, had gathered around trying to find out what had happened.

*   *   *

Barry and Jesus had been doing their best to observe the events on the ground. Their view out the gondola doorway was unobstructed. But it was too dark to make out much detail below them. They thought they'd seen Pedro and Pablo being supported and escorted through the fence. Then they'd seen the two muzzle flashes as the government man was shot. They thought they'd seen the two shake loose from their captors and head up the trash pile slope.

But two dark-haired men in purple jumpsuits didn't show up well against the darkened hillside.

Barry had an idea. He'd stripped a lot of non-essentials out of the blimp. But he wasn't a complete fool. God helped those who could help themselves. He'd kept the emergency kit.

He reached inside and pulled out the flare gun. He aimed it up over the slope and fired. The glow from the thousand plus degree magnesium shell would certainly light the way for the two disciples. The flare arced upward illuminating the scene below.

*   *   *

The blast and following concussion wave woke Lindsey and William who'd just nodded off in her bed. They both realized immediately where the disturbance had to be coming from. Lindsey grabbed her cell phone and dialed the trailer.

"No answer," she told William, her voice worried.

"We'd better check things out," he answered.

As they threw on their clothes, William thought he heard a gunshot.

"Let's get down there," he urged.

When they went out the patio door onto the pool area, they distinctly heard the second shot. They raced to the edge of the plateau. There they were joined by Liz and Hamilton who'd come to the same conclusion regarding the explosion.

Looking down, the foursome could make out the large crowd of people just outside the compound.

"Some one's blown a hole in the guys' trailer," Hamilton observed, seeing the dust cloud still pouring out its side.

"Who? Why?" Liz queried using part of the journalist mantra. The what, when and where were fairly obvious. Though exactly how was still up in the air.

"There are two men coming our way," William told them, his night vision and his hunter's instincts helping pick up the two figures in the darkness.

They all noted the Ark moving toward Mont Basura. Suddenly a bright white flash lit the whole scene.

"It's Pedro and Pablo," Lindsey informed the group.

"I wonder where Jesus is," said Hamilton.

The two couples met the refugees as they came through the decorative hedge.

"Where's your brother?" William asked urgently. This was the first time he hadn't seen them together.

Panting and winded from their escape run, both of them pointed in a general direction into the air over their shoulders.

"Calm down. Catch your breath. Take your time. Tell us what happened," Lindsey encouraged.

"They...they...they blew up our trailer," Pedro forced out.

"Miss Lindsey, William. Please help us," Pablo added.

"Who did it? Your brother?" Liz and Hamilton asked at the same time.

"Don't know," Pedro answered.

"Jesus is..." Pablo didn't get to finish.

 **Chapter XXII**

The flare had not burned out as it drifted down toward the top of the development. Reaching the end of its arc, the flare almost landed about ten feet down the side of the slope, east of Reuben's backyard. Almost, because it never actually hit the ground at all. Thanks to the methane.

Methane, chemically CH4, an odorous clear by-product of the decomposition of organic matter, a true natural gas. Mont Basura was at least one hundred and fifty feet deep, with all the different garbage by-products of urban civilization. A lot of it organic. Mont Basura produced a lot of methane, and methane is highly flammable.

How all the methane got to the places it did would probably never be known. There was more than one explanation. And a combination of reasons was most likely to blame. There was the fact that the bodies of the dead rodents and the ferrets that had chased them blocked some of the methane collectors. The fact that some of the bullets fired as cover by the escaping SWAT men, the night Hamilton's ear got clipped, penetrated the refuse pyramid and maybe ruptured some of the collectors. The fact that the collection system was new technology and possibly inadequate for the task. After all, due to excess expense it was rare to see systems overbuilt to put in added protection, especially when it came to South Florida's developers. Finally, of course, there was the explosion. The shock wave had blasted out from the side of the trailer directly into the side of Mont Basura. No telling what it had done to the underground piping and plumbing of the gas scavenging system. Whatever the reasons, the gas was now free, in varying size pockets, underneath the top of the garbage pile.

As the flowing hot magnesium settled toward the ground it passed through a vent that had opened in the side of the trash mound. Spewing out methane.

Kaboom!

Then a series. Boom, boom, boom…

Adjoining connected pockets started to ignite.

It was more than Pablo and Pedro could take. Literally blown out of their beds, crazy guerillas abducting them then shooting other guerillas, and now the ground exploding under their feet. Their world had gone mad. They were teetering on the edge of sanity. They took off running for the house.

William knew right away what it was. He remembered traversing the slope and seeing the ground bubble in front of him. And the tell tale odor.

"The methane is blowing," he yelled over the din.

The four people at the edge of the mesa were having trouble maintaining their footing. Periodic explosions kept rocking the ground under them. Multiple shafts of the flame were shooting out the east side of the Mont. Explosions could be heard erupting from the southern edge.

"The birds," Lindsey gasped.

Hamilton and William had the same thought.

"I'll get 'em," Ham yelled.

"Release them all," William directed.

Hamilton took off running for the rehab center.

Liz was torn between her professional responsibility and her heart. She felt she was smack dab in the middle of the biggest story of her career. Crazy exclusive development going up in flames, second-coming refugees as fugitives, all tied to the movie starlet and handsome Indian next to her. If she left she might be doing fluff pieces, puppy and kitten stories, the rest of her career.

It was no contest. The birds were live creatures with no one else to help them. This might end up the first of many animal reports. Besides, she was already developing a thing for the big guy.

"I'm going to help," she told the other two as she sprinted off after Ham.

Shafts of flame were beginning to shoot through the surface of Mont Basura as well as along the edges. Tearing holes in yards and streets and setting some houses afire.

The view for the protesters and law enforcement at the base of the pyramid was awesome. It was like a twisted Fourth of July celebration, random eruptions occurring almost over their heads. And like with real fireworks there was more than one color, more than just the yellow-orange of methane explosions. It had been a still night and the perfume fogging truck had made its rounds. The combination floral pine scent being misted about contained enough alcohol to ignite when hit by a jet of flaming methane. So there were occasional spumes of pink and red as pockets of perfume were touched off.

At first the group just stood stunned by the spectacle. Some oohed and aahed at the changing light show, especially as the red spectral plumes of Mont Basura No. 5 appeared then vanished. The awe quickly turned to fear and flight as an assortment of formerly buried but now blown free trash and flaming decorative foliage began to rain down on them. There was panic as everybody fled for his or her lives. Some of the camouflaged INS agents managed to escape to the awaiting Suburban. The wounded leader and his attendants, however, as well as Miguel the old commandante remained in police custody.

From the Ark, Mont Basura looked like a literal hell on earth. Flames erupting out of the ground. Ephemeral explosions of the red and pink randomly illuminating the exclusive development. The detritus of modern existence being blown into the air. And now some of the homes were starting to burn. The residents were jumping into their cars and speeding away to save themselves. Not only did most flee without any belongings, but on the southern clothing optional area of the development, many, including Florio Flores, without even clothing on their backs, or any other part of their body.

This made for several awkward situations when, later, out of harms way, they stopped for help. Several, including Florio were arrested for indecent exposure. It was enough to make some of them give up naturism.

"The apocalypse. Sodom and Gommorah. The wicked receiving their due," Barry described looking down on the spreading inferno.

"What do you mean? You started the fire with your gun," Jesus admonished.

"The hand of God. I am but his instrument," Barry replied.

"This is not God's work. Just the folly of man. Of men. Including you," Jesus stared Barry in the eye.

"If I didn't set it off, something else would have," Barry countered, uncomfortable with the thought of taking the blame for the destruction below.

"Perhaps. But it wasn't anyone else, it was you. You are responsible. And my two brothers are there somewhere amongst the flames," Jesus replied.

"We'll stay here. Do what we can to help them," Barry promised.

"Yes we will," Jesus' look let Barry know he expected nothing less.

"Boss," the pilot yelled over the noise, "We stay too close we could get hit and brought down by flying debris, and the updrafts from the heat are making her hard to control."

Barry looked at Jesus, the intensity in his eyes, "Stay here," he ordered.

"But Boss it ain't safe," the pilot warned.

Jesus gave Barry a slight nod of his head.

"Stay," remained the order.

*   *   *

From the air or the base of the trash mountain it was an amazing, fascinating, pyrotechnic display. If you happened to be on the ground in the midst of it, it was scary as hell.

Liz, in spite of four days a week in the gym plus fifteen miles of roadwork, wasn't able to catch up to Hamilton. The long legs of the seven-foot ball player and the fact he ran up and down a court for a living made it impossible. The ground rumbling beneath her feet made her stride unsteady. When a fiery fumerole blasted through the street in front of Lindsey's house she involuntarily screamed in fright. If she'd been running there she would have been incinerated. And the intense heat and smoke made it hard to breathe. Even though it was a short distance, by the time she reached the raptor rehab facility she was drenched with sweat and gasping for air.

Hamilton was already opening the pens trying to get the birds out. It wasn't easy. The heat, the noise, the sudden flashes from the explosions had the big birds extremely agitated. They were scared, almost as much as the man helping them. When approached they exhibited aggressive defensive behaviors, flapping their wings and lunging with their beaks. An osprey or an eagle was capable of tearing off a sizeable chunk of flesh.

Hamilton pressed on. He had to. He'd get behind or under the birds making big swooping motions with his arms. At least his wingspan was a match for even the largest birds in the facility. Once off their perches they went right out the door escaping into the night.

Liz watched his routine for half a minute, impressed by the way the big man got so close to the birds yet gracefully avoided their attempts to slash him while finally getting them to take flight. It was sort of like watching an avian martial arts defense demonstration.

"What can I do to help?" she called.

Momentarily distracted by the surprise of seeing Liz there, Hamilton narrowly missed having an eagle rip out his left eye.

Backing up he yelled to her, "Open all the doors for me. Maybe chase out some of the smaller birds."

Liz did as directed. The smaller raptors were just as jumpy as the larger ones. In the wild they would have been long gone from the noise and intense heat. Here the dancing flames and explosions had them beyond jittery, not knowing which way to go to escape. When they were finally herded out the door they flew straight up, the only safe way to go.

When the duo was nearly through with their task, the power suddenly went out. In a high-end development like Mont Basura it was aesthetically more pleasing to bury the phone and electric cables. Visible telephone and power lines did nothing to improve the classy ambiance. Also in a hurricane risk area like South Florida they really were safer underground.

That is of course unless underground gas lines were rupturing. A flaming methane jet had burned through the main power trunk for the whole development. Now the top of the refuse pyramid was illuminated only by the flames burning through the fissures in its surface. The good thing was that they provided more than sufficient light. Of course that was also a bad thing.

Hamilton looked over toward his house. Flames were creeping up the closest exterior walls and had already started licking around and over the eaves and onto the roof. There wasn't much he could do and no fire department would be crazy enough to try and reach the top of the burning trash heap.

Besides he and Liz still had another problem to handle. Any facility that does wildlife rehabilitation always ends up with some permanent residents. Animals too maimed or blind that, even when their injuries have healed the best they could, would be unable to survive in the wild. Some are used in traveling exhibits and as teaching tools. Many are kept because there is nowhere else for them.

The rehab center had a red shouldered Hawk missing half its left wing, leaving it unable to fly, an osprey blind in the left eye with limited vision in the right leaving it unable to hunt and a falcon with the tendon damage in both claws, leaving it barely able to perch and incapable of grasping any prey it tried to catch. The fires were getting closer but these three still needed to be saved.

Hamilton had watched the caretaker handle the birds but had never done so himself. He'd have to give it his best shot. He got two pair of the heavy gloves and three hoods out of the supply cabinet.

"Here put these gloves on," he said handing Liz a pair of gloves. "I'll give you the falcon."

She put the gloves on. He figured the falcon would be least likely to damage her because if its weak grip. He danced around with it a few seconds trying to get the hood on. It stumbled around on the perch but couldn't move that well and he quickly got the hood on its head. Once the eyes were covered the bird quieted quickly and he picked it up and handed it to a reluctant but game Liz.

The red-shouldered hawk was the real challenge. He could see and his talons were fully operational. As Ham approached, the bird bobbed and weaved like a prizefighter. Hamilton's first two attempts cost him a couple of strips of flesh. Score two to the hawk. On the third try he feinted with his left and as the bird scored its third slash he slipped the hood on. Again the bird settled down rapidly.

The osprey was easy. Ham came from the blindside and put the hood on easily.

Ham looked at the rips the hawk had given him. None was bleeding too badly. They'd heal soon enough. He slipped on the protective gloves and picked up the two birds. The hawk wasn't much, but carrying the osprey for any amount of time would require some effort. He was glad he'd spent so much time in the weight room.

"Follow me," he ordered Liz.

They exited the facility facing the ballplayer's house.

"Oh Ham. Oh God," Liz stopped and gasped.   Half of the home was engulfed in flame.

"Nothing we can do. Let's go," he replied.

He turned toward the rim of the development. There were still plenty of spaces between the fires. Liz followed. He led her over the edge and they gingerly and rapidly descended to the base.

When they reached the bottom they turned back and looked up. They had an adrenaline buzz from the tension and at the same time were weak kneed from the narrow escape. Fortunately the eruptions that had rained down old flaming trash were pretty much over and they didn't have to dodge any garbage projectiles. Most of Hamilton Patrick's house was now on fire.

Liz was getting teary-eyed feeling sorry for him.

The big man looked down at her. "Don't feel bad," he said to her. "I hadn't lived in it that long. So I wasn't all that attached to it. Heck we did the important thing. We got every one of the birds out."

She gave him a wan appreciative smile. His simple country sense of what's right was a refreshing change from big city ethical shades of gray she dealt with every day.

From the Ark, Barry, the pilot and Jesus had watched their descent. The surface of Mont Basura now looked like a fresh volcano lava flow, fires burning randomly all over. The observers had watched most of the residents of the development streaming down its side, kind of like ants fleeing a nest that had been stirred up. Several were hit by flying debris. Others were injured when they fell in their haste to beat it down the side of the trash pile.

"Where are my brothers? They went into that house and I didn't see them come out," Jesus stated.

The heat rising from below had the occupants of the gondola soaked in sweat. It periodically caused the airship to buck skyward. When that occurred their view was momentarily obstructed. It was possible they might have missed Pablo and Pedro's exit, but not likely.

"I don't know where they are. I didn't see them come out either," Barry whined.

"They're still in there. I know it," Jesus's statement left no room for contradiction.

"We can't go down there. No way to get close enough to land and go check," Barry stated the obvious.

"You got that right. Finally a little common sense," the pilot muttered under his breath.

"So we wait," Jesus commanded.

"We wait," Barry seconded.

They're both fuckin' nuts the pilot thought. As the fires below intensified and the updrafts worsened the blimp was harder and harder to control.

"If we don't crash and burn, we'll die of dehydration in this damn sauna," the pilot growled to himself.

He did the best he could to hold the dirigible on station.

 **Chapter XXIII**

Pedro and Pablo high-tailed it into the house while Lindsey and William were working out the release of the birds with Ham and Liz. As soon as the pairs separated William and Lindsey Lee chased after the refugees.

They found them huddled together, wild-eyed at the kitchen table. They were holding hands for reassurance like little boys afraid of the dark.

"They're sacred shitless," Lindsey whispered. "Let's take it slow with them."

William noticed that both men had small trickles of dried blood coming from their ears.

"They have ruptured eardrums or concussions. Or both," he whispered back.

Lindsey approached them slowly and put a hand on each of their shoulders to comfort them. They both gave a soft involuntary shudder at her touch, looking up at her with pleading eyes.

"Let's get you two cleaned up. William, would you get me a couple of wet towels," she requested nodding toward a drawer where she kept clean dishtowels.

William moistened a couple under the tap and brought them to her. She gently washed their faces and necks. The cool cloths and careful ministrations had a soothing effect on the scared young men. When she delicately wiped the crusts from their ears the sight of their own blood made them shudder again. Still, over all, they began to relax slightly.

As they settled down, William asked again, "Where's your brother? We never heard Pablo's answer."

"He's up in, how you say it," Pablo paused trying to remember the right word, his head was still foggy and his English wasn't all that good to start with.

"The blimp," he finally finished.

"What? How?" Lindsey was slightly incredulous.

"After the explosion, a black angel came down and grabbed him. Carry him back up," Pedro explained.

"Jesus was carried away by a black angel?" William was obviously skeptical and now sure they had concussions.

"Si," came the response.

"Whatever," Lindsey said dismissively. "We've got to get you out of here. The police know where you are. And this place is blowing up besides."

"Let's get moving," William ordered heading for the door leading to the garage.

The others followed closely on his heels. When the garage door opened they were treated to an eerie sight. As the door swung up they could see that the street was actually on fire. The same fiery vent that had blasted open scaring Liz had been burning long enough to ignite the tar in the asphalt used to pave the street. Outside now was an open burning maw with hellish black smoke billowing around the edges.

"Geeee-zus," Lindsey Lee gaped.

"Right. No way we're driving out of here," William said. He hit the button to close the door to keep the smoke out.

Pedro and Pablo stood riveted in place. Fear had returned to their eyes. When would the nightmare end? Were they cursed?

"Lindsey, is there anything you want to grab before we take off? There may not be anything to come back to," William asked.

"What? Yeah. Some pieces of family jewelry up in my bedroom."

"Go get 'em now," William directed.

She sprinted for the stairs with William following her. The two refugees, not wanting to be alone, were close behind.

"What's your plan? How are we getting' out of here? What we do about them?" Lindsey was more concerned about their escape and survival, as well as Pedro and Pablo's freedom.

"We're going to have to run for it. Look for a gap in the flames. Back down the side of this God forsaken dump. Then try to sneak them back on to the reservation. Least they won't get arrested," William explained his plan as they reached the top landing.

Lindsey stopped dead and the three men nearly piled into her. She turned around "What? That's it? That's all you got?"

"Keep moving," William urged. "Admittedly it ain't much. We're going to have to improvise."

"We're gonna show up like we're spot lit crabbing down the side of this heap. Every cop at the bottom will be waiting with open arms," she said over her shoulder as she turned into her room.

The three men waited in the doorway as she grabbed a ring her father had given her and a chain and locket that had been her mother's from her jewelry box. She stuffed them in her pocket.

Frightened as they were, Pablo and Pedro took a few seconds to check out Lindsey's bedroom. After all what were the chances of them getting into a movie star's bedroom again anytime soon.

"Es no especial," Pablo whispered.

"Pero, es no malo," Pedro replied.

She turned for the door, gave the room one farewell look and headed for the stairs. The men let her pass, and then followed.

As the group reached the top of the stairs the power went out. The only light now was from the eerie flickering through the windows of the flames outside. They paused, allowing their eyes to adapt to the darkness, then proceeded slowly down the steps. Liz and William led with the refugee duo close behind.

They were halfway to the bottom.

Whoosh. A jet of flame burst through the floor at the foot of the stairs.

Startled and surprised Liz and William stumbled backward. They didn't bump into either Pablo or Pedro.

Their nerves frayed like an old rusty wire cable, this was the final straw. Their last strand snapped and control and reason deserted them. They ran. Up, blindly, away from the flame.

It took a couple of seconds for William and Liz to realize they were gone. There in the dancing firelight forms behind the upstairs railing moved towards Lindsey's room.

"Come back," William yelled after them, "Stay up there and you'll be trapped. We can still get out."

And it was true. The newest eruption was only partially obstructing their escape. They could still get by. If they didn't wait too long.

"We've got to get them," Lindsey wasn't going to abandon their two wards now.

"I know," neither was William.

They sprinted up the stairs.

In Lindsey's bedroom there was no sign of them. Even in the low light two bodies would be hard to miss.

"Check the bathroom. I'll check the closet," Lindsey directed.

Lindsey found no one in the walk-in. William hoped maybe they were soaking themselves in the shower, perhaps thinking that water would add extra protection from the fires. No such luck. They weren't in the bathroom.

William and Lindsey met back in the bedroom.

"Where the hell are they?" William cursed, "We haven't got much time. You check the bed?"

"It's on a platform. No way un-," she stopped, listening to the thrum of an engine that seemed to come from overhead. "Wait."

William heard it too. They both looked up. The hatch to the widow's walk was open.

Holy shit William thought. We won't be able to get out soon; the number of seconds to escape was literally burning away. Now we're going to have to try to drag two panicked assholes down from the roof. Panic could wind up killing them all.

*　　*　　*

"I don't give a shit what you say. We're getting outta here while we can," the exasperated pilot said to his boss.

"No!" Barry commanded.

"I'm not dyin' for you two nut jobs. Fire my ass if you want. We're gone."

"Wait. There," Jesus pointed.

Barry and the pilot looked down. They saw a weakly lit rectangle of light open in the roof of the house below. Two figures came out through the opening.

"Mi hermanos," Jesus was elated.

"His brothers. The two disciples. Take her down," Barry ordered as he stepped back into his climbing harness and put the spare over his shoulder.

"I must be friggin' crazy," the pilot mumbled as he put the big airship into the slow shallow dive. The heated thinner air from the updrafts made for a bumpy approach.

Barry tossed his ropes out the door, clipped on to one and once again stepped out into the night.

"Deus ex machina!" he shouted as he descended.

"What the fuck's that mean?" the pilot said to himself.

"Is Latin. Means God from the machine," Jesus explained. He needed his help to save his brothers, but even he was beginning to wonder if Barry wasn't one or two suits short of a full deck.

"Oh. That explains it," the pilot rolled his eyes.

*　　　*　　　*

Liz and William emerged through the hatch just in time to see a winged black figure pulling himself, and helping Pablo pull himself, up a rope toward the Ark.

The two stood on the top steps of the circular staircase gaping at the sight.

"See. Un angel negro," Pedro startled them. He was standing behind the hatch door watching his brother's ascent.

"Si. A black angel," Lindsey agreed, rubbing her eyes. Not completely trusting what they told her.

Pablo disappeared into the blimp. Seconds later the ebony seraph rappelled toward the trio. The tips of the ropes were dancing around the widow's walk like spastic serpents as the pilot struggled to hover in place.

Barry landed next to Lindsey. Both she and William eyed him up and down. On closer scrutiny the angel of salvation looked a lot more like an escaped lunatic. There was a driven intensity in his eyes.

"Who are you?" Lindsey asked timidly, expecting almost anything for an answer.

"Barry Gold," a straight enough answer, "On a holy mission. Pedro put this on," he said, handing the last brother the safety harness, showing him how to put it on.

"Figured it was something like that," William nodded to Lindsey.

The two men were already hauling themselves back toward the Ark.

"You're coming back for us?" Lindsey yelled after them. The light coming up from the hatch was getting brighter as the fire in the house burned its way up the stairs.

The heat rising through the opening was becoming unbearable. William slammed the hatch cover down.

"It'll decrease the oxygen supply to the fire. Slow it down," William said.

"Did you hear the answer?" Lindsey asked. She was starting to be scared.

"No. But there's no way they'd leave us," William assured her.

Up in the Ark Barry and Pablo pulled themselves on board. Barry started to pull his lines in.

"Get us out of here," he commanded.

"What? What about them?" the pilot pointed to the two stranded figures on the roof.

"We've completed our mission. Got who we came for. The important thing is to save the holy men. Go!" he ordered emphatically.

"Wait. You can't," Lindsey screamed as the ascent lines disappeared. It was her turn to be hysterical.

William grabbed her and hugged her to his chest. There had to be another way to escape. It was too late to go back down through the house. The hatch was getting too hot to even touch.

Maybe if they took a running start down the slanted roof they could get enough momentum to leap into the pool. Of course the horizontal distance was probably a good fifteen feet. If they missed from the second story, and hit the stone patio, they'd be lucky if they only broke a few limbs.

"Don't worry. We're going to make it," he tried to sound confident. He didn't want to lose this woman or his life.

Lindsey trembled against him, "How?"

"No way," the pilot rebelled again. He didn't want to die here. But he sure as hell couldn't leave two people to burn alive without at least trying to save them.

"The adulterers will have to save themselves. Go," Barry reiterated.

"Who are you to judge them?" Jesus interrupted. He knew that for some reason Barry would listen to him. He would use his influence to save the people who'd looked out for him.

"Save them," he ordered Barry.

"But Teacher. You and your brothers—"

"We'll be fine. We can't have their blood on our heads," Jesus cut Barry off and, hoping he was still subservient, re-ordered, "Save them."

Smoke was beginning to seep out between the tin shingles as the wooden trusses and plywood roof sheathing started to ignite.

The pilot was already heading in for another pass as Barry told him, "Take us back down."

With little time left, Barry tied the safety harnesses each to the end of a rope. Then he tossed the lines out the door.

The smoke was decreasing the visibility at the roof level. But the pilot brought the blimp in right over the widow's walk. There was a temporary lull in the hot updrafts.

The harnesses smacked into the clinging couple. As luck would have it, during the filming of "Caribbean Commandos," Lindsey had used similar gear. Though her hands were shaking, she quickly had the two of them rigged up and snapped on to the ropes.

Flames started to lick through the edges of the shingles.

They pulled for all they were worth. As soon as the pilot felt the extra weight dragging down on the blimp he put the airship into a climb. He could see the fire breaking through the roof. They all needed to get out of there. The last two passengers would have to finish their ascent away from the immolated top of the heap.

Dangling at the end of the rope as the blimp cleared the airspace over Mount Basura, William saw the distance he could fall change from tens of feet to hundreds. It was then he discovered his acrophobia. He closed his eyes and clung on for dear life.

Lindsey saw him frozen in place, no longer making any upward progress. She figured out right away what was wrong.

"Don't look down," she called. "Just look at the rope above you. Keep pulling yourself up, one hand over the other. Concentrate on reaching the blimp."

William, eyes barely open, only slits really, did as he was told. Focusing to keep the rope his only field of vision, he began to climb again. Lindsey stayed by his side, talking steadily, encouraging his progress.

Finally, palms sweating, he reached the doorway where Pablo and Pedro pulled him in ahead of Lindsey.

"That was something. Haven't done a stunt like that since my last movie," Lindsey remarked as she climbed aboard, trying to break the tension and take some of the attention off William who was looking awfully pale for a Red Man.

William, huddled safely against a closed corner of the gondola quickly regained his composure, at least partially.

"What the fuck happened there?" William didn't commonly use profanity, but he was rattled. "It looked like you were taking off without us. Pulling up the ropes and all. Tell me it wasn't what it looked like," he demanded.

Four sets of eyes, the pilot's and the three holy men, turned accusingly on Barry. The black angel, who'd removed his gloves and ski mask, hung his head. Lest ye yourself be judged popped into his head.

"Sorry," was all he could mumble.

"He was trying to save my brothers and me. Not thinking through his actions clearly," Jesus tried to explain. "At least he did the right thing in enough time."

"Barely," William and Lindsey replied with unified animosity. They weren't willing to let him off so easily. It was, after all, their butts in the fire.

"The important point is we're all here safe now," Jesus continued.

The man had a valid point. After a pause William, with less tension in his voice now, asked, " Okay, what's the plan now?"

Barry, seeing a chance for some redemption, replied, "We fly back to my hangar. Then I can offer them sanctuary at my church, away from the evil influences."

There was an audible groan from the refugees. Sanctuary though it had its high points, hadn't worked out that well so far. And Barry's version, quite likely to be without the rappers, celebrities and groupies, had no appeal at all.

"That's it? That's your plan?" William was incredulous. Religious sanctuary offered less safety than the Miccosukee's sovereignty over their own lands. After all, people had been arrested in church before.

"Is there a problem?" Lindsey asked. The refugees listened carefully for his answer.

William explained his concerns.

Barry quickly offered a second option, "We can move them into the church underground. I've got people who can hide them where the government won't find them."

"Better than nothing, I guess," William commented.

The discussion was interrupted by an explosion. A small, hot, pink mushroom cloud appeared on the northeast corner of Mont Basura. The fires had heated the perfume spray tank on the fogging truck until it blew open, igniting the contents.

The occupants of the blimp's gondola watched through the door and windows in awe. What else could happen to them tonight?

They were about to find out.

 **Chapter XXIV**

The camo-clad immigration agents who'd escaped the police were in their Suburban driving west toward the turnpike. Having failed to recapture the refugees, they were in a foul mood. The man in the front passenger seat was explaining to agent Busch what went wrong and was wondering if it were actually possible to have an ear chewed off by phone.

Pointing skyward, the driver interrupted the tongue-lashing, "Look at that."

Holding the phone away from his head, he looked out the windshield, "What? Where?" He stopped asking when he saw the silhouette of the Ark blacking out a patch of stars in the clear night sky.

He waited for a break in Busch's ranting, then told him what they were watching. He also explained that at least one of the refugees was likely to be on board.

The driver noticed a pause in the conversation.

Then the passenger asked into the phone, "Are you sure?"

The driver didn't hear the answer.

"If you say so. We'll keep you posted," the passenger clicked off.

"What'd he say?" the driver asked.

"Bring it down."

"How?"

"Shoot it!"

"Is he crazy? Shoot it down?"

"Those are the orders. Pull over."

The driver did as ordered.

They both stepped out of the SUV and each took a 9mm Glock from the armament case in the back.

"Shoot for the gas envelope. We let enough helium escape and she'll come down."

They both unloaded a full clip of ammo. Though he shot in the general direction of the blimp, the driver purposely missed. It just didn't feel right.

The passenger hit the gasbag with every shot except one. That one ricocheted off the gondola's titanium frame and cut through the steering control cables. The Ark was definitely coming down. Where—was anyone's guess.

"Reload," the passenger ordered, exchanging the empty clip for a full one.

The driver fumbled for a second clip.

"We've gotta bring it down. Reload," the passenger repeated aiming into the sky again.

The two agents were suddenly illuminated by a spotlight.

"Miami-Dade police! Drop your weapons! Lace your fingers together and put your hands behind your head. Then drop to your knees." It was the commander from the reservation security detail. She'd been on her way to deliver prisoners to the county jail.

They did as they were told.

The commander and her partner walked up behind them and handcuffed them. Next they picked up their weapons.

The woman police officer came around to look them in the face, "What is wrong with you assholes? You know damn well you can't shoot up an aircraft. You're under arrest."

"But I really didn't shoot at it," the driver whined.

His partner glared at him while mumbling, "Just followin' orders."

"Yeah right. What a pair of dickheads. Our unit is full, so we'll have to wait with these morons 'til we can get someone here to pick them up," she said to her partner.

"Fuckin' dumbass feds," was his only comment.

*   *   *

They all heard the bullet spang as it caromed off the gondola's frame.

"What the hell! Someone's shootin' at us," the pilot felt it was time to get into a new line of work. Something safe that didn't involve religion.

"Whatta' ya mean? Do something. Take evasive action," Barry was slightly hysterical.

"What? You moron! This isn't an F-16, it's a blimp. I don't even know where the shots came from," the pilot responded thinking to himself—it's an airborne broadside of a barn. Easy for anyone to hit.

Everyone aboard was looking down trying to figure out where the shooter was. No one saw anything. And no one knew if the shooting would start again.

"Turn right and climb," Barry ordered having regained his composure.

Humor him the pilot thought. Right, left, one's as good as the other.

And at least going up they would make a slightly smaller target.

He tried to turn the rudder hard right.

Nothing.

He tried putting the Ark into a climb. She rose a little, but was sluggish.

"We're screwed," he whispered to himself.

"What'd you say?" William had seen his lips move and the grim look on his face.

"We're screwed," he repeated loud enough for everyone to hear.

"Watch your mouth. There are holy men here. Take us back to base," Barry ordered.

"No can do. Got no steering," the pilot replied.

"What?" Barry was a little slow on the uptake.

"No rudder. No right or left. They must' a shot out the control cable. We're going down."

"What?" Barry couldn't or didn't want to comprehend.

"Other shots must 'a punctured the gas bag. We're losing helium. When our lighter than airship becomes a heavier than airship, we'll be a no longer in the air ship," the pilot waxed poetic in his explanation.

"What?" Barry couldn't believe his plan was falling apart.

"You turning into some kinda parrot? That the only word you know?" the pilot mocked.

"Are we going to crash?" Lindsey interrupted in a dead serious tone. The question on everyone's mind.

"No."

"Can't you get us home?" Barry pleaded.

"Haven't you been listening? No."

"What's going to happen?" Jesus and William asked simultaneously.

"Look. It could be worse. There's nothing I can do to control our direction, and we could be getting blown out to sea. But the prevailing winds are out of the southeast. We're being blown inland."

They had already passed over U.S. 1 and the Florida Turnpike. And we're now drifting above the latest urban sprawl, housing developments being built in what was once the farmland of western Homestead. The farming community that was once billed as "The Nation's Winter Vegetable Capital" was now being turned into cookie cutter homes for those who couldn't afford the high life, like on Mont Basura.

"Is there anything you can control?" William asked.

The pilot looked at his altimeter. They had leveled off at just above three thousand feet, which would have been fine. A nice cruising altitude, except that the ailerons were still set in the climb position and they were no longer climbing.

"The rate of descent. And all I can do is speed it up," he replied shutting down the propeller motors. There would be less chance of fire or injury if they were turned off for landing.

Below the last lights of civilization were well astern of the airship.

The sudden quiet had a calming, almost soothing effect on the group.

"What's going to happen now?" Barry asked in a softer voice, no longer having to yell to be heard over the engines.

The pilot looked again at the altimeter. The numbers on the digital readout were now decreasing, but slowly.

"Looks like we're going to drift gently to the ground."

"Can you say approximately where?" Barry continued.

"Looks like the middle of the Everglades," Lindsey piped in.

"What?" Barry wasn't quite as calm.

"That question again," the pilot responded. "Yup. The Everglades. Snakes and alligators."

"Panthers, boars and bears, too, if we're lucky. Not to mention all kinds of birds," William smiled and sat down against the bulkhead opposite the open doorway, bracing himself and waiting to land.

The holy men were worried about the Everglades and wild animals. Also, the Krome Detention Center was on the edge of the Everglades.

 **Chapter XXV**

Liz stood at the base of Mont Basura, watching Hamilton's house and then the raptor rehab facility go up in flames. The relentless destruction of the tongues of flame was horribly entrancing to watch.

"Gruesome and awesome," Ham commented. "You better call it in."

"Huh?"

"Call it in. You gotta get your news truck and chopper out of here. This is a helluva story. Great visuals while the fires are burning. Like Reuben says, great visuals can make or break a story. And these are awesome."

"Oh. Right," Lindsey pulled out her cell phone.

The night crew at the station had been monitoring the police and fire scanners and the remote broadcast truck was on the way. They were so delighted she was already on site able to scoop the other stations that they even forgot to ask why she was already there. The chopper was more of a problem. They had called and paged the pilot and his cameraman and so far only the cameraman had responded.

Liz and Hamilton slowly worked their way around the perimeter of the trash pyramid's base. It was slow going in the low light and litter-strewn ground. They reached the access road just as the remote truck rolled up.

The uplink antenna was raised. The cameraman checked his connections and feed to the station. Then he gave Liz the rolling sign.

The report was fantastic. Picked up by the big three networks, as well as several cable news channels.

Liz had decided not to wipe the soot and grime from her face. It added to the authenticity. The fires still burning briskly atop the garbage mesa over her head in the background, the microphone in her right hand and the hooded, injured hawk perched on her gloved left hand made for a gritty and gripping opening shot.

In a controlled and commanding voice she told about being awakened by the explosion at the refugees' trailer. About coming outside in time to see the flare from the blimp start the chain reaction of fires now consuming the exclusive housing development. How the Heat's brave rookie center, with a small amount of help from her, had managed to save every one of the birds in the rehab center. And how they'd barely escaped with their lives. During her delivery, the hawk quietly shifted its weight back and forth, its head cocked toward her, apparently charmed by her voice.

She also mentioned witnessing the miraculous escape of the holy men and her friends, William Panther and Lindsey Lee Olsen delivered, from the flames in a daring rescue by the Ark.

Finally she described her own exhaustion and feeling of helpless futility while standing at the bottom of the slope watching the development go up in flames, unable to do anything more to help.

When she finished, tears had traced tracks through the dirt in her cheeks. They were real, unaffected. And they sure played well on TV. Offers from the major news organizations would be rolling in by the end of the day. The doughty newswoman would have her pick.

As soon as they were done recording, Liz contacted the station. After accepting their praise for a job well done, she asked, " What do you hear on the scanners? What's going to happen here? Any updates on the location of the blimp?"

The overnight news director replied, "No fatalities, lots of injuries, in the fire at your location. Plan is at this time to just let the fires burn out. If I could get hold of the damn copter pilot we could still get some great aerials."

"Have you tried his boyfriend's house?" Lindsey interrupted.

"No. Good idea. You don't happen to have the number?"

Liz gave it to him. She and the chopper pilot were buddies.

"I'll try it soon as we're done," the director continued.

"As far as the blimp is concerned, there was brief chatter about somebody firing shots at it. It was last seen heading out over the Glades. Say, what were you doing out there in the first place?"

"Following up a lead," she deflected not wanting to become any bigger part of the story.

"It's almost three in the morning. Go home and get some rest," the night director ordered.

"Nah. Think I'll head out west to the Indian casino. It might be a good place to be based in case the Ark is down in the Everglades somewhere. If it's OK I'll take the sat-truck. Be ready to broadcast."

"Fine. Follow your nose," he knew her instincts had been dead on so far.

"And get yourself a room. It's on the station. Try to catch a couple of hours sleep."

"Fair enough. I'll call with the room number when I check in if you'll promise to wake me if anything breaks."

"You got it."

She and Hamilton, who'd hidden discreetly out of sight during the taping, and the birds all loaded into the truck. Along with the cameraman, they headed out to the Indian casino on Krome.

On arrival, they dropped the birds off at the recently finished state-of-the-art rehab facility. They checked in, getting two rooms, one for Liz, and one for the two guys. Liz called in her location, took a quick shower, and was out like a light.

In the other room, the cameraman from the remote truck, a night owl and not particularly sleepy, had lots of questions for Hamilton. He didn't get many answers. The big man also took a shower and went right to bed.

Liz was awakened by a phone call at 6:05 am. The station's chopper was waiting for her on the casino's helipad. She quickly ran the room's iron over her clothes from the last night. They didn't look too awful. Thank god for polyester.

At the helicopter she was joined by Hamilton and the cameraman who looked at Ham then gave her a questioning look.

She put her finger to her lips, the shhhh sign.

He gave her an affirmative nod.

All three squeezed aboard with the pilot.

"Morning John," she greeted. She knew he'd ended up shooting the aerials of the fire alone using the chopper's automated traffic cam.

"Thanks for giving me up last night," he grunted.

"Oh, Jimmy understands."

"Yeah, yeah. Let's go," he replied.

They strapped themselves in. John pulled back on the stick and the whirlybird lifted off. They banked south over the Tamiami Trail, then headed southwest toward an area of the Everglades known as Shark River Valley.

"So what do we know so far, John?" Lindsey asked into the mic that allowed her to communicate with the pilot.

"They found the Ark," was all that came over her earphones.

The sun was just over the horizon, beginning to erase the shadow from the River of Grass.

"And...?" she prodded.

"And that's it. All I know. We're s'posed to fly out there, try to figure out what's going on and report it."

She wasn't going to get anymore from him, so she asked to be patched through to the station. John obliged.

In another five minutes they'd reached the crash site. They were informed by radio that, since an active investigation was underway, they would have to maintain a 250-yard "no-fly" zone around the area.

What they saw was the blimp with its passenger compartment, the gondola, resting on the edge of the hardwood hammock, a slightly raised island of trees in the midst of the sawgrass plain. The silver fluctulant, semi-flaccid gas compartment draped over the treetops was rippling in the morning breeze.

On the ground near the wreckage was a dark, blue helicopter with NTSB, National Transportation Safety Board, stenciled in white on the fuselage. A team of inspectors in navy blue jackets with the same logo was inspecting the crippled airship.

"Notice what's not here?" the pilot said into his mic, his curiosity aroused. Over the years, land and sea, he'd flown to a lot of crash sites.

"No. I...don't," Liz replied, scanning the area.

"Think," he goaded. Inspite of being torn away from his partner in the middle of the night, he liked Liz. He knew she was smart and had the makings of a good reporter. She listened, so he wanted to help her do well.

She looked again. What was missing?

"Hey. There's no emergency personnel."

"Bingo. Normally on something like this you're gonna have either the Coasties or Metro-Dade Air Rescue down there, too. Paramedics either pulling out the injured or bodies. We got no stretchers, no body bags."

Liz called the station to get an update from those monitoring the scanners. Her report was on the air live by 6:45 am. The visual cut from her speaking inside the helicopter to telephoto views of the crippled airship on the ground.

The verbatim audio went, "Early in the morning the FAA received a signal from an emergency-locator transponder. It indicated a downed aircraft in an area of the Everglades known as the Shark River Valley. A reconnaissance flyover of the NTSB located the wreckage of the airship, Ark, a blimp owned by the religious group Semites for the Son. The airship was last seen coming to the rescue of several people trapped by the fires burning atop the exclusive development, Mont Basura Harbor. The first NTSB investigators to arrive on the scene found no sign of the passengers or crew. At the present time no one has received any word from Barry Gold, his pilot, movie star Lindsey Lee Olson, Miccosukee chief William Panther, or the fugitive refugees: Jesus, Pablo and Pedro, referred to locally as the three holy men. As of this report, the whereabouts of all these persons is officially unknown,"

When she'd finished, the pilot clicked his mic and asked, "So whatta you wanna' do now?"

"Head back to the casino. I've got a feeling we're not done out here."

John radioed in to okay it with the station and was told to give her whatever she wanted. He smiled to himself. Whether she knew it or not she was on her way. He headed the bird back to the casino's parking lot.

*　　　*　　　*

The Ark's pilot gave the compartments' occupants periodic readings of the altimeter. When it got below three hundred feet, he flipped on the emergency locator radio beacon, sat down and braced himself against the wall for the crash landing.

There was no moon, only starlight. It was hard to judge where the ground was as the aircraft closed on it. But through the door and windows somehow the blackness seemed to get blacker.

Each person was silent with his thoughts as impact approached. Barry reached toward Jesus for comfort. The oldest brother took his hand and held it.

The first thing that happened was a swishing and scraping sound as the bottom of the gondola touched the tips of the sawgrass. The blimp was moving sideways, to port, with the gas envelope acting as a sail in the wind.

As contact and friction increased, the airship healed over slightly on its left side. Their motion slowed as the drag on the passenger compartment grew. The landing was actually quite soft; the tall grass a perfect cushion. Eventually they slid to a stop.

And started again. The gasbag in its capacity as a sail would catch a wind gust and gently bump them along again a couple of hundred yards. They came to a final rest when the blimp's sail got caught in the mahogany and cypress trees in the hammock.

Barry let go of Jesus's hand.

"Every one Ok?" the pilot asked when it was apparent they weren't moving any more.

All affirmatives. Other than a few bumps, no injuries reported.

"What was that button you pushed just before we landed?" Barry asked.

"Emergency locator."

Barry was educable. He finally didn't say, "What?" However he did say, "Why'd you do that? Now the Feds'll find us and this all will be for nothing."

The pilot had had it with the whining, "Because you fucking idiot, pardon my French to the rest of you, if the landing hadn't gone well and we're all laying here broken and bleeding, you'd be sure as shit glad somebody might find us and bring help."

"Oh," was the glum reply. "But now we're all going to be caught."

"Have a little faith," William smirked. He stepped out of the gondola then said, "Everybody follow me."

As they exited out of the blimp's doorway, they stepped down into water about six inches deep. They grouped around the hatch until the last person, the pilot, came out.

"All the other crap I been through tonight. Now I'm up to my ankles in swamp water. This is just freakin' great," he groused.

He turned and along with several of the passengers started heading toward the higher, dry ground of the hammock.

"No. Stop. Not that way," William ordered.

They froze in their tracks.

"Why?" What's up there? Something bad?" The pilot didn't know what to expect. Didn't want to get bitten by some hungry swamp creature. His closest contact to the wild was watching Animal Planet on cable.

"No. That's not it," William explained. "You wanna get outta here, right?"

"Right," a unanimous chorus agreed.

"You also didn't want to get caught, right?"

There were fewer "rights" in agreement this time. Several members of the group were scared enough that they didn't care who rescued them.

"Look. We don't want to leave any footprints there for the searchers to find. We gotta leave them guessing. Think maybe we even got off somewhere before the Ark crashed. Make 'em search a bigger area. Not sure of where to look for us."

"How do we do that?" Barry sounded hopeful. Maybe they could still keep the holy men out of custody.

"Follow me." William turned in the opposite direction from the hammock and pulled out his cell phone. The damn thing could be useful after all. He punched in the number and waited. He whispered special directions to the man on the other end. Then hung up.

"Let's go. Form a line behind me and don't straggle."

The Ark had flattened a thousand yard long swath of sawgrass into the water as it bounced to a stop. William proceeded to lead them back down the landing strip. The going was slow. The Shark River bottom, and river is what it was, miles wide and extremely shallow, was covered with a spongy muck called periphyton, formed from decayed plant materials. So the footing was less than firm. The water's depth varied from ankle to armpit deep. Occasionally there were solution holes, erosive pits in the underlying limestone, where feet could get stuck and shoes lost.

Lindsey, right behind William, asked, "You know what you're doing?"

"Oh yeah. I'm in my element now. No problem long as everybody keeps up." He knew exactly where they were.

She took some comfort in the fact that he was unconsciously humming to himself, actually seeming to enjoy the situation.

There was also the fear to deal with. The five men at the tail of the aquatic conga line each clung tightly to the person in front of him. And the pilot hated being last. He kept up a steady chatter of questions to distract himself.

"Hey chief. What about alligators around here?" he called.

"Not likely. Too much work for the big ones to maneuver through the grass. And you're too big for the baby ones to try to take a bite. Same with the crocs."

"Thanks. I feel much better. How about snakes? Any poisonous snakes?"

"Well, the Glades have all four types indigenous to North America. But coral snakes, copperheads and rattlers don't like water all that much. Generally don't swim 'less they have to."

"Stop. You're going to scare him. You should be trying to keep him calm," Lindsey hissed in William's ear.

"I thought I was. Knowledge cancels the fear ignorance breeds," he whispered back.

"Hey chief, that's only three. What's number four?"

"Cottonmouth water moccasin. Pretty obvious from the name they don't mind water. Good swimmers in fact. But we're making enough commotion to scare them out of the way," he continued merrily.

Lindsey gave him a little swat to the side of the head.

They'd covered about three quarters of the distance when William halted. There was a low droning to the east. As they waited in waist deep water the sound was getting louder.

The crazy night leading up to this, up to his gut in a god forsaken swamp full of killer creatures. The pilot couldn't take it any more. He pissed his pants. The release and warmth in his groin actually felt good. Pedro heard an "ahhhh" behind him.

"Damn. It's a helicopter. We're caught," Barry moaned, dropping his hands from Lindsey's waist.

"No. It's not. Just wait," William seemed very relaxed.

Within two minutes the sound went from a distant drone to a low hum to an overpowering din forcing them all to cover their ears.

Shortly afterward they were all caught in a bright spotlight as a large airboat swept to a stop in front of them.

"Uncle Jesse. I knew I could count on an old frogger like you," William called out.

"You're right there, but what the hell you got goin' out here, boy? That ain't like no group of tourists I've ever seen."

William was Jesse's favorite nephew. But looking at the group he was with—one beautiful woman, a kook in a Batman suit, three beards in pimp coveralls and a guy in an airline uniform—he was wondering what the boy had gotten himself into.

"Long story," William shouted back over the growling engine. "Right now we need to get out of here. You didn't leave any tracks?"

"Boy, who taught you everything you know about poaching?" Jesse yelled back in an offended tone. "Came down the open branch of river and turned up on the flattened grass. Just like you said. Go back the same way. No one'll ever know we were here."

"Good enough," William smiled. Though he'd never done it himself, his uncle had taught him how the old time Miccosukee hunters, the one's who didn't think it right that their activities be confined to reservation land, would sneak into the national park to get what they needed.

The group happily climbed into the airboat. Jesse handed them all ear protection and then put his on. He cranked up the engine, shut off the spotlight, put the boat in gear, fishtailed around 180 degrees and sped away in the dark.

In a short time they were safely delivered to William's chickee south of Frog City. Spread out on the floor of the platform and in the hammocks, the exhausted band was soon sound asleep.

The first of them to awaken, William and the three brothers, began to stir long after dawn. To pass the time and not disturb the others they went fishing in the pond where William had thrown the frog carcasses just two days ago. They soon had a nice stringer of perch.

While the boys cleaned the fish, William started the cookfire and put on a pot of coffee and one of cornmeal.

The smell of the coffee woke the rest of the group and shortly after 11:00 am they sat down to share a nice brunch of fresh fish and grits.

Several hours rest and no imminent threat of arrest or bodily harm had reduced tensions tremendously. Topics of discussion were mostly mundane; the immediate thing being that everyone wished they had fresh clothes to wear. William managed to scrounge up a pair of jeans and a shirt from a cache in the chickee. He gave them to Barry so he wouldn't have to look like a failed caped crusader any longer.

"So what now? We can't stay here forever," the pilot stated what was on everybody's mind.

"Well, you're on Miccosukee land again. Real reservation. So you can't be arrested here either. But you're right. It isn't set up for long term accommodations for seven."

"Chief Panther, do you have a radio here?" Barry was deferentially using William's title out of respect and gratitude for being saved the night before.

"Yeah. Use it to track the weather when we're hunting," William replied, pulling out a beat-up old boom box.

"Let's get the news. Hear what they're doing about us. Then decide what to do," Barry suggested.

William tuned in an AM all-news station. First they got the local forecast. Then the traffic reports for the impending lunchtime rush. Finally the local news.

"Authorities are continuing their search for the seven occupants of the blimp, the Ark. They were last seen when the airship was used to save them from the tragic eruption of Mont Basura. Wreckage from the blimp was found this morning. But there was no sign of the passengers or crew. Investigators are back-tracking the probable flight path searching for any sign of the missing persons," the broadcaster intoned.

The present residents of the chickee had heard helicopters flying back and forth well south of their location.

"Eruption! Makes it sound like some kinda natural disaster," the pilot interjected.

"In other news, Judge Herbert Spahn IV…"

"Well, I guess…," William said starting to turn the dial to off.

"Leave that," Lindsey cut him short. "He's the judge on our guys' immigration case."

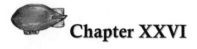 **Chapter XXVI**

Judge Spahn had made his decision regarding the refugees. And was releasing it in time to make the television noon news cycle.

A man with a meticulous and strict constructionist legal mind, the judge had researched much of the case himself. He and his clerk did a thorough job of reviewing applicable case law.

And Judge Spahn took it one step further. He went over to South Beach and observed sandbar formations. Then he checked the tide tables for the approximate time of the incident.

His decision—at the time of the refugees' arrival the sandbar was indeed well exposed. Enough so that a rational man would consider it dry. And the sandbar was well within U.S. territorial limits, American soil.

That coupled with the American legal tenet of innocent until proven guilty, forced him to decide the government's case was without merit. Their feet were dry. Therefore they were not guilty of illegal entry. And hence the government's arrest and detention of the refugees was in error, as were any future legal problems deriving from that erroneous arrest.

The refugees, wherever they were, were free to go.

 **Chapter XXVII**

It was over.

At least as far as Jesus, Pablo and Pedro were concerned.

"We're free!" they yelled, jumping up and down, slapping each other on the back and hugging.

The other four were grinning, watching their celebration.

There were still a few details to work out now, as well as a massive amount of destruction to be dealt with later.

"Can I borrow your phone? I better call Reuben. There may still be some processing for the guys to go through before the government let's them go completely," Lindsey asked William.

"I doubt they're going to screw with them much more. Probably say good riddance. But here," he said, handing it to her.

She dialed the scrappy attorney on his private number.

The six men could only hear her half of the conversation.

"Hello, Reuben."

"Yeah it's me, Lindsey Lee. We're all here. No one's hurt. We're all fine."

"Yeah, we heard. It's great news. Whatta we do now?"

"We're a few miles south of the Tamiami Trail."

"Yeah. In the Everglades."

"We can meet you at Frog City in say an hour and a half."

"Okay. Fine. See you then."

She turned to the group, "He says the government is just going to leave you guys alone. But he still wants the press there because they wouldn't dare try anything else on live TV. And because, well, he's Reuben. Can you get Jesse to give us a ride back?"

"He doesn't like getting' up in the middle of the day. But he'll do it for me," William took the phone back and called his uncle.

They killed an hour discussing the future.

Lindsey Lee's immediate problem was that she no longer had a home.

William offered her the use of the chickee and a suite at the casino.

She said yes, as long as he stayed with her.

Barry needed to replace the Ark. At least it was insured, and the positive news coverage would bring more converts to his church.

The pilot still wanted a new job, something firmly planted on the ground. He didn't say anything out loud. But maybe the chief could get him a position as a poker dealer at the casino.

William knew a shake up was coming with the tribe. Rex had put his ass on the line with the Bayside reservation and it had blown up in his face. William didn't really want to be the Big Cat, but would wait and see what the Tribal Council decided.

Finally there were the refugees, no longer fugitives. The exile world was there to conquer. Quiet, easy jobs with occasional public adulation would be fine. But they'd tasted the big time. And enjoyed it. Barry detailed for them a very interesting proposal. It wasn't completely crazy. And they didn't say no.

At 2:00 pm the news crews in the camera trucks parked between the abandoned gas pumps of the defunct Frog City gas station heard the approaching drone of the airboat. A few minutes after the crews heard the engine shut down, the saintly seven, an eponym bestowed on them by Reuben when they went missing, came trooping out from behind the derelict general store. Spontaneous applause broke out from the small crowd waiting.

Lindsey ran over and hugged Liz and Hamilton. The last time she'd seen them they'd been running into the fire.

Hamilton went to William and offered his hand. William took it and gave him a bear hug.

"Got all the birds out safe," he said as he was released.

"Great work, big man," even greater you two are okay, he thought.

Reuben took over, and none of the saints seemed to mind.

"The government has dropped their case against my clients," he addressed the media, "And it would be wise not to persecute them any further. In fact, reparations are likely in order," he continued.

The press quickly got the gist of Reuben's message and pushed for what they really wanted.

"Let us talk to the survivors," they chanted.

"Fine. Fine. A short Q & A with me standing by for advice if needed. Remember they've just been through a harrowing ordeal."

While the three holy men were being interviewed by a separate network, and articulating their traumatic experiences well in both English and Spanish, Lindsey snuck off with Liz who took her back to the remote truck.

"What's going on?" Lindsey asked. "You looking for an exclusive?"

"I wouldn't mind one, but that's not why I brought you here," Lindsey said, reaching inside the truck.

She pulled out a clean and stylish white linen blouse and a cerulean blue linen skirt.

"Oh my god. Thanks. How'd you know?" Lindsey gushed.

"Like you, I left without packing last night. I didn't get anything clean 'til around ten this morning. I had 'em bring me something from the wardrobe at the studio and figured if we got to you first you might want something fresh. I took a best guess on the size."

"You're an angel."

"There's fresh undies in there, too. You can close the door and change," Liz said helping Lindsey into the truck.

"Honey you got the exclusive and anything else I can do for you," Lindsey promised as she closed the door.

Five minutes later Lindsey Lee Olson, movie star, emerged from the truck. Thanks to the wardrobe change, a few fresh wipes and a hairbrush, she felt and looked a hundred per cent better. She returned ready to face the cameras.

There was a momentary silence as she walked back into the throng of reporters. William had a surprised 'how'd that happen?' look on his face.

Several of the news professionals stopped their interviews with the men in mid-sentence and clustered around Lindsey Lee.

Liz watched and giggled softly to herself. Sometimes men were so damn predictable. Let' em push and ask their questions. Lindsey was playing them. Besides, Liz knew that Lindsey would deliver on the exclusive.

The questions and answers went on for about another ten minutes, until Reuben cut everybody off.

Then, as if on cue, two white limos from the casino with the tribe's logo on the side pulled up into tiny Frog City, actual population zero. Their chauffeurs got out and beckoned the Saintly Seven.

"Tell Rex, nice touch," Reuben whispered in William's ear as he walked past.

"He didn't send them," William turned around and winked. "I've learned a few things watching all of you."

Reuben laughed.

William and Lindsey stepped into the lead car.

Barry, his (unknown to him) former pilot, and the three free men got into the one behind.

The two cars pulled out in a line and headed east, back toward civilization.

Most of the broadcast media filmed the limos departing, using it as the closing shot in their coverage of the latest only-in-South-Florida escapade.

Then it was time to pack up.

On to the next story…

 **Epilogue**

Six Months Later...

Captain Larry watched as the mate finished hosing down the boat, prepping it for the day's charter. The kid, his nephew Eric, had actually forgiven him for pushing him overboard. Seemed to understand the necessity of using him as a skipping decoy. At least that's what he claimed.

Actually, Larry thought, Eric would do just about anything to get back on a boat. The kid loved the water and didn't need much of an excuse to go out on the ocean.

And what a boat. A brand new forty-five foot sport fisherman built by Bertram Yachts right here in Miami, the Salt Air. Captain Larry had gone legit.

The smuggling business had lost its appeal. He didn't much relish the thought of getting shot at again. And all the crap his last fares had been put through after their arrival. He didn't want to stick anybody else into that kind of situation. So he took his profits, invested them in the new boat, and was in the charter fishing business now.

Today's group was a little different from the usual tourists who either wanted to catch a bunch of good eating fish, or catch and release a trophy marlin or sailfish that they could get their picture taken with. Today's group was only a little about fishing and a lot about reunion.

"What's our count today, Eric?" he asked the boy.

"Ten passengers. The four religious guys, the rapper and his girls, and the movie chick and the Indian she's dating."

In fact, the charter had been Larry's idea. He had discreetly contacted the three refugees after they were free and finally given them his name. He offered a trip to them and any friends they wanted to bring to help make up for not getting them to shore.

"Big group. Only a couple at a time can fish."

"Uncle Larry, it didn't sound like they were all that interested in catching anything. Just more like they wanted a nice boat ride."

"Well, we can sure offer 'em that," Larry said from the dock, admiring his own boat.

He looked toward shore. Two of the charter customers were coming down the dock.

"Ms. Olson, Mr. Panther," he greeted them.

"Permission to come aboard?" Lindsey replied.

"Granted. Eric, the mate will show you where to stash your things inside the salon."

The couple, holding hands, stepped onto the aft deck and followed the young man inside.

Seedy and the handmaidens came aboard a short time later. William couldn't recall ever seeing the young ladies dressed so modestly. All wore loose fitting white cotton blouses and conservative, tan, Capri pants. Mr. Player had come attired to catch fish, wearing a white polo shirt, tan heavy khaki pants, deck shoes, and a fishing hat with long bills to protect both the face and the neck. Incongruously there was a silver garbage truck logo on the crown.

The six friends stayed inside the cool confines of the air-conditioned cabin while waiting for the last members of their party.

"So, chief, I thought there'd be a few more folks comin' on this cruise. Where's that big gold mine, Hamilton and Liz, that reporter he's been hangin' with? And what about Reuben?" Seedy asked.

Lindsey, as sometimes happens with couples who've been dating awhile, answered for him, "Ham is in L.A. with the team. Doing pretty good, too. Made triple- doubles in two of the last three games. You still selling those silly ponchos with bullet holes in the hood to let the water in?"

"You bet," he laughed.

"He and Elizabeth are still together. She flies to New York Friday nights to do the weekend morning news shows on ABC. During the week they spend as much time together as they can when they're both in town."

Liz's success was in no small part due to the prime time interview she'd conducted with Lindsey Lee. The two beautiful women and a good story with explosions and fires was a ratings smash.

"What about Mr. Elias?" Magdalena inquired.

"I'll take it," William said. "He's got a full plate. He's had to settle things for the three refugees."

"Yes, we know," interjected one of the Marias.

"He's also still looking out for Rogelio Negro. You can imagine the number of lawsuits that were filed in this town after a development for the rich and famous blew up, then burned to the ground."

Four heads nodded in agreement.

"You'd think that catastrophe by itself would keep him busy for years. In fact, he called in a corporate liability defense specialist, Knut Stephenson, from the west coast to help him. But you know he's always got something interesting going. He's taken on an age discrimination case to keep himself in the spotlight."

"Some old people getting' fired or not hired 'cause they're old? Doesn't sound all that interesting," Seedy commented.

"You're right. Reuben wouldn't take anything so regular. Pay attention. Try to understand the logic on this. It's a ten year old boy suing the state to get his driver's license."

"But that's way too young," the other Maria complained.

"Normally. But try to follow. The boy was born from a frozen embryo. One that was implanted in his mother after being stored for five and a half years. You add five and a half to nine months' gestation and you're over six years."

"So?" Magdalena still couldn't see where it was going.

"I'm not finished. The kid's a devout Catholic. For Catholics life begins at conception. To him, he was conceived, then on ice for 66 months, developed in his mom for nine more and now has been out of the womb for ten years. Add it together you get sixteen plus years. And in the state of Florida you can get a driver's license once you reach sixteen."

"Ain't that some shit," Seedy was laughing so hard his eyes were tearing. "Anybody can pull that off, it's Reuben."

They felt the boat rock gently as the last four passengers stepped on deck. They were more than half an hour late.

"Here half a year and they've already learned Cuban time," Magdalena gave a disgusted look at her watch.

"Good morning everyone," Barry Gold greeted them cheerfully as he stepped inside followed by Jesus, Pablo, and Pedro.

What a difference six months had made. The young men seemed transformed.

It wasn't just that they'd gained a little weight. Or that their beards were neatly trimmed and that their long hair parted down the middle, looked professionally styled yet Biblical. They were resplendent in what appeared to be tailored casual wear. Jesus all in white. His brothers wore the same heavy linen white shirt as his, but matching ecru polished cotton slacks instead. All three also wore brown leather TEVA sandals. Their raiment fairly screamed profession packaging.

Seedy and the girls rose as the group entered the cabin. Barry and the rapper shook hands then embraced. The girls each went to one of the refugees and greeted them with hugs and chaste pecks on the cheek.

William gave Lindsey a questioning look.

Captain Larry stuck his head in the cabin, "Is that everyone? Ready to go?"

Barry answered, "Cast off captain."

Eric untied the dock lines, while Larry cranked up the twin Cummins diesels.

Everyone stepped out on the deck to get the view as they left the marina in downtown Miami. On their way to sea they passed Star, Hibiscus and Palm Islands, three privates gated enclaves, where some of the areas biggest movers and shakers as well as national celebrities made their homes.

"I put a bid in for you boys on the ten bedroom place on Star Island," Barry said. "Should be enough room for all of you."

"Sí, but only temporarily. Until Mr. Negro can get our new house built."

"What?" It was Lindsey's turn to ask Barry's favorite question.

There was a moment of silence as they passed the Coast Guard station where the three refugees had first been held. Conversation resumed when the boat turned east out Government Cut toward the ocean.

"What, what?" Barry mimicked enjoying himself.

"They're buying a place on Star Island?" she asked knowing that houses there started in the high seven figures and that eight figures wasn't uncommon.

"Let me tell you, as their representation, things are going quite well for them."

Lindsey'd heard through peripheral contacts in the entertainment field that Barry had become their agent and that they were doing well in the Hispanic Evangelical and motivational speaking fields.

"I'd say so," she replied.

"Look, they have a great story to tell. And I've been helping them with Bible study so they can make the religious connection. They're the hottest thing in the Spanish market right now. And their English is coming along well enough we're going to try some crossover next month. Be part of some big southern revival shows."

"There's that much money in it?" she couldn't help herself.

"You're kidding, right?" They easily command in the six figures for one night's appearance on these group motivational speaking tours alone."

Lindsey just shook her head. She had no idea.

William was more interested in what Jesus had said. "What was that about Rogelio building you a new home? Isn't he up to his elbows in lawsuits?"

"Funny thing about that," Barry said.

"Yes. Let me tell him," Jesus interrupted.

"Go ahead."

"As you know Mr. Elias took care of my brothers and me. And he also represents Mr. Black. I mean Mr. Negro. But I'm trying to understand how things work in this country. So I asked him to explain all the legal…" He paused looking for the right word.

"Implications. Ramifications," Pablo surprisingly suggested.

"Right. Thanks brother. Well it seems that as he was going through the process of getting our immigration matters straightened out, the government came to Reuben with a proposal for Mr. Negro."

"But why?" William asked.

"This is where it gets interesting," Pedro interjected.

"Well of course the whole mess was the government's fault for holding us in the first place. And there was Mr. Patrick's getting shot, probably by some type of government agent."

"Yeah, but nothing was ever proved on that. And the federal government has legal immunity for its actions," William said.

"True. But, as you well know the ATF investigated the bombing of our trailer. However, did you ever hear anything about the outcome of the investigation?"

"Beyond that it was the work of radical exiles. No?"

"You ever hear of anybody being prosecuted even after arrests were made?" Jesus continued.

"No. Rex said something about the Feds replacing the trailer as a small reparation for the trouble the tribe had been put through. But no, nothing on prosecution."

"But you know that they had the head of this group, commandante Miguel in custody and that he shot the immigration guy. Twice."

"Right. And I never heard about anything happening to him. But what's this got to do with Rogelio?" William thought the whole story was getting pretty far off track.

"I'm getting there. It seems that the smart old commandante was shrewd enough to secretly tape the people who gave him the explosives to blow up your trailer. He didn't trust them."

"And they were government agents," the explanation was becoming clear to William.

"Including the guy he shot," Jesus continued.

"So if he keeps his mouth shut, the commandante skates on the charges." William knew how the system worked.

"And the bombing was strongly implicated in the subsequent destruction of Mont Basura Harbor from the shock waves it produced," Jesus encouraged William to finish the story.

"So the Feds, not wanting to be publicly outed for their part in this, offered Rogelio a deal."

"You got it. He keeps quiet, they'll cover any restitution he has to make and help him rebuild."

"Son of a bitch. And you boys would want to move up on Mont Basura?" William asked.

"Fond memories. At least in some ways," Jesus replied.

"And if we like the Star Island place enough maybe we'll wait for Basura II."

"Basura II?" Lindsey asked.

"There's a lot more people living down here now. The second Trashmore will probably be filled to capacity in five to six years. And Rogelio had negotiated the development rights to it when he originally made the deal with the county," Barry explained.

"He always knew how to work it," Lindsey said.

"And he thinks he's got the methane problem beat for next time. Instead of collecting and storing it to pipe into the housing, he's going to run it into gas street lighting. Give a nice look to the new development and easier to monitor the flow and burn rate," Barry added.

"Calculating. Working the angles. That's our boy, Señor Negro," Lindsey smiled. "Didn't mean to break the eggs. Just tell everybody you'd always wanted to make an omelet."

"Anyone ready to try some fishing?" Larry called down from the flying bridge. They'd reached the Gulf Stream, Miami and Miami Beach barely visible on the western horizon.

"Sure," William and Seedy replied, the only two real avid fishermen in the group.

Eric helped them set up their rods.

During the trip out the two Marias and Magdalena had changed into relatively modest one-piece suits. Now they came out with their large towels to sun themselves on the foredeck.

As they passed by, William asked, "Seedy, what's going on. The girls aren't dressed, you know, so sexy?"

"Appearances my man. The ladies are dating the holy trio. A certain propriety must be preserved."

"You're kiddin'. Remember I was there for the initial meeting," William was skeptical.

"No. They're serious. The ladies are singing choral music at the religious shows. Magdalena thinks she may get a proposal soon."

"Really? You turned a new leaf too?"

"Prefer to think it as branching out. Gospel rap. I've done a couple shows with them. Big untapped market there."

"The American dream," William smiled.

"Amen brother."

After William and Seedy each landed a good size dolphin, the other men and Lindsey took turns fishing. Eric filleted one of the fish then pan-fried chunks of the fresh meat and served it as sandwiches for lunch. Throughout the day the group caught several more dolphin and some decent size, fifteen to twenty pound yellow fin tuna.

Those who weren't fishing or kibitzing with angling suggestions traded stories. Catching up on news and getting details of future projects.

The group learned that the tribal council had removed Rex. He was reduced to night desk manager at the swamp casino. His efforts at providing security followed within hours by the trailer explosion had left the Miccosukees embarrassed.

On top of that the EPA had had to come in after Mont Basura blew to determine the environmental impact of the garbage hurled onto the reservation. In the process they had discovered a threatened species of fern, an endangered species of crab, and a new subspecies of mangrove tentatively named the Basura Brown. This effectively ended the development of the casino and marina for the foreseeable future.

The tribe had asked William to become the new leader. A job he didn't really want. He would be glad to offer advice but didn't want to be cooped up in an office looking at figures and reports. He delayed giving an answer by taking another job.

He was the technical advisor for Lindsey Lee Olson's new project. She and Reuben, who seemed so busy he must have had no time to sleep, had put together a screenplay of the whole refugee story. There were bios for either a TV miniseries or a full-length feature movie. Lindsey would play herself. And Reuben hoped to play himself. They were opting toward the movie version because the bigger budget would allow for better special effects with the explosions and fires.

Barry suggested that his clients at least be considered for cameo roles. And that perhaps the soundtrack include music from Seedy Player and the Heavenly Sisters.

Lindsey didn't say no. Her technical advisor thought- why not?

Around 4:30 Captain Larry told Eric to have everybody reel in. It was time to head back.

Jesus was up on the flying bridge to check out the view. Twenty feet above the waterline the area was used mainly for observation, to look for flocks of birds or patches of seaweed and the fish that would be under them, or to watch a guest fighting a big gamefish and figure out which way to steer the boat to help land it.

Looking down toward the bow, Jesus saw the three young women picking up their towels and books. He was enjoying the brisk salt air and the fresh sea breeze.

"It's beautiful up here," Jesus remarked conversationally.

"Yes it is," Larry agreed wryly having seen him look at the young women.

"No, really?" Jesus laughed, now looking toward the eastern horizon.

"Yeah. It really is," Larry agreed. He couldn't think of anywhere he'd rather be on a day like this.

Jesus thought he saw a movement in the distance. Something bobbing in the water, driftwood, maybe porpoises, it was too far to tell.

"Do you have any binoculars?" Jesus asked.

"Whatta you see?" Larry said handing him a bright yellow waterproof pair.

"I'm not sure," Jesus replied adjusting them for his eyes, then focusing on the area in question.

It was a raft. Someone was trying to stand and wave at them.

"Turn the boat. Quick. There's people out there," Jesus ordered.

Larry looked over his shoulder making sure that the lines were in. Then he swung the wheel about and pushed the throttles forward.

Technically it was a large rowboat made out of plywood. There were four men on board. And two oars. Actually one and a half. One appeared to have snapped in two, losing its blade. If they'd had any provisions they were gone now.

William, Jesus and his brother quickly pulled the men aboard. It was doubtful they would have made it under their own power.

"Take them into the salon," Larry called down. "Keep them out of sight 'til we get them to dry land." He didn't have to tell this group why.

In the cabin the women brought them moist towels to cool their sunburned faces and cracked dry lips. They were given bottles of water and Eric brought them leftovers from lunch. They relaxed a little in their seats, grateful to be alive.

Jesus stood back and looked at them. All were gaunt, bearded, with long straggly hair. There seemed to be a family resemblance in their faces. Another set of brothers?

"Florida?" one croaked weakly.

"Soon. Luego," Jesus answered in both languages.

"What are your names?" Barry asked

Four blank stares.

"¿Sus nombres?" Jesus asked.

"Mateo."

"Marco."

"Lucas."

"Juan."

9671809R0017